L

A

Teresa Hamilton's brilliant debut novel, *Choices*, made history being the first book to be sponsored by advertising since the nineteenth century. Interspersed with teaching for over twenty years, Teresa flew as cabin crew for a major airline. It was the diaries she kept that provided the inspiration for LOVE, SUZI x. Teresa lives in East Sussex, UK, with her husband, 3 children, 2 dogs, 1 ancient cat and a fish. She also owns a webstore, East is East, selling unique home accessories. For more information about Teresa please go to her website: www.teresahamilton.co.uk

ISBN-13 978 1491236369
ISBN-10 1491236361

www.teresahamilton.co.uk

Twitter @THamiltonwriter

LOVE, SUZI x

Teresa Hamilton

For Joanna, Ellie & Harry
The world is out there waiting for you...

Acknowledgements

Years ago when I was teaching I was summoned to the school office one day to take a phone call. Little did I know the adventures that lay ahead of me when I accepted the job as cabin crew. I skipped back along the corridor to my class room like one of my seven year old pupils. The subsequent diaries of my adventures were used to write this. Which ones are based on reality and which are entirely fictitious I'll leave you to decide.

During my 'flying years' I was lucky to go on trips with my friends Sally Broadhead and Lynette Atkinson. My love and thanks to them for sharing, not only the other end of the trolley, but some hilarious moments with me. But special love goes to my dearest friend, the late Tracy Fourés, the first one of us to take to the skies and whose encouragement made me fill in the application forms in the first place.

Love and thanks always to Sally Griffiths and Richard Stevenson for their invaluable editorial advice. Also to Helen Oliver and Hilary Caddick for their continued support.

When Suzi started to take shape on my blog it was Dr Korinna Stiebahl's enthusiasm to read more about Suzi's exploits that encouraged me to continue. Without her, Suzi would not be the girl she is today. My love and thanks to her.

Final thanks go to my fundamental support group:- Deborah Holman, for always encouraging me; Jo Hamilton, for her invaluable contribution in keeping me up to date with the mind of a twenty-something and as always, Nick Williams, for your encouragement, editorial advice and most of all, just being you.

Prologue

'My husband's dead!'

My mind mentally scanned the training manual that I had been studying so fervently for the last few months. Nope, I couldn't remember any page where it advised me how to cope with this eventuality. Mind you, this was pretty exciting stuff for my first flight as a bona fide stewardess.

'Let me come and see, madam,' was the best I could come up with, flinging back the galley curtain. I followed the woman up the darkened cabin, picking my way through arms and legs that were sprawled out into the aisles, like children at a sleep-over, the passengers were watching films after being fed and watered.

The woman clambered unceremoniously over her 'dead' husband slumped in the aisle seat. I racked my brain for what to do? The manual had said that as the first crew member on the scene I must make a decision and act but it was so dark it was impossible to tell if he was just deeply asleep or indeed dead. He was a large man and there was no way I could lift him to lay him on the floor for mouth to mouth, if that was necessary. I ran my tongue around my teeth and found a little something stuck in the groove of a molar. I had only just finished a tuna roll. What had he just finished? I shook my head. Mouth to mouth was definitely unnecessary. I shook his shoulder. No reaction. I shook him harder whilst shouting

1

in his ear. Nothing.

A. B. C. – 'Clear the airway,' came flashing into my mind. This is what I had to do in an emergency. A stood for airway, B for breathing and C for circulation. These steps are fundamental when assessing a person for signs of life. Well, this *was* an emergency. I instinctively started to undo the tight belt around his portly waist. I looked across at his wife anxiously clutching her knees to her chest and staring at me.

'Is he on any medication?' I questioned her. 'Or had a lot to drink with his meal?' She shook her head, her eyes wide in the darkness.

I struggled with the catch. It wouldn't pull tight enough to unclasp the hook. I tugged again, pushing his bulging flesh in slightly with my other hand.

I didn't get very far.

'What do you think you're *doing*?' he shouted. His eyes fluttered and opened as he grabbed my hand to stop me undoing his belt. Interfering with the man's trousers had brought him round from wherever he was – pleasantly, I hoped. I quickly backed off and released the leather belt. I opened my mouth to explain but the cries of joy from his distressed wife overwhelmed him as she clasped his face to cover it with kisses.

It's not every day you bring someone back to life (his wife thought I'd performed a miracle) and keep up the cabin crew reputation for customer satisfaction.

All in a day's work, eh?

7th February - Disused Hangar - Heathrow Airport (LHR)

Dear Eve

You won't believe it, but I've got our dream job - flying round the world, staying in expensive hotels and getting paid to do it. Remember how we used to pretend that we were one of those glamorous stewardesses that we'd seen on the TV adverts? Well, without a hitch I passed the interviews and now I'm long haul cabin crew and it's just as good as we'd always hoped.

How I managed to get through though I'll never know. You know what a clumsy idiot I was when we were at school? Well, I'm no better now but somehow I managed to convince them I could do this job. Or maybe it was fate. You always said I was lucky. Well, you were right this time. I met other candidates who had spent years re-applying after failing the interview process. I sailed through everything, even when I fluffed an interview question to name the Education Minister. Don't know why they wanted to ask that? Maybe in case he's on one of my flights and I spill a drink down his suit?

I've got to tell you about my training. Some of it feels as though I've been dropped onto a disaster movie set. I'm mid-way through and it's the practical safety part. I'd heard whispers from the other recruits about how exciting it would be so was prepared to be thrilled beyond my wildest dreams. It *had* to be better than the endless mock-up scenarios we'd endured. One word, dull, dull, DULL (okay that's three, but you get my drift).

The first week of the training was residential. We were

3

closeted together in a hotel for six days and nights; maybe to see if any cat fights would break out amongst the females? Much of the course consisted of role play (and not the kind that springs to mind, trust me). They obviously saw that I was a closet actress bursting to tread the boards but would never make the Royal Shakespeare Company so took pity on me. I have pretended to be: 1) a disabled passenger so that I can appreciate their needs, and 2) an angry passenger so my cabin crew partner can learn how to shut me up, which means that, working on the theory that it takes two to argue, you just smile and empathise. They should definitely try telling my boyfriend, Matt, that!

The days were spent in the classroom learning our way around the stowages and dark corners of the aircraft galley, interspersed with practising our cabin technique of sashaying between the aisles, pushing and pulling the trolleys with the greatest of ease. One day I wondered if they'd made the right choice in recruiting me when I tipped a tray laden with plastic containers and food all over one of the others. I didn't think my hips were that wide but I'll have to learn to manoeuvre them more carefully – if I'm that clumsy on the ground, heaven knows what will happen in the air with unexpected turbulence. I'll have to announce my entry into the cabin with '*EVERYBODY TAKE COVER! Stewardess with loaded tray on the loose.*'

On one of the training days we were dispersed to various airports around Europe. Ruby, my buddy for the day, and I were dispatched to Amsterdam. Easy you'd think and after getting there we thought we'd nailed it too. There were just so many exciting shops to look at. They briefed us to really get into the whole travel experience so that we knew how the passengers felt. Surely that meant checking out the duty free; spraying on as many perfumes as necessary until I smelt like a mixed floral bunch and squeezing out those sample packages of face cream until my skin was baby soft? And don't get me started on the sunglasses, accessory and bikini shops.

'Have you seen this?' Ruby asked. She was standing by the designer swimwear rail and holding up a tiny, lime green, bandeau style bikini. 'It's *the* colour this season. I'm going to get it.'

'I thought lime was last year. It's yellow now, isn't it?'

'For God's sake, Suzi. You're going to have to keep up better than that. It's all about the contrast with the tan.'

I looked at my pale, cream skin. That was me out of the game. It took me ages to tan and even that was after two coats of burn and peel first. It was obviously not only all about the tan but all about the language as well. Seems I was way behind on cabin crew speak. Ruby disappeared to the till clutching the lurid material. I caught sight of my watch.

'What time does our plane take off?'

She rummaged in her handbag. 'Not sure, I'll check.' She pulled out a piece of paper along with her purse. 'SHIT!' she screamed, glancing at it. 'Now! RUN!' Ruby dropped the bikini on the counter next to the bemused assistant and weaved her way through the maze of clothes rail to the entrance.

'They'll wait for us, won't they?' I asked, letting go of the three swimsuits I'd been deciding on so suddenly they fell in a heap on top of the stand.

'Come on, Suzi! Don't be an arse,' she yelled at me over her shoulder, starting to run as though from starting blocks towards the departure gate. 'Of course they won't wait for us.'

The rest of the training group told us later we were

only supposed to walk through the airport, turn round and catch the returning flight. Now I know what it's like to run at breakneck speed to your departure gate, shouting profanities at your partner while wearing high heels. Only to be told that the gate has closed and the plane is about to depart. I'd say that was pretty much a comprehensive passenger experience. I'm not sure the tutors took the same view though. We sat patiently right outside the gate the whole time after that and were allowed to board the next flight. I hope this doesn't mean a black mark against our names nor is an indication of things to come.

My training manual is so large it needs a chauffeur, like a politician's red box, just to transport it. I can hold a tray of *'chicken or beef, sir'* plus extra nuts for the passenger in 24B and my hat sits at just the right jaunty angle to look professional but not pudding-bowlish when I swish through the airport terminal, smiling all the time of course – teeth need to be on maximum show without appearing psychotic.

We've now progressed to this disused hanger somewhere on the outskirts of Heathrow Airport. We've been put into two groups to take turns and there is a lot of waiting around, hence I've got time to write this. Various kinds of aircraft are surreally propped up along the walls –but only half of each kind of plane, cut length wise. This allowed us to climb the steps to board the plane but with only one side looking over the ground, while the other faces a wall. My group went first. We were led towards the 747 and walked up the stairs behind to enter the supposed 'aircraft'. Like lambs to the slaughter we found our seats and sat patiently. There was a mixture of experienced and new crew as passing this test is an annual safety requirement for everyone. Then the trainers arrived and at random we were chosen to play the role of the cabin crew or passengers.

Pick a disaster, Eve, any disaster and they can simulate it from their control desk. It's a bit like a mixture of the films '*Snakes on a Plane*' and '*Airport,*' anything can happen. I sat down and prayed that they wouldn't pick me to be a crew member immediately. I didn't want to be the one to let everyone 'die' through my incompetence. I got a reprieve the first time and was given the delightful role of playing a passenger – being instructed to wait till I was told what to do. I decided against demanding a blanket, drink and playing with my seat back - perhaps it wasn't the moment to be juvenile.

The lights were dimmed. The cabin started to fill with smoke. My hands started sweating. It was only a mock up I reminded myself.

'You alright?' the girl next to me asked. She indicated my white knuckles gripping the arm rest between us. 'First time eh?'

I nodded. Smoke began to fill the immediate area and I could see the 'crew' fumbling to retrieve a fire extinguisher and then rushing about.

'Don't worry,' the stewardess next to me continued. 'They want you to pass. Think of all the money they've spent on training you.' Small comfort but I clung to it.

Someone barked at me to leave my seat and make my way to the open doors. We both got up and squeezed between the seats taking our turn in the queue that had formed in the aisle.

'They only kick you out if you do something really stupid,' she concluded over her shoulder at me. We reached the open door. She turned and leaped out.

I stood on the threshold of the doorway. This was more like it. I was standing at the top of the biggest yellow slide I'd ever seen which stretched out in front of me. I jumped, arms folded across my body – quite the perfect passenger in my opinion. No stilettos to pierce anything, no manic scrabbling to save my duty free and no sitting down on the lip of the chute to take it gently as though I was at the local park. But I leapt with such enthusiasm, if it hadn't been for the two crew members waiting at the bottom to help me up and the mattress stuck to the wall opposite, I'd have broken limbs I went so fast.

I climbed the steps to the aircraft again. The stewardess's comment crossed my mind. What if I did do something stupid? How stupid is enough to get you kicked off the course and out of the airline? I mustn't let a throwaway comment like that get me flustered. I can do this job and I can do it well. It'll just take a bit of time to get the hang of it all. I've been devouring that training manual every night when I get home; more than I did for my school exams.

I found an empty seat and sat down. My new friend dispensing advice was now sitting in the row in front of me this time. She turned, poking her face through the gap between the seats.

'Wasn't that bad, eh? It's the exam tomorrow that you need to worry about. You can only get five questions wrong or it's curtains for you.' Thanks. No pressure then I wanted to reply, but the cabin fell silent. We were debriefed. Note to self: the previous 'crew' forgot to turn up the cabin lighting so that they could see where the fire was coming from. Basic but useful point to remember.

Time for another scenario.

'Suzi Frazier!'

My name was called. This was it. My heart pumped so hard I could feel it thumping in my ears. I was told to take the crew seat behind the 'passengers' at the rear door. It was going to be an emergency landing complete with flash lighting and sound effects but I wasn't to know if we were supposed to be on fire or broken in two, three

8

or millions of pieces. This was my moment. All I knew was that I had to wait until the Captain announced which doors to evacuate from in case there was a hazard outside I didn't know about.

And…action!

Arghh. Nothing came over the intercom system. I waited... The trainer looked at me. The captain hadn't announced that we should open the doors. Should I wait and perhaps we'd all burn to death or do I use my initiative and start shouting at everyone to evacuate?

Evacuate! You never know the Captain might have been knocked unconscious up there. They wouldn't be able to write about my heroic antics if I waited too long for him to give the commands and we were all burnt to a cinder. I looked through the small window. Nothing hazardous that I could see. I looked at the trainer. His dead pan face was not going to give me any help as to what to do next. He wrote something on his clipboard. I turned the handle and heaved open the aircraft door shouting orders at everyone to get out of their seats.

Blimey! I hoped they would move quicker in a real emergency. I was supposed to be the last one off after checking the cabin was clear. I'd be toast if they dawdled like that. The power went to my head.

'Jump! Jump!' I shouted at them and start pushing them off. 'No! Don't sit down. JUMP!'

A stewardess I hadn't seen before was cowering at the back.

'I'm pregnant,' she offered. Pregnant or not, sorry lady you will be a goner if I left you behind. But then a thought struck me, Eve. Was she pregnant for real or was she a ringer to test me? Her face was pale but I couldn't see an obvious bump. Could I cope with the guilt of making her miscarry if she was really expecting? The trainer barked at me to clear the cabin. The stewardess

9

stood screeching at me not to force her to jump. I grabbed her arm and pulled her towards the door. She continued pleading with me and pulled back into the aircraft. I had to decide. Obviously in a real emergency I would just manhandle her out through the doorway. The cabin was empty. I had to make a decision. It was me or her.

I left her to her mock death, turned and leapt down the chute to save myself. Perhaps they could leave that bit out in the news article?

Love, Suzi x

28th February - San Francisco (SFO) 1,000ft - hotel

Dear Eve

You know what? This job has really come along in the nick of time. It's Matt. He wants marriage and babies - the whole shebang, but something's making me hesitate. I know I've got to see what else is out there first. There's nothing wrong with what he wants mind, I'm just not sure if now is the right time, or come to think of it, if Matt Murphy is the one. I'm so confused, Eve. I wish you were here to help.

More excitingly, I've just had my first flight as a supernumerary. The Captain generously allowed me to grace his presence. I sat right behind him on the jump seat in the flight deck of the 747 as it approached the runway. It was amazing to watch the early afternoon sun dazzle us through the cockpit window. I was able to peep over the Captain's shoulder. I kept as quiet as a mouse though. I'm not even sure he remembered I was there; he was too busy concentrating on talking to the control tower and flicking numerous switches and dials.

10

I couldn't believe how quickly the ground came up to meet us. You can't feel a thing from up there in the cockpit. Not like the crash, jolt and oxygen masks coming down as the wheels touched the ground of a heavy landing when I was sitting down the back going on holiday once. This time it felt as though we'd just gently stepped out of the sky. I bet the pilot thinks he's fantastic if he lands like that every time. I wanted to congratulate him after witnessing that landing but he was so busy as we taxied to our parking space that I didn't have the chance. I don't know that I could bring myself to do it anyway. Too embarrassing. I did pluck up the courage to speak to the First Officer later though as we were waiting for our bags. He told me that those heavy landings are necessary sometimes when the weather is poor to, '*make sure the plane is firmly on the ground. Doesn't do to kangaroo jump along the runway.*' I'd never thought of it like that.

No wonder the Flight Deck are treated like Gods by the rest of the crew. A lot of the female flight attendants I've met are gagging to get a ring on their finger from one of them. That is the ultimate prize apparently. I can't see why. Perhaps if I was looking for a father figure or free flights on the jump seat forever, I might be tempted. Or maybe the attraction is the power element? One of the other girls was going all giggly whenever the striped God came onto her radar (they have stripes on their epaulettes so you can recognise what rank they are). The Captain's word is law aboard the plane. Nothing happens in that silver bird without his say so. It would have to be a case of *Mutiny on the Bounty* if the crew wanted to disagree with his commands. Bit tricky to eject him into the Pacific from 35,000ft, but you get the drift.

San Francisco, Eve. I'm actually here. What could be better for my first flight? The Caribbean? Kate and Lucy from my training course opened their rosters to find they were being sent there. Okay, so I was a tinge green around the gills but I am grateful. Really. Word has it that there are a lot worse places to go than San Francisco and I'm sure as a newbie I'll get more than my chance to find out.

Aaron, my partner on the other end of trolley, and I were brewing up in the galley before the customers boarded. 'What're you going to do in San Francisco, Suzi?' He asked me.

'No idea. I am completely open to suggestions,' I replied. 'What do most of the crew do?' I asked looking up from pouring the tea.

Aaron looked at me. 'You won't see many of them.'

'Why?'

'You're not serious?' he questioned. The blank look on my face replied for me. 'Most of the stewards have requested this trip?' he continued. The penny didn't drop as far as I was concerned. 'It's San Francisco? Suzi. You do know about San Francisco, don't you?'

Apparently there's more than 'one gay in the village' in San Francisco. That's why the crew was top heavy with male members. I could feel my cheeks colouring up like a furnace and had to pretend I was desperate to check the toilets at the back of the aircraft till they returned to their usual pale tone. Doh... I'd better man-up. Shows how sheltered I've been in 'Twinklesville,' cosseted with Matt all these years. I feel like Sleeping Beauty waking up to realise there's a big, bad world out there. Oh, when I say 'Beauty', that's not after a long night sector back over the Pond after sightseeing, of course.

Love, Suzi x

8th March - Home

Dear Eve

Thank god for Aaron. He helped me complete my paperwork for landing into Heathrow, otherwise I'd have had to request another round trip to get it done in time. We have to reconcile any duty free sales with the stock that we had originally. Taking into account currency exchange rates there is a little room for error, but not the amount I seemed to come up with on my first reckoning.

'Arghhhh. This can't be right. Not again,' I wailed as I buried my head in my hands. 'Shit, shit, shit!' Picking up the full money bags again I tipped their contents out onto the galley work surface. I started to put them into piles to count. A few coins fell on the floor and rolled under the bin. I pulled out the bin and got down on my hands and knees. A stray ring-pull from a can of coke dug into my flesh. I felt my eyes start to water.

'What's up Suzi?' Aaron asked as he pushed the trolley he'd been manoeuvring into the galley and waited for me to get up. I rubbed my knee, swallowed hard and wiped my eyes. It had all seemed so easy when we'd practised doing the paperwork in training. But now we were near to landing. I had to let senior crew know that the documents were all signed and the trolleys sealed before landing into Heathrow. I'd need to dip deeply into my pockets to square up my figures.

'Do you think the Captain would circle the airport for me so I can get this done?' I asked Aaron. He put an arm around my shoulders. 'I just can't seem to make it match.

I don't want to be handcuffed and led off the plane because of inadvertent embezzlement or accusations of smuggling.'

'Here. Let me take a look,' he offered kindly. 'You count this lot and I'll check your figures.'

It's my own fault; I probably tried to do too much whilst I was in San Francisco and was knackered. Well, you would go for it in a big way, wouldn't you, when it's your first time in a city? We only had a day and a half off. There was another new stewardess too so four of us hired a car. Luckily they didn't ask me to drive. Probably had something to do with the fact I kept looking to the right each time we crossed a road. Aaron had to grab my arm more than a couple of times to prevent me stepping out into the traffic. It would have been far too confusing with the driver's seat the wrong side. We took ourselves off to the see the Golden Gate Bridge amongst other places. It was amazing. We went down a street famous for being the crookedest street in the world and ended up having buffalo stew at a diner the others knew about.

I had a great view of the city from my hotel room. It was on the twentieth floor with huge picture windows that looked out onto the streets below. Rows and rows of houses and shops were laid out in regimented form before me. As the sun went down the streetlights began to twinkle like a row of fairy lights in a long line as far as I could see until they disappeared over the hill.

I think I'm going to enjoy the hotel part of the job. Crew are always accommodated in tip top hotels. It will make a change from the usual two star bed and breakfast Matt and I are used to. He whisked me away one weekend and I thought I had captured a spontaneous romantic. (Do they exist?) We ended up checking into a dingy B & B somewhere by the coast. Damp sheets and a ceiling that 'rained' every time the man in the room above didn't pull his shower curtain across properly. I tried to see the funny side of it, be considerate and say it didn't matter. But I did think it would have been better to go camping; at least I would have been wrapped in my own bed linen, even if it was still my old purple sleeping bag that you and I used to share on our sleep-overs.

Everyone has an opinion on flight attendants. Many see it as no more than a glorified waiter or waitress. Well, fair enough, but glorified or not, after the flight home from San Francisco I was exhausted and there was no milk in the fridge. I'm now sharing a house with three other girls. Sarah-Jane Andrews (brunette and a bit scatty) is so loved up with her new man at the moment she can't see past his backside (granted it's a cute backside, but still). Samantha Greene is busy trying to impress her boss to get a raise. I know she's seriously considering propositioning him and, Debbie Willis. Well, Debbie is sans job. Unless you count sitting on the couch all day watching soaps. But then again, you can afford to if your parents are as well off as hers. Harsh but fair. Instead of a rug to keep her warm she uses her crisp and sweet wrappers as a Technicolor blanket. Only one of us seems to have passed our exams in housekeeping and making sure the fridge is well stocked with essentials and guess who that is?

Matt thinks I should be considering settling down. But how can I? I'm only twenty-four. Look at all the people I'm going to meet. Anyone would think we were in our late thirties and time was running out. Matt may be older than me but my biological clock hasn't even started ticking yet, let alone flashed up a warning of my sell-by date.

I do try to understand where Matt's coming from. His younger sister's married and had her first baby by the time she was twenty-two. I know he sees his life going that way too. We've been together for so long now. He was delicious when I was leaving school and snagged him. It made all the other girls jealous that I had a boyfriend six years older than me. I admit it did give me a thrill. He seemed so much more experienced and different from all the boys my own age. He had started working, had a car and seemed to know so much, but since then we've just drifted along. I didn't realised he was such a plodder. No wild plans of seeing the world for him. I used to think we were a match made in heaven. Perhaps I'm just getting older? I'm beginning to realise although he's a lovely man, maybe he's just not the lovely man for me?

It's not only him but his family seem to have adopted me. I'm in up to my neck and sometimes it feels like a noose (a tightening one at that). I know they all think I'm the 'one' for him but there's got to be a bit more out there, surely? I know you'd understand. I really miss talking things over with you. What am I to do? Catch the next flight out of here, I reckon.

Love, Suzi x

14th March - Heathrow. Just finished a New York (JFK) - Heathrow (LHR) sector - now waiting for the crew bus

Dear Eve

The man in 32k nearly drove me BONKERS. Before he'd even found his seat he demanded a blanket, pillow, water and all that was on the menu. He didn't stop wanting my attention. I, of course, smiled sweetly and told him that I would get everything as soon as I could. His last request before he settled down to watch a movie was for a large whiskey. That seemed to sort him out because when I checked later he was fast asleep. Talking of movies, you know me, Eve. Still obsessed. It's great that there seems to be so many re-runs in the hotels round the world. There's always a film to fill those wee small hours of the night. I get excited whenever I see the lion roaring on the screen and settle down with glee. They're a life-line to counteracting loneliness, I can tell you.

Thank goodness, we picked up a really good tail wind on the way home, which was a relief after a four hour delay in JFK. It was a good flight – so much easier when it's a shorter one. Time seems to whiz past. By the time we'd served the drinks, got the dinner out and followed it with 'tea or coffee?' twice, we were well on our way.

It was all going so well I felt I'd cracked this stewardess malarkey. I had just strapped myself in after the signal that landing was imminent; three pings over the tannoy system, code for '*get your arses on your seats, crew, I'm bringing this big bird down*'. There are strict

17

directives on landing protocol. I have to let the crew at the front of the plane, who in turn let the Captain know, that the cabin is secure for landing. It's a bit like Chinese whispers over the intercom, except that it's all in code and we can't mis-hear the message otherwise all hell breaks loose. 'Cabin secure' means that the punters must all be strapped down as well as everything stowed securely in the galley. Can't have a coffee pot falling out on someone's head.

I looked up. A woman two rows in front of me in the middle seat was pushing past the person next to her.

'Could you please sit down, Madam?' I asked politely. 'We are just about to land.' She ignored me and reached the aisle.

'Madam!' I raised my voice to just a respectable level of authority (about the same as that teacher who scared us once when she discovered us smoking in the school toilets). I strained forward against my five-point, harness seat belt to press home my point. 'You must sit down!' Jeez. She may have a death wish but I don't see why she should take me with her. She ignored me again and kept on walking towards me, a small bag in her outstretched hand.

I then had a choice. Either undo my harness and hope we didn't crash on landing and accept what she was offering me or, sit tight and let the stupid woman fend for herself. If we did crash and I wasn't strapped in, who would open the door and get everyone out? Always supposing I wasn't killed in the crash in the first place. I looked though the window in the door next to me. I could see the ground coming up to meet us fast. Whatever was in that bag had better be worth it. I quickly undid my buckle, took a few steps forward and grabbed what she was offering me. It was warm.

'Now, sit down!' I commanded. Oh, the power of a

uniform. The woman returned to her place, squashing past her fellow passengers. I perched on my seat.

I didn't need to open the bag to realise what it was in it. The man sitting opposite me smiled in sympathy. Sitting with someone else's repulsive stomach contents on my lap was not an option. I've always had that rebellious streak in me. Remember that time I made you climb the trees at the back of our house when Mum said we weren't allowed because they were too high? Just as I felt the first touch of the wheels on the ground I flung the small bag towards the galley bin and strapped myself in. The loosely sealed bag wobbled precariously on the top of the pile of rubbish as the plane jolted and landed heavily on the tarmac. Yuk. Such a glamorous job.

Love, Suzi x

15th March - Home

Dear Eve

You'd think Matt would be happy to see me now I'm back. Headline: *Girlfriend Returns After Being Away For Days*. A bit of rushing up with flowers, protestations of undying love, offers of dinner? Nope, nothing. A simple '*tell me all about it*' would be nice. I'd cooked him his favourite Thai chicken curry to set the mood when he came over straight from work. Instead he sulked all evening talking to me with more grunts than words, sat on the sofa picking his dirty nails (did I tell you he's a mechanic?) watched TV, drunk my diet Pepsi and then went home early. Arghhh…

Still, life carries on. I've had a few days at home to catch-up. I hate doing ghastly chores but in order to keep that insatiable blue suitcase full with my clean underwear, it has to be done. Also, someone has to clear the grime from the shower plug hole before it overflows like a river and onto the lino. Queen of Cleaning; that's my title. I hate seeing the house decline whilst I'm out of the country. I won't live in a pig sty. I'm under no illusion as to why my house mates are so keen for me not to move in with Matt. Who wouldn't want a mug like me clearing up after them? We should have lived together, Eve. Although, on reflection, maybe not. I remember your bedroom, you always had your clothes scattered everywhere so I could never find anywhere to sit down except on top of them. I wouldn't have minded clearing up after you though; I could have teased you about it.

Love, Suzi x

20th March - 35,000ft, LHR - Barbados (BGI)

Hi Eve

'Quick, go and have a look at the woman in 35A. Her dress is up round her waist, you can see her knickers,' my colleague urged me on the flight to Barbados.

I grabbed a plastic bag and sashayed down the aisle pretending I was checking for rubbish. I could clearly see the couple in seats 35A & B getting stuck in. I hurried back to the galley.

'What should we do?' I asked naively. 'I can hardly go up to them and say excuse me sir/madam, do you think you could stop all that sexual activity. Or for God's sake, get a room?'

'Well, no one else has complained yet, so offer them a blanket,' Karen replied.

'You know the guy sitting behind them is her husband,' I dropped casually into the conversation.

'No!' Karen said clasping her hand over mouth.

'Yes, they told me when I was serving their meal. Apparently the one she's groping is his employee. Hubby's even paid for the trip.' We both stifled our giggles.

'How much have they had to drink?' Karen asked. 'I served them a couple of doubles earlier.'

'Tons.'

'Go and have another look at what the husband is doing,' Karen ordered pouring hot water into the pot. 'Cup of tea?'

I grabbed a pile of blankets and wandered casually down the aisle.

'He's asleep,' I reported on my return. 'But I managed to pass the two lovebirds a blanket although I don't know if they noticed, he was too busy with his tongue down her throat and his hand up what's left of her skirt. I can't believe some people.'

'Well they'd better hurry up and finish off,' Karen said matter-of-factly. 'Mike's just been down to say to get ready for the next meal round.'

Love, Suzi x

Eve

I've been naughty. I've discovered that I have a dark side, Eve. One that is released unexpectedly and can get out of control. But it wasn't entirely my fault. Let me give you the recipe that led to my downfall.

1. Land in paradise. Gasp (remembering to shut mouth afterwards, not an attractive look) at the heat of the Caribbean, the beauty of the beaches and the luxury of the hotel.

2. After check-in, arrange to meet rest of crew in designated room for party.

3. Foolishly agree to go with everyone the next day on the Jolly Roger boat trip after getting carried along with their enthusiasm that '*I would love it.*'

4. Arrive sober at the dock and cast off at midday on a beautiful schooner fashioned like a pirate ship. Crew dressed up, tall sails and a long plank placed over the side, threatening to be walked.

5. Remember accepting first rum punch. Started to sip it as I'd been warned it was lethal but it only tasted like fruit juice.

6. Remember accepting second rum punch. Soon forgot crew's advice. Sips turned to gulps as it was so hot.

7. Just about remember dancing seductively in my red and white bikini sandwiched between two stewards. One who feigned concern that I didn't burn while massaging sun cream on any bare skin that wasn't moving.

8. Remember nothing else.

The next thing I recall is waking up in my bed not knowing how I got there.

'Suzi? You in there?'

I rolled over and groaned.

'Suzi? Come on. It's time for sundowners on the beach.' A voice called out to me. 'Come on, Suz. We need another aerobics session.'

Apparently as I found out when I finally surfaced hours later, while on the boat I was practising my grapevine aerobics moves, cajoling everyone to line up across the deck while I played teacher leading them in time to the music. Karen told me that I was a huge source of entertainment. I became bossy and assertive insisting on repeating the formation until they were all in step with one another and anyone who didn't toe the line was made to drink a forfeit. Eve, I've no idea where this person comes from. I've never been a party animal and certainly would never make a spectacle of myself, it must be something deeply buried inside me. When I became overbearing the ship's crew decided I should walk the plank but at that point I rushed to the loo and managed to get out of it. I don't know whether the shock of hitting the clear blue water would have sobered me up or finished me off. Before we left one of the more sober stewardesses had to tie my bikini top in a knot at the back to stop me removing it when everyone started shouting 'Off! Off! OFF!'

It's so unlike me! But at least I only had a hangover to contend with for my sins and not complete humiliation or a visit to the hospital; one of the stewards got back and dived into the hotel pool, hitting the bottom. He was sporting an egg the size of the dragon's on his forehead afterwards. He had a very prominent brow to start with, the bruise only made him look more like a Klingon from Star Trek. Note to self : restraint is a good thing. Oh, and

23

definitely a story to tone down for Matt (and my Mum).

With love, Suzi x

26th March -Home

Dear Eve

Matt's still a bit off with me and I didn't even mention the rum punches incident. Strange how I was so content with him before I started this job. He has such a good sense of humour and they say that a GSOH always wins the girls. It certainly worked on me. I rang him as soon as I got back to see if he was free and he made out he was busy when I know it is only meeting up with his football mates that he sees every week. Surely he could easily give them a miss? Jeez, they're almost conjoined anyway. They say women can't go to the toilet on their own on a night out but Matt and his mates remind me of concertina men made out of paper all holding hands in a row. One picks up his pint and it's a signal for the others to do the same.

'I have to make an appointment a week in advance just to see you,' I managed to get out of him in the end after 24 hours of asking him 'what's wrong?' This revelation popped out in the car on the way home after he had eventually agreed to go out; and that was to the cinema so he didn't have to talk to me. I had a massive urge to empty my unfinished popcorn bucket over his head but it would only have been a waste. What could I say? I'm trying to be understanding of his situation but it seems I'm moving on and he isn't. Maybe we can't keep going in this relationship? He loves his job and I admire him for that. But surely my job is important too? I wish he would show even just a little bit of interest in it. I know it's not easy for him with me popping in and out of his life but if we don't sort it out now, how will it work long term and make us both happy?

When Sam came home from work, she was pleased to see me. I know I went on a bit about Barbados, but it's all so exciting and when I showed her the photos on my camera she kept asking questions. We sat on the sofa with a big bag of pretzels. What a sweetie. I didn't mention how attractive one of the stewards was though. He can serve me rum punch any day. Feel better after my rant. Off over the Pond next to Seattle. Better take an umbrella – I've heard it rains a lot there.

With love, your best friend, Suzi x

1st April -LHR - Seattle (SEA) - Vancouver (YVR) - 184ft - hotel

Dear Eve

Such a long flight to Seattle. I didn't think I'd make it. I've got to get used to being on my feet all the time. Even in my break it's hard to switch off and sleep on a day sector. The rest-area on the plane usually smells gross anyway by the time everyone else on the crew has been and gone into the few bunks we're allocated. Hardly conducive to sleeping.

I decided to stay up as long as I could when we got into Seattle to adjust to the time change. When it was suggested we go up Space Needle for a meal, I jumped at the chance. It's a tower that revolves whilst you are eating, so by the time I had munched the recommended amount for perfect digestion, I had seen round the city without having to move from my seat.

I mooched around the market down by the quay on my own the next morning. As you would expect there were loads of stalls selling a vast array of fish but there were also some selling clothes. I found one with cute children's clothes; all miniature hoodies with slogans on them. Not something I should tell Matt about. It rained all day and although I didn't get completely drowned, my hair ended up looking like a bird's nest. Not at all attractive, nor cabin crew quality.

The next day we had to work a shuttle sector to Vancouver. Most of the passengers had already got off in Seattle so there was only a handful left. When the flight is like this it's a lot more relaxed. Carly, my partner had been flying for a couple of years so she had more idea what to do.

'Why don't you go up to first class and see if there's anything left over from the food round?' she suggested. 'I'll look after this lot.' She motioned towards the half a dozen passengers left in our sector who were contentedly plugged into the in-flight entertainment system.

So I made my way up the aisle and swept into First Class. The stewardess was in deep conversation in the galley with the Captain.

'Got any ideas what you want to do in Vancouver?' she broke off and turned to ask me.

'No idea at all?' I replied. 'It's my first time so everything's exciting.'

'Fancy an adventure?' the Captain asked.

Blimey, Eve. I didn't realise that the Gods mixed with the rest of us.

'Sure,' I replied as the stewardess offering me a canapé she had been arranging on a plate. 'What have you in mind?' I placed the brown mushy mixture in my mouth. It tasted like vomit and had the consistency to match. The Captain and stewardess were facing the other way as he was showing her a photo on his phone. I spat what ever it was out in my hand and quickly hid it behind my back.

'Victoria Island.' The Captain announced holding up his phone for me to see the picture as well. I leaned backwards and squeezed the half chewed soft canapé remains into a napkin I could feel behind me on the counter.

'Like another?' the stewardess asked holding up a whole plate of the dark poison.

'No thanks,' I replied. 'They were lovely, but ...' I hesitated. 'What were they?'

'Not sure,' she replied smiling. 'Something put on for one of the special diet passengers. I can't stand them.' I turned round and wiped the remains from my hand and put the tissue in the bin next to her.

'Need a drink now?' she continued laughing as she poured me a cup of water.

We were going to be in Vancouver for a few days. The next morning six of us got up early to catch the ferry to Victoria Island. Not a large P & O cross channel ferry with all mod cons that I'd been on that time when I was eleven over to France, but a smaller, tatty, just-bigger-than-a-tug-boat ferry. I love being new in this job. There's always someone else who knows what to do and is keen to show off. It means I can just tag along and this time we had the ultimate prize with us - the Captain.

Now I know I've been rather forthright in my view of Captains in previous letters Eve, but let me say that this one was a darling. Think of a granddad taking his family out...think of your granddad before he went deaf. Because we'd got up at the crack of dawn, once we were on board we had breakfast round a big table with the waiter attending to our every request. It took a few hours to get there but when we arrived on Victoria Island, Carly and I went exploring. We'd arranged to meet the others at lunchtime down by the quay. When we got there a small sea plane was parked alongside the jetty. The others were already in the restaurant so we sat down with them and after looking at the menu, ordered our meal. Groups of people were coming and going in and out of a small office beside us on the quayside.

'What do you think's going on in there?' I asked Carly. She put down the knife she was using to spread the butter on her bread and looked over to where I was pointing.

'Haven't a clue,' she replied.

I hadn't given a moment's thought to how we would get back to Vancouver but whilst we were deciding on desserts, the Captain got up and left the table. He disappeared into the office. A short while later he came out smiling and announced he'd bagged us a ride back to Seattle. I like to think their conversation went a bit like this:

'Hi, I'm a Captain. My 747's got four jet engines. I've left it parked back in Vancouver. We're in a bit of a fix- I've got the kids with me. I see you've got a small, two prop engine parked over there, not as big as mine of course, but, mind giving us a lift back?'

The contrast between the jumbo and the sea plane was incredible, Eve. The prop engines were so loud you had to shout to one another and hang on as it was a lot bumpier. Luckily my lunch had gone down otherwise I had the feeling I might be seeing it again more quickly than I'd want to. You could see all the colours of the water and watch the fish swimming silhouetted against the rocks just underneath the surface as we skimmed along. We eventually got back to the hotel the next morning at 6 am and I slept all day. Keen not to end our adventure we'd gone on to a concert and a club when we arrived back in Vancouver. It seemed rude not to tag along to that too.

Might change my opinion of hanging out with flight deck – there are advantages; I don't have to fancy or sleep with them but if I'm with the main man, that Jumbo's not going to leave for home without me.

Love, Suzi x

15th April - Home

Dear Eve

Matt seemed pleased to see me when I made it back to England. He gave me some flowers and took me out for a meal at my favourite restaurant. It's where the fish and chip shop used to be. Remember we used to pool our bus money and get a bag of chips on the way home from school? Extra salt for me and all swimming in ketchup to keep you happy. When the fish people left it became a Chinese takeaway but that didn't last long and since then it's been a brilliant Italian.

It was a pleasant evening, which means there wasn't any arguing, but he didn't ask me anything about my job. After I'd ordered my usual Four Seasons pizza with extra onions he chatted away telling me about events at work. Only once did I change the conversation to my recent trip to Vancouver but Matt quickly steered us away from that topic by telling me he was in line for a promotion. I'm really pleased for him that his career seems to be taking off. I took the hint and listened patiently and didn't mention my work again. If he doesn't want to acknowledge my new lifestyle then perhaps I shouldn't force it on him? But we will have to face it at some point. What I must face is do I want to be with him anymore? If the answer is no, I've got to tell him sooner rather than later. Just not sure how to do it without hurting him.

Had to leave this for a while before I could finish it.

Wow, feel as though I've been hit by a sledgehammer. I didn't realise Matt had it in him. After the flowers and meal date, I went round to see him the next day. He was behaving a bit strangely but I just ignored it. I just thought he might be tired. He often works long days with few breaks if they have a backlog of cars to fix. It all kicked off on the way back from seeing his sister who's just had a baby. I did feel a bit suspicious as to why he was so insistent we go round, but I let it ride. The baby was such a sweet little thing and so well-behaved, but his sister looked exhausted. She was worse than some I've seen on a long night sector, and I've seen a few rough sights I can tell you. I'm beginning to know what it is to work nights now and have your body clock all messed up, but at least mine isn't a life sentence. Anyway he told me in the car that he was thinking of buying his flat and wanted to know whether I would go in with him. Whoa... I hesitated as I was trying to think of a way to say 'no' nicely as he'd obviously been building up to this moment. My not-jumping-at-the-offer was enough for him though. The conversation went something like this...

'What is wrong with you? Don't you want to settle down and have a family?' *Voice raised.* I thought we were going somewhere, Suz... why've you changed?' *Long pause to really make me feel guilty.* 'It's that damn, stupid job. We were fine before you started it.' *Voice nearly at squeaking pitch and large vein on forehead beginning to gleam.*

'Were we?' Silly comment by me. Might as well have lit a touch paper. It turns out that settling down and having a family is all he's ever wanted. I'm the one and now it's my fault that I've messed it up. Arghh…

I don't like arguing it's so tiring. I could definitely do with some Evie advice right about now. We used to think it would all be so easy, this falling in love and settling down malarkey. It was in all those films we watched. After a few troubles the hero and heroine always made up and got together in the end. Maybe these are my 'troubled' times with Matt. It's just that I can't see myself walking off with him into the sunset in the end.

I know I'm running away but thank God I'm off again soon on another trip in that magic bird.

Love, Suzi x

19th April - Muscat, (MCT) 50ft - by the pool at the hotel

Evie

This is more like it. I was waiting for the glamour bit to kick in. I've been rostered on a trip to the Gulf and back. The hotel is amazing. The foyer leads into a central atrium. Plants cascade down, spilling over the balconies so that when you look up from the ground all the floors seem to blend into each other in a green haze. It's incredibly hot outside but the swimming pool was built so that some is under cover giving a slight relief from the heat. Beautiful gardens surround the hotel, all lush and green from the many staff continually watering them so I went exploring. I found a small gate along one side of the garden walls which opened onto a beach. It had the tiniest pink sea shells mixed in with the sand. It took me quite a while to pick up a small bagful.

I only packed enough clothes for one night which made Mandy in my galley laugh.

'You're obviously new, Suzi.' Mandy observed. 'To have such faith in scheduling. You'll soon learn never to leave home without a complete wardrobe for all climates. The Gulf is on the routes down East, we'll be lucky to get home without being turned around and sent to Australia.' I stared at her. My mouth must have been open in disbelief like a fish gulping air because she continued with her advice.

'Anything can happen. You may think this is a three day trip but we could get a call at any point turning it into three weeks. It only takes something to go wrong elsewhere and London will have to change our itinerary.'

I bonded quite nicely with the steward who was working in my galley. We found ourselves together holding the fort seated on a trolley in the galley on the flight out. Somehow it all spilt out. He was very sympathetic about my dilemma with Matt. I've been turning it round in my head for so long that it was good to get a male objective view on things. Matt's made me feel as though I am being totally self-centred. Anyway, Chris said he didn't think I was and has been very attentive. I was beginning to think I was invisible to men but from Chris's reaction it seems there might be hope for me after all.

It's when I have time waiting around at these hotels that I reflect on where my life's going. It's baking hot. Hotter than I am used to so I laid out by the hotel pool under the shade. I've tried to read but I can't concentrate. I keep thinking about Matt and what he said. I suppose I should look at it from his point of view too. He never knows when I'm around so how can he plan his social life either? Why couldn't I have just stayed in my old job? I was doing well at working my way up in the company. I started as an office junior after leaving school. By the time I left I was in charge of another member of staff and running the small office. The hours were easy and I'm sure they would have accommodated me if I wanted to go back part-time after having a baby. So you see Eve, it was all there waiting for me. It's that rebellious streak rearing its ugly head again. I don't like doing what's expected of me. When I saw the advert that the airline was recruiting, something made me send off the application form and see it through. I never expected anything to come of it but the fact that I sailed through the two interviews must surely mean that it was meant to be? You and I were always determined not to sink into a life of drudgery, Eve. We always said that we wanted to be pioneers, not just one of the crowd. Somehow without you reminding me I lost sight of that along the way.

I'm going to talk it all through with Matt when I get back. He's got to face up to the way our relationship is changing. If we're taking different paths then it's up to me to make the move before I end up making us both unhappy. Wish me luck.

Love, Suzi x

27th April - Home

Dear Eve

Argh … Stand-by. I hate it. You start off by being located only one and a half hours away from the airport. This means being in a hotel for 48 hours, suitcase packed with hot/cold/wet/dry clothes because you could be off to anywhere, for any amount of time. Then, if you make it through that without being summoned from on high, a bit like those stupid game shows where you have to get through the first challenge only to be given a harder one, you get … *Bing!*… yes, you lucky person… you get four hour Stand-by. At least I find that easier. You don't have to be on red alert, but can usually go home as long as you are near a phone and can easily get to the airport in time, booted and suited.

I'm not good at getting a call that means: '*skedaddle your arse over to the airport as a crew member has just gone sick and your plane has to leave in an hour otherwise the whole crew will go out of hours, the plane will be delayed whilst they get a fresh crew, the passengers will complain, we'll loose millions of pounds in revenue, blahdy, blahdy, blah.*'

I picture myself chasing the aircraft down the runway, flinging my suitcase to Indiana Jones, who is hanging out of the hold trying to grab my outstretched arms. Too much TV in the middle of the night down route, maybe?

The phone's ringing, it might be a call out - I'll have to finish this off later…

MCT - hotel - again

I got through the first one-and-a-half-hour standby period and was towards the end of the next four hour, just thinking scheduling must have forgotten me and whooping with joy when I got called out to go East. One minute I'm at home making a cup of tea, the next on my way to the airport to go to Muscat again. The first stop on a twenty day trip. Apparently scheduling decided after looking at my previous rosters that I hadn't been to Australia before so it was time I should go. One of the

crew was pissed off with me as her friend was on stand-
by too and they wanted to work together so had asked for
her to be called first. Not my fault. I only had time to
ring Matt and my mum and tell them I wouldn't be seeing
them for a while. He didn't sound pleased but at least he
didn't launch into a diatribe. It might do us good to have
a longer break. So déjà vu – Muscat, but this time it was
off to Singapore and beyond afterwards. Yippee.

My yippee was short lived when I got on board to see a
full flight. I didn't have time to think.

'I'd better go and sit at my door. We're just about to
take off,' Karen, the stewardess in my galley said just as
we were taxing to the runway. From initial impressions I
think I should be able to bond with her. She's fairly new
too and is keen to explore all the way to Australia and
back again. 'Would you put the milk away for me?'

I nodded, picking up the jug to pour more cold milk
into my tea so I could drink it down in time. The call light
above our heads suddenly flashed on. John James
McCullum, or JJ to his friends, six-feet two, blond, single
and definitely *not* gay walked into the galley.

'40B wants some water. I'll take it on my way down
to my seat. Have you checked the other side of the cabin,
Suzi?'

Christ! I'd been so busy getting settled, clearing up the
galley and making a cuppa I'd completely forgotten to
check that the bloody passengers were strapped in for
take-off.

'Shit no. I'll do it now.' I thrust the milk jug onto the
shelf in the full fridge, just managing to close the door
and rushed out into the cabin.

The engines roared. I just got everything done, sat
down and strapped myself in before I felt the rush of
power and the aircraft race along the runway. I looked

35

over towards the galley. The latch on the fridge door strained as the front of the plane lifted. Suddenly the door burst open as we climbed. I, along with several of the passengers seated around the doorway, watched as the milk jug wobbled. It slid forward towards the edge. I grimaced. There was nothing I could do. To undo my harness now would be dangerous. They had impressed on us in training that take-off and landing were the most likely times for emergencies to happen. Then, as though something had given it a final push from behind, like children playing about at the edge of a swimming pool, the jug overbalanced and landed upside down on the cabin floor spewing out its contents; the creamy, white liquid leaving a meandering trail up the aisle. The man in front of me started to clap. Soon more passengers started giving me a round of applause as they noticed what had happened. I gracefully took a half bow in my seat and waited until the Captain released the crew and I could mop up my mistake as best as I could.

The rest of the flight passed in a case of '*chicken or beef, sir? More tea, coffee? Yes, just one moment and I will get it for you,*' for the whole bloody time it took to get there. I'm the only one feeling plucked onto this trip. The rest have had it rostered for ages so are looking forward to it. Certainly my recent taste for brown milk helps to mellow me into the party mood. (Never particularly liked Tia Maria and milk before but I'm finding it a good mixture to stomach even in the early hours of the morning when my body clock's all over the place). Everyone on the crew has his or her own special tipple. My lips are sealed though about where we get our supplies. (Haven't mentioned that to Matt - another change he'll use as ammunition. Hell, he's not my keeper).

Still in Muscat but now the next day. The phone rang before I could finish off before. It was Karen saying they were going out.

Eve, I think you should know, I am now officially worth two camels. Whilst sitting minding my own business waiting for JJ and the others in the foyer of the hotel at Muscat, a man came up and sat opposite me, legs spread wide apart. I was going to the beach but had dressed appropriately for the journey in long top and linen trousers so barely had any flesh showing, but the sight of a single, western woman was obviously too much for him. Placing his hand in his white robe pocket and jiggling, I don't know nor care to think what, he propositioned me.

'How much?'

Naturally I ignored him (really, I couldn't believe my ears, the audacity of the man). Ten o'clock in the morning is a bit early to ply your wares surely? Or maybe not, not being in the prostitute business, I can't say what time it usually all starts kicking off. Anyway, obviously not one to be put off, he said it again, a bit louder.

'How much?'

What is a girl supposed to do? I tried ignoring him again but his eyes were boring holes in my body. I reckoned I had two choices. Stand and face him, causing a fuss that could escalate and get me locked up, especially if he turned out to be someone of influence, or go back to my room and hope he didn't take it as a signal that I was keen for business.

Luckily for me JJ and the others appeared and I rushed into his arms making a great show that he was my boyfriend, whispering 'get me out of here' as I explained all. Naturally, the others on the crew used this as a fine opportunity to conclude that I shouldn't give up the day job as I would only have been worth two, possibly two and a half camels at a push anyway.

Matt texted me to say he's got something he wants to ask me. I haven't given him a single thought since leaving England. How mean is that? I'm supposed to be in love with this man. Surely I should be missing him a bit more? JJ asked me if I had a boyfriend, so I told him about Matt. It doesn't seem to make any difference. When I rushed up to him in the hotel foyer after the propositioning incident he kept his arm round me all the way to the taxi and didn't move from my side all day. Hmmm… I must admit he does look good in shorts. Everything looks well toned right down to his toes.

At the beach it was suggested that we have a go at water skiing. Well Eve, I may not be able to water ski but I've perfected the art of giving myself a sea water enema. JJ and the others showed me how to water ski, even some smart arses mono-skied, but I showed them. I showed 'em…one cheek, two cheeks or even one cheek and a boob on display. I could do it all, any combo they fancied. I'd worn my pink all-in-one swimsuit especially to retain a little dignity and hold everything in place but unfortunately had left the necessary skills behind. There's only so much humiliation a girl can take in one go. JJ had arranged for the speedboat to have the beginner's static pole sticking out of the side so that I could start off slowly trying to get out of the water with the instructor at my side on the deck yelling orders at me.

'Now slowly does it, Suzi. As the speed picks up when you're ready, try and straighten your legs and stand up.'

Stand up! It took more than a few goes to make it past the crouched toilet position. I always thought I was quite co-ordinated and sporty. Remember how I used to beat you at netball Eve, when we were in the school team?

Even when I'd mastered the right amount of leg pressure to get up from the crouching to standing, it was another thing to progress to doing it at the end of the rope. Each time the boat slowly moved forward I ended up torpedoing forward and being dragged along, face down like a fish on the end of a line. After hours of being flung about like an octopus, orifices filled to the brim, I decided to give up and admit defeat. I know I shall have the piss taken out of me for the rest of the trip but at least I know I've had a good wash - inside and out.

Love, Suzi x

2nd May - Singapore, (SIN) 65ft - hotel

Dear Eve

I do love the little old ladies that we get on the flights. They sit in their seats and treat the 24 hours down to Australia as though it's a bus journey. The one on the Singapore sector hadn't even undone her coat by the time I found her in my section. She was visiting her sister for the first time in years and hadn't realised that she could get up and move around if she needed to as she '*didn't want to be any trouble and get in your way when you're so busy, dear.*' Everything I did for her was so appreciated. I walked her around the plane and made her get comfortable, kept her drinking loads of water and showed her how to work all the gadgets in her seat. Hats off to her for going all that way in the first place.

You would love it here, Eve. Singapore is amazing. I knew it was something different the minute I stepped out of the airport. The heat and smell hits you; a mixture of a Chinese restaurant kitchen turned up to boiling point with a tape of musak sounding like crickets running permanently in the background. I thought Muscat was good but this hotel is incredible, even down to the plush carpets in the lifts; green with the crest of the hotel embroidered in the centre. Note to self: learn to shut mouth and stop going 'whoa' when I see something interesting.

There's no rest with this crew. The four of us changed out of our uniforms and went straight out after we'd checked in. JJ and Karl (a steward from First Class) were keen to show Karen and me around. I nearly tripped over my mouth it was open so much. We had made our way to a popular tourist street and found a bar with tables outside. The pedestrian way was thronging with all nationalities as people pushed their way past street sellers and market stalls. JJ and Karl sat down at one of the tables pulling out chairs for Karen and me. A beautiful woman walked past and I gasped at her as she disappeared along an alley way.

'Lovely isn't she?' JJ commented.

'Yes,' I answered as another equally beautiful woman sashayed past.

'You know they're men don't you?'

I stared at him.

'Lady-boys,' he stated triumphantly. 'Haven't you heard of them?' I shook my head and stared at another woman as she walked past. No way was she a man. She was just too beautiful. I tried to see if there were any giveaway signs. Nope! Nothing I could see. She had boobs in the right place, a small waist and endlessly long legs with nothing that looked out of place in between.

'Look more closely,' JJ instructed as he called to a woman who had been chatting to the owner of the stall opposite.

Karl leaned forward and whispered in my ear. 'Look at

their Adam's apples and hands.'

The woman JJ had beckoned came over. I stared at her trying not to make it too obvious as she sat down. She perched daintily; her arm slung casually around his shoulders and raised a perfectly plucked eyebrow at me. I realised she'd caught me staring at her throat and quickly looked away. JJ ordered some drinks for us all and I proceeded to steal surreptitious looks at her whenever I thought she was preoccupied. She was so meticulously turned out with nails long, beautifully shaped and polished. I quickly looked at my hand with its broken nails from trying to get the trolley into its stowage before landing and hid it under my legs. I looked at her again. Thin kohl lines that swept gracefully into a point at the corner of each eye stared out at me within exquisitely applied make up. I rubbed my eye as a droplet of sweat crept down from my forehead leaving a smear of mascara on my hand. How did they manage to turn out so stunningly dressed in forty degree heat? I lifted an arm and watched as a ring of perspiration that had started to stain my T-Shirt in a circle under my armpit. I could do with taking a few grooming lessons. They looked better than a lot of women I know. It was just a shame about the Adam's apple and large hands. I could see what Karl meant, they were hard to disguise even with a seductively draped scarf. Like a child spying on grown ups necking in the park I tried to look away as JJ encouraged her to stay with us while winking at me behind her back.

'What you looking at?' the woman barked at me. I replayed the sound in my head. Was it low like a man or higher pitched like a woman? I went on a charm defensive.

'Your nails are beautiful,' I replied meekly.

It was obviously the right answer as all her aggression dispelled and she immediately turned away, ignoring me and carried on smiling and chatting to JJ and Karl. I turned my attention to the rest of the street.

The whole place was a feast for the senses. Everywhere I looked there were fake CD's, sunglasses, bags, watches. It was buzzing; people bartering, stalls laden with goods, a real wonderland. I felt so naive. There's this whole other world out there with cultures, customs and lives so different to mine. It doesn't matter that I've seen it on TV and movies, there's no substitute for being there and feeling a place.

We finished our drinks, got up from our seats and started looking at the stalls. JJ gently but firmly excused himself from the company of his new friend then wandered over and stopped beside a man crouched down frying something that looked like noodles in a wok over a high flame. It was a while since we had eaten and my stomach had been rumbling. JJ motioned for the man to sell us a portion.

'What is it?' I asked coming alongside and staring at the mixture being tossed regularly in the air. Strips of something that looked like red and green peppers and noodles all cooking in a brown sauce, continued to sizzle in the pan.

'Try it and see,' JJ winked at me taking the small container the man had filled and held out to him. He speared a forkful and put it in his mouth.

'Delicious.'

'JJ don't be annoying. What is it?' Karen reiterated.

'Well, it can't be anything too bad,' I interjected. 'He's nearly finished it.' I grabbed the fork from his hand and put it into the remaining mixture, twirling the strings of noodles round to secure them. Putting the forkful in my mouth I started chewing. 'Hmmm. Bit chickeny but more chewy.' I swallowed most of it down. 'Not bad,' I reached for another forkful and put it straight in my mouth. 'What is it anyway JJ?'

'Snake.' JJ answered. 'Delicious isn't it?'

It wasn't the fact that this mouthful suddenly tasted bitter Eve, more the thought of that slippery, slimy creature being rolled around my teeth that made me spit out the half chewed contents of my mouth right beside JJ's flip-flops.

'Eewwwwww…' Karen squealed. With a toothless grin the food seller shook his head and laughed as JJ paid him.

We're making quite a team the four of us. The boys knew of this amazing shopping mall. I was looking for a dress to wear to my friend Katie's wedding. She hasn't replaced you as my best friend, she's more the inherited kind from Matt. She and Ashley are getting married shortly after I get home from this trip. She had asked me to be a bridesmaid as Matt is best man, but I declined as I wasn't sure I would be able to make it. It was also a bit too cosy for my liking. I didn't want Matt to get anymore ideas about us getting married soon and the whole bridesmaid thing could kick it off.

So we wandered around this department store with JJ picking out a few dress suggestions for me. The three of them then sat around patiently whilst I tried them on. When I came out of the changing room with a tight fitting black and white number on JJ's eyes lit up. I walked back to the changing rooms and caught the look he gave to the other two in the reflection in the mirror. He'd put both thumbs up and was almost panting with his tongue out. Must admit my heart skipped a beat. It's a long time since I'd caused that reaction in anyone. I know I shouldn't be so excited at the thought. Oh dear.

Love Suzi x

9th May - Adelaide, (ADL) 160ft - hotel

Dear Eve

People never cease to amaze me. It was dark outside and I was patrolling the aisle of the plane on the flight when a passenger stopped me.

'Are we turning right?' he asked.

'I'm not sure sir. I'd have to check the navigation system on board. Why do you ask?' I replied.

'Oh, I was just looking out of the right hand window and I saw the yellow light flashing on the wing.' I just smiled Eve, and explained that we always had our navigation lights on in the dark, a bit like a car's headlights. Satisfied and not at all embarrassed at asking such a daft question he just nodded and turned round to walk back to his seat.

We're staying in a lovely hotel in Adelaide, all pink and grey décor. This place reminds me of the Witterings in Sussex. We used to go there for holidays every year when I was a kid. You came down once with your family for the day. My grandfather used to trail my sister and I behind him laden with fishing nets, buckets and spades, along the beach to the shops to get an ice cream.

There are loads of bungalows here. Looks like it's Grannysville. Pretty though. The trouble with this job is that I only ever get a snap shot of a place before I'm whisked away again to the next stop. It's hard to make a proper impression of a city based on that and I probably get it entirely wrong.

We've only got a short stop here. The four of us went out drinking again. This is most unlike me but I'm beginning to realise it is part of the flying lifestyle. Matt said that I'd changed. After his comment about the makeup, he'll no doubt have an opinion about the drinking as well, if I tell him. I don't mind about the makeup. The aircraft lights make you look so washed out in the middle of the night. The last thing a passenger wants is to be served by someone looking like the living dead when that's probably how they're feeling anyway. As for the drinking, I can't go to a room party or bar and sit with lemonade each time. So what if I'm changing, who says it isn't for the better? Everything within reason. I want to make sure I get as much as possible out of this experience.

Talking about getting as much as possible, JJ manoeuvred it so that he and I ended up trailing behind the other two on the way back to the hotel. Karen and Karl seem to be getting on just fine and didn't notice anyway. She told me she fancied Karl and was quite happy to see where things went. I on the other hand, fancy JJ, but unlike lucky Karen can't afford to just see what happens. I haven't told Matt that I'm thinking of breaking up with him yet. I can't start something with someone else before I do. So when JJ took my hand, twirled me around and drew me so close that I could just catch the sweet aroma of beer on his breath as he embraced me, I gently pushed him away. He was pressed up against me so firmly I was under no illusions as to his intentions.

I will not feel guilty. Nothing happened. Not that I didn't want it to but I like to know my men for more than a few days before I jump into bed with them. It's difficult to think of Matt in England when I'm away and everything is so exciting but I have my boyfriend and must sort things out with him first.

Love Suzi x

Perth, (PER) Australia

Dear Eve

We passengered over to Perth. I didn't realise but sometimes crews have to fly as passengers on other airlines over to cities or countries to pick up their next sector on their roster. The scheduling department in London can see the whole picture, like a huge jigsaw. They can manoeuvre us around the world so that each crew slots into place to make the whole operation run smoothly. Little old me has to do as I'm told even if it doesn't seem to make logical sense. So although I'm officially working, I'm in fact just flying to my next destination as a punter. Usually when other airline crews know they've got fellow cabin staff on board they give them a bit of extra special service. No, not anything wild or illegal just extra drinks, food and giveaways. I ended up stuffing a load of champagne into my bag along with some miniatures. I drew the line at the remains of my afternoon tea like some of the others, however delicious it looked on its crisp white table linen.

JJ has friends in Perth so when we arrived the four of us were invited to their house. It changes the whole perspective of a place when you meet someone who lives there and they can show you around or tell you a bit about their lives. I really liked Perth but would it still be as good if I wasn't having such a good time with good company? I'm not sure. We all ended up in a club until very late, or early, depending on how you look at it. Everyone looked so young, or maybe it was just me feeling very old. We have to work down to New Zealand next.

Love, Suzi x

15th May - Auckland (AKL) - 1,000ft

Dear Eve

I'm on the other side of the world. New Zealand! Weird time change and the night sky doesn't look right. I don't know the names of many constellations back home but looking up at the Southern Hemisphere's dark sky and not recognising the Great Bear or Orion's Belt only goes to make England seem so much further away. We had four days off before we had to report for duty again so JJ suggested that we go skiing. He managed to persuade a sister hotel on South Island to the one here on North Island to swap our rooms so we caught a flight there. Karen and I dashed out to the shops to see if we could find anything suitable to wear.

'There. This will do,' Karen said holding up a fluorescent orange pair of ski trousers we'd found in a small store.

'Only if you want to frighten the Yeti,' I concluded putting them back on the rail.

'We may be on the other side of the world,' Karen replied indignantly. 'But even I know the Yeti is in the Himalayas not New Zealand.'

We eventually settled on a cheap pair of waterproof trousers each concluding that we would wear layers of tights, trousers and jumpers underneath to keep ourselves warm rather that splash out as there was nothing we liked. After that we had to find a launderette. What the hell am I doing washing my thongs in Auckland? Mad. Mad. Mad.

We all got up early and caught a flight over to South Island. The boys took charge and hired a car. This time I did offer to drive, although my offer was rejected. At least I felt I could cope with familiar road signs and driving on the left. Unfortunately Mount Hutt, our skiing destination was closed due to the high risk of avalanche so the boys took us on a tour of the countryside instead stopping at a great pub where we played pool. The whole time difference caught up with me. I tried to keep going but ended going to bed at 6pm, like a toddler and slept round until 7am. Unbelievable! What's that all about? The weather was so atrocious the next day there was no skiing so we caught a flight back to Auckland. I've started to get a cold and my left ear really hurt on descent.

Love, Suzi x

Sydney airport (SYD) - waiting for ground staff

Oh Eve

MYGOD! The pain in my left ear is excruciating. We'd taken off from Auckland and I was supposed to work a two-sector flight to Perth via Sydney. As we approached the descent into Sydney I was nearly on my knees with pain.

'Here put these over your ears,' Karen said handing me white plastic cups stuffed with pads of hot, wet, cotton wool at the bottom.

'Why?' I asked doing as I was told.

'The vapour and heat collecting in the cups are supposed to help relieve the pressure in your ears.'

'I look ridiculous.'

'Well, you do look like you're trying to communicate with someone on a boy scout's telephone,' JJ laughed as he came into the galley. 'It's an old wife's tale. It does nothing, just gives everyone else a laugh.'

'It's soothing,' I remonstrated pushing him out into the cabin. 'At least Karen cares enough to...'

'...make you look silly,' he laughed as he disappeared up the aisle.

I raided the first aid kits on the plane to see if there was anything in there that could help but could find nothing to ease the pain. I decided I couldn't take another ascent and descent in my current state, worried I might burst an eardrum. I couldn't pop my ears and wanted to hit anyone that came near me, the pain was so bad. Not ideal customer relations. So the senior crew member decided I was a liability and arranged to off-load me in Sydney. They would have to fly one crew member down to Perth. I was so looking forward to the weekend there. JJ's friends are having a party and we're all invited.

I felt terrible having to say goodbye to the crew and walk off that plane. They'd become my surrogate family and I felt all alone as I waited for them to rescue my bag out of the hold. It didn't take long; the crews' bags are usually placed up at the front of the plane so it wasn't as though they had to rummage through 400 odd bags to get mine. Saying goodbye to JJ was dismal. I told myself I was being pathetic and to man-up, but it wasn't much help. I'm waiting for the Duty Officer to take me through the airport. I want to cry. This is all my fault. I'm being paid back for my ungirlfriend-like behaviour. I bet Matt has a doll of me and is sticking pins in it.

I feel like shit and am alone in Sydney and I don't know how long for.

Love Suzi x

Dear Eve

'I know you're in there.'

'I know you're in there.' There was banging on the door but this time louder. Vaguely I came to, looked around another hotel room and tried to work out where I was. Everything was dark.

'Open up! Let me in,' came the demand from outside the door.

My ear was aching. I remembered that I was in a hotel room in Sydney. Quickly I got out of bed and looked at my watch. 1. 45 a.m. What the hell was going on and who was that outside my door? I rushed over to have a look through the spy hole. A suited man of about thirty was standing outside.

'Let me in!' he demanded again. I reached for the door handle, and then some self preservation clicked in. I stood away from the door and took a deep breath. What the hell was I doing? I was off-loaded here and the Duty Officer sorted me out with a room. It's not the usual crew hotel which was full, so he's hoping to move me tomorrow. Nobody knows I'm here in Sydney except my crew who have flown on to Perth without me.

I went over to the bedside table and rang down to reception.

'Can I help you?' the calm voice enquired.

'Yes, I have strange man banging on my door demanding to be let in. I'm alone here in Sydney and know no one. Please can you send security up to deal with it?' I was amazed at my self control.

'Are you sure you don't know him?'

'Certain. Can you please hurry as he's making a lot of noise?'

'Of course, I'll send someone up straight way.'

I went back to the door and put my eye up close to the spy hole. The man was leaning against the door frame. Suddenly an eyeball came into my view – like Sauron's all-seeing eye on the top of the tower in Mordor from Lord of the Rings. I jumped backwards, nearly knocking into a chair.

'I know you're in there,' he repeated. 'I can hear you.'

'Go away!'

'Let me in darlin'.' He slurred banging on the door again.

'I'm not your darling and I'm not letting you in,' I said emphatically. 'You're drunk. Go away!'

'Oh don't be like that, darlin'. I've only had a couple of beers with the boys.'

'I told you,' I repeated. My voice growing louder with each sentence. 'I'm not your darling. I don't know you. And I don't care how many beers you've had.'

'Just let me in and I'll make it up to you.'

'I'm not letting you in.'

'Awww… not even if I do your favourite thing?'

I smiled. 'Not even if you do that,' I concluded.

I looked through the spy glass cautiously. He was now standing propped up against the opposite wall, the beer bottle hanging loosely in his hand by his side. Even if he knew what my favourite thing was, he was incapable of delivering it.

The phone beside my bed rang.

'Excuse me madam,' the hotel security man asked. 'This man outside your room says that you're his girlfriend.'

I looked again. The man hadn't changed nor had my recognition of him. He was now accompanied by a man in uniform with *Security* written on the jacket pocket.

'I can assure you, I've never seen this man before in my life. I've just arrived in Sydney this evening and know only one person, the Duty Officer at the airport. I will not be letting this man into my room so please deal with him.

I still don't know why my suited 'boyfriend' picked on my room to hammer down the door. Who knows what would have happened if I had let him in? Would he have done my favourite thing? I'll never know. Thankful that I seemed to have escaped unscathed, I replaced the security chain across the door lock and went back to sleep.

The next morning I rang JJ in Perth but it only made me feel worse. He was having a fantastic time with the rest of the crew and I was stuck in Sydney, with one totally blocked ear, the other partially blocked and all on my own. I went down to the hotel reception and complained about the lunatic last night banging on my door. They knew nothing about it, typical; the night staff hadn't mentioned it. I could have been attacked or worse if I'd opened the door and no one would have cared. I feel a bit sorry for myself, Eve. It is weird being stuck in Sydney; a bit like being abandoned. I wish you were here with me.

When you go into the briefing room at the beginning of a trip you are faced with unknown faces. It's a bit like the first day at a new school except that if you don't like anybody you won't be going back to the safety of home at the end of the day. The success of the trip often relies on whether you can find anyone in that room to bond with. The company is so big it's rare to meet a friend in there unless you've requested the trip together. So each time I have to find someone amongst the crew that I can get on with otherwise I'm Johnny-no-mates. It gives speed dating a whole new meaning. So finding JJ, Karen and Karl to hang around with was magic. It's easier for male stewards; they can go out for a drink at night in any city in the world but for us girls, it's hard sometimes not to feel vulnerable on your own.

The Duty Officer came and moved me to the usual crew hotel. He started hitting on me which was a bit weird, saying that he could show me Sydney if I wanted. When I met him he told me he was married. He must think air stewardesses are easy game. Wouldn't mind if he was tall, dark and handsome but he's shorter than me and a bit paunchy –hard to resist I know, but hey...

I'm damn well going to make the best of it here. Operations in London want to know when I'll be fit to work again so that they can make me join another crew. Can't have me wasting their money on the other side of the world. I have to make a trip to Kings Cross to see the crew doctor. Probably not the first place that I would have chosen to visit whilst in Sydney but there you go.

I asked the front desk to let the incoming crews know that I was stuck in the hotel on my own, in case anyone I knew turned up. Not likely seeing as I haven't been flying very long but, you never know. In the meantime, I'm getting out there. I went to the Opera House. It's amazing, what vision the architect had to create a building so beautiful. Afterwards I strolled around the Botanical gardens which were vast and clearly very popular. Then I caught a hydrofoil over to Manly where there's a pretty beach, just great for people watching. Thought I'd take the harbour trip another time. I hung around too long though and only just had time to do a quick bit of retail therapy by buying some cute shoes before I had to come back. I haven't had much money before so it was fun to think 'what the hell.' I wish I could stretch to some Jimmy Choo's but maybe that will be for another day. I'm not really that into labels, but I do love shoes. They always cheer me up and it's true - they never make you look fat.

London's nagging and wants me fit and well in a day so I can join another crew. I rang Matt to tell him my problem. The way it's going I won't make it back in time to go to Katie's wedding. He'll have to go on his own. He wasn't very pleased but managed to sound sympathetic. I appreciate it's not nice going on his own but I can't help being ill. So I rang JJ and got a much better reaction. The crew are just leaving to go on to Mumbai, the next sector on their way home. Of course, he was missing me (he would say that though, wouldn't he?).

When I got back from one of my morning escapades I walked into the hotel lobby at the same time as a new crew was checking in. I recognised one of the girls from my training course but she completely blanked me. Goodness knows what I did to her? Anyway there was a message for me from another crew member I didn't know, asking if I wanted to go out to dinner that night with him and his mate. It restored my faith in human kindness. I thought I'd take him up on his offer. It would be nice to sample Sydney at night at least once while I'm here.

Love, Suzi x

25th May - Still SYD - hotel

Oh Eve

I've never been so bored in my life. Imagine the scene. A smart restaurant in Sydney, a couple of 'best friends' and me. They had requested the trip together and clearly didn't need anyone else. Okay, I know it was very sweet of them to take pity on me and I did my best to appear grateful but quite frankly, and it sounds so mean, but I'd had more fun in my room inspecting my navel.

I learnt all about their life together back in England, how they love their Alsatian, 'Chloe' and have been lucky enough to have a close circle of friends. Mind you, I did notice that Derek clocked another guy sitting at a table behind Keith a lot. So maybe the sun isn't shining quite so hard out of Keith's behind as he likes to think. The last straw was when one of those photographers came round the restaurant trying to tout for business. My new best friends insisted that we all had a picture taken and then gave it to me.

I decided to plead with London to let me go home. I've been in Sydney a week. I must be costing them a fortune for my hotel room and expenses and me doing nothing. It would make sense for them to get me home. I missed their deadline to join the other crew and my ear is still blocked. I'm no use to anyone. If I could just get home without bursting my eardrum I could sit it out. I spoke to Matt again. He says he'd done a lot of thinking too whilst I've been away. Maybe he's going to give me the push and make it easier for me. I do hope so. If he called it a day I wouldn't feel so guilty.

Although JJ is really nice, he's only a bit of fun. I'd realised that there were plenty more fish in the sea. No way am I ready to settle down with anyone just yet. Karen confided that she and Karl got it together whilst in Perth and she is supposed to be engaged back home. I'm too nice. Other people don't seem to have trouble manipulating a few boyfriends at a time; perhaps I need to wise up and give it a go.

I can go home! The Duty Officer rang. As soon as I get the okay from the doctor, London say I can passenger home. They've obviously had enough of my whinging and wanted to get shot of me. As long as I don't claim overtime.

Love Suzi x

28th May - Home

Dear Eve

So that was it, back to the doctors I went and a general fluttering of eyelids and blowing of nose commenced. If I could get the all clear from him, the next flight to Heathrow would get me back not only in time for Katie's wedding but I would pick up my original crew for the last sector. Although my ear was still blocked, if I blew a lot I could just about get it to pop eventually. Hopefully that would be enough.

I got the required piece of paper to say I was fit enough to travel, but not work, home. I packed ready for the evening flight and the Duty Officer whipped me straight through the official channels of the airport, still saying he would have shown me Sydney *and* the Blue

Mountains. Yeah right, his wife must have been visiting her mother's. But the bonus was that I got a seat in business class for the journey home. Thank God for painkillers. The doctor gave me such mega ones they knocked me out and I slept for the first two sectors, through Sydney to Dubai.

I picked up my crew on the last part of the journey into London. JJ seemed pleased to see me and told me to call. How much he meant it though is another matter. I've learnt enough about crews, Eve, to realise that once you leave Heathrow on a trip, anything can happen. It's a bit like a time machine. You get into the metal tube and you're transported to another world where all the normal rules can be broken, but once you touch down in England, everyone slips back into their real life and it's basically hush, hush. I'm not bothered; JJ was just the catalyst to make me see the light.

I've had plenty of thinking time recently and I've decided that as I'm back in time I will go with Matt to Katie's wedding and not rock the boat. I'll just have to make sure we're not left alone. We won't be able to have an in depth discussion there. There'll be so many things going on I will be able to put off the inevitable for a bit longer. Yes, I know I'm being a coward but I wish you could look me straight in the eye, Eve, and tell me you wouldn't put off something like this too. I could have just sent Matt a text telling him it was over. At least I'm facing up to things; I'm just waiting for the right moment.

Love Suzi x

5th June - Home - day after the wedding

Dear Eve

Why do they do it to you? It was all going so well. The wedding was a dream. Katie looked so beautiful, all glowing and happy. She'd asked me to do a reading during the ceremony. I read from Captain Corelli's Mandolin by Louis de Bernieres – one of my favourite books. The bit where the Dr Iannis is telling his daughter, Pelagia the true meaning of love. I just adore the image of love's roots entwining and growing together underground until they are one tree not two. Okay, call me a romantic, a sentimental fool, but I had to work it to make sure I only looked at Katie and Ash. One glimpse at Matt and I'd have gone red from guilt and everyone else would think it's because of my love for him. Blimey, I only kissed JJ once. Well, pretty much just a kiss anyway. There might have been a bit of lustful groping but it was all above board. There were four of us on that bed anyway. (Did I forget to mention the waterbed Karl had in his hotel room in Oz? Such fun, I thought they'd all been punctured in the sixties. Anyway by the time the bouncing had stopped...I could go into more detail but a lady doesn't kiss and tell).

I got through my poem. There were a few nodding heads and I was on the home straight, congratulating myself on a master class when Matt manoeuvred me outside onto the lawn in the moonlight after the ceremony. He got down on one knee and only bloody proposed! Dark blue velvet box with sparkler sitting daintily inside it. A solitaire as well. The Full Monty. Worse still, our friends on the terrace having a smoke saw what he was up too and cheered. Arrrrrrgh... what was I supposed to do? I felt completely trapped by the short and curlies. Everyone was cheering and clapping... and waiting. I could feel a cold sweat on the back of my neck and started breathing heavily.

I hadn't had a chance to speak to him on his own since coming back from Australia. I never expected him to do anything like this. This is Matt we're talking about. Safe, predictable Matt who takes years to make a decision about whether to change his hairstyle (and quite frankly there's not a lot of change you can make to curly brown locks except a No.1 all over). How long had he been cooking this one up? I've only been in the new job a few months.

All these thoughts flashed through my mind as he waited expectantly for my reply, one knee getting a damp mark from the grass on his wedding suit. Suddenly I remembered Jane Austen. Remember we were always the wierdos who loved her at school, although we didn't quite understand the language? All that repressed emotion and swooning and having to be revived by smelling salts. I thought it was the only way I could get myself out of this and save face for both Matt and me. You'd have been proud of me Eve. Might be a little old fashioned but worth a try as nothing else was pinging into my head to save me.

So I pretended I'd had too much to drink and swooned. Gracefully of course, as I didn't want to hurt myself on the way down, and it was only a slight stagger, not a full on faint and collapsed in a heap on the grass at his feet.

But, Eve, it worked! The attention was taken from my answer to my health. Matt heroically leapt forward to steady me. I insisted that I needed to go home, quoting my recent ear infection, jet lag and the excitement of the day as reasons. God, I felt shallow. Matt seemed to forget he'd ever asked me. The pace picked up. There was all hustle and bustle from various friends and it was decided that someone else should give me a lift home as Matt didn't want to leave. I, of course, continued in role and remained 'fragile' (I wasn't Rosalind in the school production of 'As You Like It' for nothing). I know it was only delaying tactics but I needed to speak to him on his own.

I've been keeping my head down since. It was late when I got back from the wedding but Sam was still up. She could see something was wrong so I ended up spilling it all out to her over a glass or two of Merlot. Well, a whole bottle in the end and that was just me. I didn't realise how I'd been storing it all up. Once I got it off my chest and took a long hard look at the whole situation, I could see that my relationship with Matt was futile. I was just clinging onto it for old time's sake. Sam's a good listener and she made me feel that I wasn't being the bitch I felt, but true to myself. She also told me to man-up and deal with it by telling Matt once and for all and stop delaying. That was a bit harder to take. I don't like being told what to do, especially when I know she is right, but I took it on the chin.

The next afternoon Matt rang to ask how I was feeling. See, he is caring, kind and a nice boyfriend. Why isn't that enough for me? Anyway I tried to arrange a time to meet him in the week. Because I went sick in Australia my rosters have all been cancelled and I've been put on the dreaded 'stand-by' until scheduling can slot me back into the system. I've only got a couple of days left before I go back to work. Matt, however, couldn't fit me into his very busy diary and then it unexpectedly kicked off. I had a grilling, Eve, or more like a shouting-down-the-telephone-at-me kind of conversation. Oh my god! I imagined he was going to burst that prominent vein on his forehead gushing blood and brains all over his carpet. I've never heard him so riled. He says it's all my fault and I am still the selfish one who doesn't care about him… hmmmm. I did say I thought we ought to take a break from each other but I'm not sure he registered it, he was so wound up.

I will not be dictated to, nor bullied into making a life long commitment that I'm not ready for yet. If he doesn't want to live a little before he turns into pipe and slippers man then so be it. His little performance has only made me more determined to move on.

Love (a relieved) Suzi x

10th June - Home

Dear Eve

Anyway, life goes on. Two days later I was called out on stand-by to do fire watch. This was a new one on me. I couldn't remember seeing it on any page in the training manual. The upshot was that an empty plane was stuck in Manchester. They had already dealt with the passengers and transferred them to another flight. So sandwiched in the back seat of a car, in between the Captain and First Officer, (bloody hell, think grumpy old man and his son for 5 hours!), we were driven up to Manchester so that we could fly the big bird back to Heathrow.

My role was vital. I had to parade around the cabin looking out for any problems, oh and serve the 'Gods' refreshments don't forget, they can't be expected to make their own doily-encased sandwich.

The Flight Deck, although hugely talented, don't have eyes in the back of their heads and while pressing all those switches and dials on the panels to fly the beast (and yes, I can confirm they do know what each switch does, in answer to a previous, curious passenger) they wouldn't know if the toilets at the back had gone up in a puff of smoke if I didn't yell to tell them. Weird wasn't the word. No one but me and the roar of the engines and the whole of an empty 747. No babies crying, punters demanding drinks nor lecherous business men trying to 'accidentally' touch my bum. I had to sit down at the very back for take off, but as soon as I was released out of my seat I skipped along the aisles singing at the top of my voice and yelled at all the non existent punters to get their own bloody drinks as I rested my feet in first class. Adventurous, aren't I?

I tell you what though, anyone would have thought we'd come from Hong Kong by the time we landed, it took so long circling around Heathrow waiting our turn. Full planes or empty planes, air traffic control rule the skies.

Love Suzi x

16th June - Barbados (BGI) - 200ft - hotel

Dear Eve

There is a God up there! After that enlightening trip down from Manchester with two pilots all to myself (I know you're thinking lucky, lucky girl) I opened my new roster to read I'd been scheduled a Barbados trip. How good is that? I didn't reply to any of Matt's texts or phone calls on my days off but went and visited my parents instead. From what friends tell me Matt's still got smoke steaming from every orifice after our last conversation. I need him to calm down a bit. Anyway, Mum hasn't got any phone signal at her house, nor has dad although he wouldn't know what it was even if it jumped up and bit him on the bum.

The flight to Bridgetown was good; everyone seemed in holiday mood. I think it's weird that a long haul flight is turning into just another day at work. We're not in Barbados for very long. This is a two-parter. One night here then back to England for one night, then over to Chicago. Same crew. So a short stop on the island without moving from the hotel. Well, when I say not moving from the hotel I mean, not moving anywhere except from room to bar and to beach. White sand, blue sea and rum punches. Yessss! Just what the doctor ordered.

I need to make the most of this - I'm sure it's a fluke. Like snow on schooldays, trips to the Caribbean don't seem to come my way very often. Being relatively new, I probably have to work my way up the scheduling department recognition list to get good rosters, either that or find someone there to sleep with. Hush my mouth. Might be something to aspire to though and better than looking for a Captain. Even on this trip the stewardess in first class is fluttering her way around the Flight Deck. Silly girl, I heard from one of the stewards that the Captain's not interested in her type at all. It was so amusing to watch her leaning on the bar next to him, boobs out on display like a ripe bowl of fruit and flicking her hair about (well, I did spot the odd flaw in the pears, the start of a wrinkly cleavage but who am I to judge, the girl's working it). Can't wait to see her beach performance.

I've got my sights on someone much more manageable. The steward working on upper deck. He's really cute, seems interested but has got a girlfriend who also flies. Could be fun… I haven't got long. Headline: *Tottie On The Pull.* Upper deck steward watch out.

A day later in London - hotel

I rose early the next morning. Being in paradise the sun was up and had already put its hat on. It was so lovely to have the warmth seeping into my bones. Made me feel confident and attractive for once. So there I was, walking along to the beach with a huge grin on my face like some idiot when hey presto, guess who was lying on a sun bed?

So casually (casually for me means I didn't kick sand on his recently oiled, six-packed body) I sauntered over and parked myself within talking distance. I tried to lie decorously on the lounger but yes, you've guessed, the bloody thing tipped up one end and dumped me in the sand. Fortunately I hadn't put sun cream on so didn't get sticky like an ice cream with those hundreds and thousands all over. Just felt a right numpty. After giggling (men like a girl who can laugh at herself, right?)

I recovered my composure and managed to lie down with my shades, bikini and magazines all in the right place, more gracefully the second time.

I don't know where everyone else was but it didn't matter because he looked up from his book and smiled at me. Yesss! Not to waste a second I asked him what he was reading and that was it. Connection made. He put down his book, swung his legs off the lounger so he could face me and started chatting away.

What do you think? Not bad for someone who has been out of the game for a while, stuck with a boyfriend who thinks romance is watching footie on telly holding hands. So after a discussion of Peter James's *Not Dead Enough* with Tom, which luckily I'd read, he asked whether I'd had breakfast yet and hey presto the next thing, we're sauntering along the beach to find a small shack serving food. Not arm in arm, but he was pretty close.

I'll have to practice draping and tying my sarong effortlessly though, like they do in the adverts. He didn't seem too bothered by my failed attempts to be seductive, nor did he laugh at me. Even catching the wispy material as the slight breeze tried to whisk it away. I made sure our hands touched when he gave it back and tied it so that I had a fair bit of cleavage on show. No, I'm not becoming one of the wrinklies (I'll explain later, Eve) nor being hypocritical. Mine is subtle seduction. In fact it was so subtle he didn't even notice.

What a difference not to face an unshaven, blurry eyed Matt across the table whose only thought is to get that spoonful of Shreddies into his mouth and swap him for someone bronzed, interested and responsive. Perhaps I'm being unfair but having the clear waters lapping up the beach beside you and the warm sand to dig your toes into whilst engaging with an attractive guy with deliciously blue eyes (okay, I know, I've swallowed a Mills and Boon) does somewhat cloud your judgment. This part of the job I like.

After breakfast we walked back to our sun beds to find that some of the crew were also up and about. There was the usual mixture of sights on the beach. People think that you have to be young, slim and gorgeous to be cabin crew but judging by one or two of the examples spread (and I mean spread) all over their towels it clearly isn't the case. Once you're in the crew club, that's pretty much it. I've even heard talk of one stewardess who grew so large she couldn't walk down the aisle on the plane straight on but had to turn sideways. Word has it her manager told her to do something and she told him where to go and not in her best stewardess manner either! Just mix many years of customer service with sun damage and you end up with the 'wrinklies'. This is the name given to those somewhat older stewardesses who obviously haven't been paying as much attention to their sun protection regime as they should.

Enough bitching, before we got settled into sunbathing mode with the others, Tom suggested taking a boat out. I jumped at the chance. Not so keenly that he'd think I was gagging for it but enough to let him know I was interested. We were just leaving to go when one of the other stewardesses piped up from her prone position. I thought she was buried in her magazine but she wanted to come. I swept straight into work mode and smiled sweetly between gritted teeth as I was rather hoping it would be just a cosy twosome.

Tom led the way to a small dingy and manoeuvred it out into the water. It did cross my mind that it might be his usual seduction technique, but I dismissed it as me being too cynical. Before I knew it the three of us were casting off from the beach. I laid myself up the front so that I could face him and keep an eye on Melanie. He, naturally and very manly I might add, drove the thing. Yes, you might have guessed - I'm not a sailor. No technical boating terms to be found here I'm afraid, but I'm sure you get the drift. Ha ha.

I enjoyed watching Tom's rippling muscles pulling this and pushing that and smiled whenever I caught his eye. I dangled my hand in the water now and again and cursed at having left my shades on the beach but it was good tanning time. Whereas Melanie didn't stop talking the whole way. We heard all about her parents' divorce, best friend's fabulous boyfriend and her life long ambition to be cabin crew. I wanted to deck her by the time we got back quite late to an empty beach.

Melanie came over all fluttery as she thanked Tom, even raising on her dainty, manicured little toes to peck him on the cheek before she walked off. I stayed until he had sorted everything out with the boat and he walked me back to my hotel room. I unlocked my door and turned round to thank him to find him standing right behind me. He obviously decided the time was right to make his move as before I knew it he had his tongue down my throat. I managed to drop all my beach stuff at the surprise of it, including my bottle of sun cream which landed (painfully) on his toe.

Not the best reaction I've ever had to being kissed as he hopped about the corridor and cursed that I might have broken it. After he had recovered he tried again. Talk about fast worker once he got going. I found myself being gently pushed backwards into my room, our mouths locked in a bit of tongue wrestling and pinned against the wall by his body.

But Eve, it was as Tom started to undo the clasp of my bikini top with one hand, his mouth covering mine that I came to my senses. What was I doing? I didn't want to become just another notch on his belt. I'm so confused. This wasn't me. It was all happening too fast. How many had he impressed before me with his handiness with a boat? Let alone his handiness with a bikini top which, I can tell you, was not going quite as smoothly as he must have hoped.

I'm not that desperate I need a quick session, standing against the wall in my hotel room. Nice as the thought of it may be. He was pretty fit and all that and I can't say I wasn't tempted, but a) he had a girlfriend, b) I still hadn't told Matt it was all over and c) if I was thinking of a 'c' whilst he was fumbling so much with a simple catch that he had to use two hands to undo it then it obviously wasn't the '*Affair to Remember*' for me.

So just as my red bikini top imploded and hung from its halter strings around my neck and down the centre of my boobs like a splash of tomato ketchup between two fried eggs (I *am* pleased with how my tan is coming along though) I pushed Tom gently away. After a bit of a struggle, as the material was all tangled up, I fixed my top, secured my dignity and was able to face him. Shame, he did taste so delicious - of salt and sun and was obviously getting all hot and bothered in anticipation. But best to stop it there. I reasoned he'd had a good eyeful of my boobs so maybe that would compensate him a bit and make him think it hadn't all been a waste of time. I told him that now wasn't the right time and that with pick-up only a short time away I needed to get showered and packed. He offered to shower with me. Give him full marks for trying but I persuaded him that it was best left as it was and eventually I got him out of the door.

I showered, packed and got down to the lobby in time for check-out and ready to get on the bus with the rest of the crew. Tom was right behind me and pinched my bum as I was boarding so at least I know there's no hard feelings. We've got a night in London then off over the pond to Chicago next.

Finishing this off in the hotel in Chicago (ORD)

I didn't know what I wanted to happen after spending the day on the beach with Tom. Maybe further encounters on the Chicago part of the trip? But I was feeling up-beat on the flight home. I'm so out of practise at this game, Eve. Being with Matt for so long, I've forgotten how the whole seduction/dating malarkey goes. Sometimes that's exciting when you're away from England, but it's also a bit scary. Part of me is restrained and sensible but it fights with the other very naughty side of me that just says, to hell with it - go for it girl. It's a good job you and I are not flying together as that would definitely mean trouble – you were always getting us into trouble.

Men are so funny. Tom's girlfriend is also crew and on the last sector from Barbados to Heathrow we carried her as a passenger. When I heard she was on board I couldn't help but wander upstairs to have a look. I asked him which seat she was in and I could almost see the sweat pouring off his brow as I sauntered along the aisle pretending I was checking the cabin so that I could look her over. She was in a window seat. I know I shouldn't have but I couldn't resist leaning over to ask her if everything was okay. I could almost feel his panic as he was out of earshot watching from the galley. Why he should be playing away from home, I don't know, she looked lovely. If I was in the sisterhood I would have confessed to her and revealed what a cheating rat he was, how he'd had my top off and would have gone the whole way if I'd let him. Poor girl, she deserves better.

When I saw Tom on the flight to Chicago the next day, I realised I might have blown any chance of even a

69

friendship. He took some persuasion that I hadn't said anything untoward to his girlfriend on the flight back from Barbados. Apparently, she laid into him when they got home. He's obviously got a roving eye.

Chicago is turning out to be a bit of a disappointment. Not the place itself which is lovely, but I've gone down with a cold, along with half the crew, so I didn't feel like exploring. I stayed in my room only foraying down to the beach by Lake Michigan for some air. Tom isn't a happy bunny and doesn't hold quite the same appeal with a puffed up red nose so everything's fizzled out to nothing. Good job we'd had the Barbados sector first to liven things up.

Waiting in the crew bus to go through customs. LHR

The flight home from Chicago was a struggle. We encountered a particularly demanding set of passengers that took all my efforts to keep my regulation stewardess smile in place. I think a clown's painted smile would be a help in those situations-scary, but then I wouldn't have to move a muscle. Not sure if it would go down too well with the passengers though.

One bit of excitement though. You'll never guess who we had on the flight. Part of my job on this trip is to take care of VIP's, mothers and babies or young children travelling alone. I was told that I had to stand at the gate and wait for a VIP, making sure that they didn't bring more than the required size hand baggage on board. You can imagine these celebs think they can do just what they like. Well, not with me they can't! I was all ready to stop a trolley load of trunks coming on board when who should totter towards me but Joan Collins. Well, I think it was her as she was so swathed in furs from a Cossack hat down to a floor-reaching coat that I could only make out an immaculately made-up pair of eyes as she swanned past me. I was so in awe checking all the details of her outfit that by the time I'd finished, her companion had entered the plane, turned left and was busy stowing Ms Collins's half a plane's worth of luggage. I got a slap on the wrist for that.

We all took turns to go up and look at her throughout the flight. She was inspiringly, gobsmakingly gorgeous. I don't know how old she is but if I look half that good later on I'll be pleased.

Love Suzi x

20th June - Home

Dear Eve

When I got home from Chicago, I was just checking my future rosters which had arrived and spotted JJ's name on one when the doorbell rang. I picked my way through the contents of my suitcase strewn all over the floor and opened the door. Matt stood there. A humongous bunch of flowers in his hands. Bloody hell, he looked like a florist's delivery boy. Well, instead of rushing into his arms as he thought I was going to, all I could think was, what a waste of his money. I only had three days at home before I was off again. They would have died by the time I got back and I could hardly put them in my suitcase to take with me. I was really tired but managed to switch into stewardess mode, knackered stewardess mode mind you. Smiling, I made all the right noises as I ushered him in. Took him twenty minutes to get round to telling me he wants to have another go at 'us'. Aghhh…. I thought I'd made myself clear the last time.

Cue more screaming and shouting, when the vein on his forehead started doing it's red to purple sticking out and throbbing trick. Eventually, two stiff gins later (and the sun wasn't even half way over the yardarm), I think I got through to him that there is no more 'us', only a 'me and him'.

At last I've done it. After all my procrastinating I've finally told Matt how I feel. Have I done the right thing? Only time will tell, but the thought of meeting up with JJ and going down route with him excites me more than a mixed, orange and yellow floral arrangement, however large. Bloody chrysanthemums as well, I hate them with a passion. After all this time Matt still can't remember my favourite flowers. He eventually calmed down and came round to my way of thinking and nodded his head in agreement when I suggested that it was over. Of course I said we would remain friends and he could contact me if he wanted but really I think my phone might have a malfunction whenever his name comes up. I need some space.

Love Suzi x

25th June - Los Angeles, (LAX) 130ft - hotel

Dear Eve

So there I was on a trip to L.A. The longer the flight went on the calmer and more rational my thoughts about Matt became. Even the family with the two obnoxious children who wouldn't stop kicking the back of the seat in front so that the woman in it started having a go at me, were less hassle. Matt had actually thrown his slippers in frustration at me at one point. He'd left them in my room the last time he'd stayed and just happened to trip over them as he was pacing in anger, trying to think up more reasons why it was all my fault. Just goes to show, never trust a man with moccasin slippers. Definitely dodgy. I just couldn't help thinking that I'd had a lucky escape. Imagine being married to someone who puts moccasins on his Christmas and birthday lists just so he's got ready ammunition. I want a partner who can make me laugh - but not at him. Give me a man who can go through life without slippers, and I'll show you a risk taker and adventurer.

So I'm in Los Angeles. We used to stay down-town but are now put up in a hotel in Santa Monica by the beach. I haven't bonded with anybody on the crew so I'm pretty much Jonnie-no-mates. Still the weather's good and there's so much to see. I went for a walk along by the Palisades. It's like a prom that runs alongside the Pacific Coast Highway. It's really pretty with palm trees and pathways that weave through the grass and neatly tendered flower beds. There's a great view of the ocean on one side. By the time I'd walked along and back I was ravenous. But I had to pass through Venice.

Venice Beach Park is a place that makes walking along the front at Brighton seem like the starter. If you think Brighton has got a few dodgy characters it's nothing compared to the likes here. Everyone comes out to show off their own particular brand of peculiarity and to soak up the rays. And it wasn't just the men. I saw sights that shouldn't be allowed out during the day. You get the usual bearded wonder doing his Taekwondo or a very precarious Sun Salutation in risky shorts but who in their right mind would go roller-blading in a thong? Well, she did for a start. Mind you, if my butt was that taut I'd want to show it off too.

It's a shame it's such a short trip, I could do with

exploring some more. At the back of the beach are stalls selling all sorts of tat, plus I could have got my hair braided with Stars and Stripes (very becoming with the uniform, but I managed to resist).

I stopped off for a late breakfast to watch as the world and his wife came out to play. Just as I was tucking into my eggs (over easy) with a humongous portion of hash browns on the side, glad that I wasn't sitting in a thong as it would not have stretched to cover anything by the time I'd finished my plateful, along walks Katie, the stewardess from First Class with a tall, bronzed, brown haired man beside her. My jaw nearly dropped my mouthful of eggs back onto the plate he was so gorgeous. She obviously had been brought up beautifully and taught to share as she noticed me sitting on the terrace and, to my delight, asked if they could join me.

Breakfast had suddenly got even better. Turns out the fitty's called Ed and he's her friend from another crew. Well, he didn't show any signs of being her boyfriend nor gay but she did let it slip towards his second coffee refill that he was a First Officer. He was so funny and entertaining and had me laughing so much I nearly spat a mouthful of toast over him; I could just about forgive him for being Flight Deck. Neither of them seemed in a hurry to move on so we ended up sitting there until they started serving lunch. Ed seemed to know everywhere and everything and had a knack of making even the most ordinary topics hilarious. When Katie moved away onto the beach to take a private call on her mobile, I suddenly found myself tongue tied when Ed asked me how I was getting on with the job at the same time as gently leaning across the table and removing an eyelash from my cheek.

'Oh.' I uttered as I sat still unsure at first what he was doing. He held out his finger to show me. Thank goodness it wasn't a bogey or anything unsavoury. 'Fine.

74

Thanks for asking.'

'You don't sound too sure.'

'No, really. Everything's okay.' He didn't realise, it wasn't his question that was causing me a problem but the intimacy of his touch. Brushing me with an electric bolt would have caused much the same reaction. And the way he looked at me, Eve; straight in the eyes. I felt my insides go to mush and slosh around, dousing the butterflies fluttering in there. Thank goodness Katie came back at that moment so I could excuse myself and go and find the toilet, giving my cheeks time to calm down. Turns out he's stopping over in San Francisco next. Shame he's not flying me home, I could have found many excuses for visiting the cockpit otherwise.

Love Suzi x

30th June - Home

Dearest Eve

When I got back to the house from L.A, knackered from such a long flight, all hell had broken loose. Apparently Sarah-Jane's new love had dumped her and Debbie's parents had announced they were getting a divorce and that all the money was going to be divided between them so there wouldn't be a steady supply for her anymore. Her father had mentioned the forbidden word. He'd told her that, horror of horrors, it was about time she got herself a job. Just as I walked in the front door I could hear Sarah-Jane crying in her room and Sam was trying to placate a hysterical Debbie in the kitchen.

I dumped my suitcase in the hallway and, after getting a brief update from Sam, took two strong coffees and a box of tissues up to SJ's room ready for the flood. Ahh... how lovely to be man-free. After hearing all about what a bastard SJ's old love was because he'd been having an affair with someone at work, I persuaded her that men weren't worth it and she was best off having a break for a while. I don't think she'll take any notice of me though.

I snuck into bed for a few hours restorative kip as soon as I felt it was safe and by the time I dragged myself out from underneath my duvet the house was quiet. I found out that Sam had gone to work; SJ had bathed her puffy red eyes with cold water so that she could face her world at work and Debbie had got as far as switching on the computer to look and see if there were any jobs out there to suit her. Despondent that there wasn't one waiting for her in her in-box, she was in denial, back on her usual spot in front of the TV covered in her coat of many crisp wrappers. I don't think there are many employers wanting people whose only achievements in life are knowing the TV guide to daytime television off by heart or being able to hum all the theme tunes to the soaps – but I may be wrong.

I had a few days at home to recuperate. Matt was clearly licking his wounds and didn't come round and thankfully didn't ring either. I don't feel guilty, Eve. Why should I? I'm just being true to myself. This is a time of transition and he will have to come to terms with it. It does feel a bit weird to be at home and boyfriend free. We've been together for so long. When I'm abroad it's usual to be on my own but so many things here Matt and I have shared.

Sarah-Jane has been looking for companionship too so we've been out for a bit of retail therapy, been to the cinema and to a club. It's really been okay. Bit like going on holiday. I'm not sure how I'll feel after months on my own though. Why is life so difficult, Eve? Why do we get fed all that 'boy meets girl, they fall in love, boy marries girl and they live happily ever after' rubbish? They've left out how you have to meet a load of boys before you find the right one and how do you know it's the right one when you do eventually meet him? I'm so confused. I wish you were here. I know you would have the right spin on it and make it all seem logical.

Love you, Suzi x

1st July - Jamaica, (MBJ) 20ft - hotel

Dear Eve

The silver time machine has done its trick and landed me in Montego Bay. After a few days of Debbie's histrionics at the house I was glad to leave and come away. Being able to escape from home life is worth all the hassle from the passengers on the flight. Even the one who really should perform his colonic irrigation *before* he boards the plane, not when he's on it. Guess who had to investigate the blocked toilet and shut it off? Nasty business.

Still, my mood couldn't be dampened. We discovered when we arrived at our usual hotel that they had made a huge cock-up; double booking our rooms so they couldn't fit us in. After much ranting and raving, not mine, of course, I'm too junior to cause a fuss, we were up-graded along the road to the most gorgeous couples-only hotel. The bed in my room was the biggest I've ever seen, covered in loads of romantic petals and chocolates. Boy, this is the place to have your honeymoon. As I dumped my suitcase on the stand and leapt onto the bed springs (not at all squeaky either) my heart did give a little lurch. Unless I went out and grabbed the first man I saw on the other side of the door, it would be just little old me in the vast white sheets. Would a little of Matt be better than loneliness in my old age? What if no one else comes my way?

A knock on the door brought me out of my self-indulgent reverie. Mandy, the stewardess I had been teamed up with on the plane, was standing there. She had a bottle of plonk in her hand, wearing just her bikini and a huge grin. What was I thinking of? Out damn thoughts.

'Have you seen the infinity pool?' she exclaimed, tapping her bejewelled foot with impatience, waving the bottle like a tour guide. 'I'll give you two minutes to get your kit off and join me.' Now that was an offer I couldn't refuse.

I love England but waking up to scorching sunshine and a deep blue sea that only dares to ripple occasionally, does make the grey choppy stuff on the South coast seem like the poor relation. Last night the whole crew met up and had sundowners on the beach. Flight Deck as well. They're not usually in the same hotel as us mere mortals. The stewardess on the upper deck, a vivacious redhead, definitely had her sights on the First Officer. A lesson in seduction ensued. Hilarious wasn't the word. She tried every trick in the book starting with hair tossing and full-throw-back-the-head laughing at his every utterance, to playfully touching his arm and brushing that imaginary fluff from his Hawaiian shirt.

It must be the atmosphere of this place. It makes you think romantic thoughts but even I could spot seduction overload. Isn't anyone subtle about it these days? Surely men don't want it offered on a plate? Or do they? Mind you, she hasn't got long before the trip is over so, why not?

The F.O. seemed to enjoy the attention and it made amusing viewing for the rest of us. Mandy nearly wet herself at their antics especially when Red Head 'accidentally' spilt her drink all over his shorts and rushed off to get something to wipe him down. He was sitting in a beach chair at the time and she ended up genuflecting at his side.

We've planned to climb the Dunns River Falls and the two love birds are coming. Should be fun.

Eve, it was so exciting. The Dunns River falls are the most beautiful thing I've seen so far. I wish you could have been with me. Cascades of water flowing down over huge boulders to the beach. You start at the bottom and you have a guide who leads you on a route up the waterfall. We'd left the hotel early so as to miss the hoards of tourists that swamp the falls so it wasn't overcrowded when we started to make our ascent. I was very sensible and wore a swimsuit with boy-leg cut so that I wouldn't give anyone a nasty shock of my bum. There were parts where you do have to have your head almost up the person in front's ascending buttocks. Not pleasant. I could only hope that the person in front of me wasn't in a thong. When I saw Mandy also suitably swim-suited I carefully manoeuvred myself behind her. After a bit of jostling where I saw Red Head (not at all suitably swim-suited but in a very skimpy bikini, tut-tut) make sure that she was next to the F.O. the seven of us snaked our way over the huge rocks and up towards the top.

Some of it was quite slippery but I'd been warned so I wore my very cheap, plastic, pink jelly shoes. Ok, so they weren't the latest in footwear but I'm not proud. There were all sorts of sights. I saw some sensible guy wearing his navy blue, wetsuit shoes. His footwear may have been secure, just a shame he hadn't given the same thought to his very small, tight Speedos. There was definitely the risk of a couple of things peeking out that shouldn't have.

Half-way up there was a natural slide where you could slip off the top rock into a small pool of water. Red Head went all girlie and insisted that someone catch her. Ha-ha! Guess who it was? The F.O. manfully positioned himself at the bottom and we suffered a long performance of how she was so nervous she couldn't let go. Shame I'd already had my go as if I was still up there behind her I would have pushed her off myself, the fuss she was creating. Unfortunately for her, her bikini top didn't stay as it should, so the F.O. had to catch something else as well to maintain her dignity. What a joke? She should have just whipped it off and gone topless down the slide– would have been more exciting. Meow.

By the time we'd climbed to the top of the falls and stopped for refreshments at the ideally placed café it was lunchtime. When we got back to the hotel I found that I'd got a text from Matt. All the excitement of the morning disappeared. I didn't want to think of him and my life in England. We're supposed to have finished. I love that delete button on mobile phones.

Love Suzi x

11th July - Home

Dear Eve

It was early in the morning when we arrived back at Heathrow. It seems blasé to say that the rest of the trip was uneventful but nothing could touch the magnificence and excitement of the Falls. Even a quick over-night stop in Antigua only meant another room party with sundowners followed by a morning on the beach. I know the girls back in the house think I'm the luckiest girl in the world having a job like this, but as my grandpa used to say 'all jobs have their boring bits.'

I was desperate to catch up on sleep but couldn't rest before the flight which turned out to be full. I was so looking forward to getting into my bed when those wheels touched down. I think it was quite understandable when I got to the crew car park and turned my key in the ignition and absolutely nothing happened, that after opening the bonnet and not seeing anything untoward, kicking the damn tyre seemed justified.

I was just about to break down in tears at the injustice of it all when a sleek, dark blue car drew up beside me. I can't tell you what kind as I'm completely useless at recognising makes, but I *can* be sure of the colour. A fit God-like creature got out and I nearly hugged him with joy when he said, 'Hi Suzi, what's the problem?'

It was Ed, Eve. Remember that attractive F.O. I'd had breakfast with in a café at the back of the beach in Venice, California, a couple of trips ago? Well, like a saviour from heaven he was standing in front of me, suited and booted in his uniform. He lifted his Oakley sunglasses (the real McCoy, I'm sure, no fakes for him) and smiled at me. He's still as gorgeous and makes my heart flutter just to look at him. In my knackered, emotional state I was so pleased to see him I could have kissed every inch of his delectable body.

He suggested that it was probably worth trying to give me a jump start and in true saviour spirit got out his jump leads. After driving his car up to the front of mine and fixing the cables he started his engine and connected us up. I can't fault him just because nothing happened. The man was trying his best. Perhaps because he could see I was close to tears he whipped out his phone and rung a mechanic friend of his (I didn't tell him I also had a mechanic ex-boyfriend) who agreed to come and look at my car.

'So what shall we do while we wait?' he enquired still smiling at me. 'Steve says he'll ring me when he's on his way.' I was convinced he would have abandoned me at this point but no, after locking up my car he insisted I got into his. I duly did as I was told (must be the uniform - it demands obedience) and slid into the leather front seat beside him. Before I knew it I was driven for twenty minutes until we pulled up outside the sweetest little cottage. One of a row of four, all set back from the road.

'Is this yours?' I asked like an idiot as he walked up the gravel drive and unlocked the front door.

'For the moment,' he replied turning to usher me past him and into the small hallway. 'It's on the market. I'm thinking of selling up to buy a bigger place with my girlfriend.'

Damn, damn, damn. He'd kept that quiet in L.A. I may have just found my soul mate and his soul is already attached to someone else's.

'Oh, that's nice,' I replied. 'Not wedding bells though?' God, could I have sounded more desperate?

'Nooooo,' came the reply. He took his jacket off and slung it over the back of a wooden chair and threw his keys on a small table. 'Now what can I make you? Coffee? Bacon sarnie? You must be knackered. It might take a while for Steve to get back to me.' And he walked off towards the back of the house.

A God who can cook. I looked around the living room and leaned over the fireplace to scrutinise a photo of Ed with his arm casually around a petite, blonde girl. Ed was facing the photographer with a half full pint glass in his other hand. They must have been at something formal as his girlfriend was squeezed into a red silk suit. She had a large-rimmed hat which had slipped to the back of her head, holding it in place with one hand as she gazed adoringly up at him.

Although the room was small it didn't scream of being a man's house. The pale yellow walls bounced the light around from the bay window that looked out onto the neat front garden. I finished inspecting his limited but very expensive looking photo frames and ornaments (wouldn't do to let him think I was sizing up his housekeeping skills) and joined Ed in the kitchen. The kettle was on and he was humming to himself as he unpeeled a pack of bacon and laid the slices out individually on the grill pan.

'Nice place you've got Ed. Been here long?'

'Thanks. A few years. I love it. Really convenient for the airport and everything. It's great for one but…'

'…now you are about to become two,' I ended his sentence for him. I really needed to get to the bottom of his relationship with that blonde. How long had they been an item and if there was any chance of an opening?

'Put like that it sounds serious,' Ed admitted. 'It's not that serious. Just that Candy needs to move out of her place. Seemed the obvious thing to do,' he explained.

'Doesn't sound as though you're too convinced,' I suggested. Yes!! It obviously wasn't his idea. He didn't sound *that* committed. She must be the driving force in the relationship.

'Is she crew?' I asked innocently.

'No, works on the ground.'

No wonder she was worried and wanted to get her feet under his table. I would too with someone like Ed for a boyfriend. I watched him expertly cut the brown bread and place it in the toaster. There's not been many times in my life, Eve that I've been star struck, but I concluded that Ed McEwan was definitely someone a bit special.

It was just as I had the bacon sandwich poised between my pearly whites to take a huge bite that the phone went.

Steve, the mechanic was on his way to look at my car. My annoyance at having to leave must have shown on my face because Ed once again quickly took hold of the situation and jumped up from his seat at the kitchen table.

'You stay and finish that,' he commanded. 'I'll go and meet Steve and let you know what he says.' All I could do at that point was nod as I chewed furiously, trying not to spit out tomato ketchup in my rush to clear my mouth and speak. By the time I'd finished he'd downed the last of his coffee and was picking up his car keys.

'I'll need your mobile number though, Suzi,' he said matter-of-factly.

Result! A legitimate way of him having my number without me having to manoeuvre things.

'And I'd better have yours too,' I replied scrabbling through my handbag at my feet for my phone. Nailed it! I'm getting good at this game.

'Don't worry now,' Ed replied. Damn, that'll teach me to be cocky. 'Wait till I ring you, then it'll be in your phone. It may take a while with Steve. Make yourself at home,' he offered as a parting shot as he opened the front door. 'There should be plenty of hot water, take a bath if you want. Be back as soon as I can.'

Brilliant! I had the run of this gorgeous guy's house with permission to use the facilities.

I wasn't snooping. Honestly I wasn't, Eve. It was just that after I'd finished eating and cleared away, the least I could do after all Ed's hospitality couldn't have him coming back to a dirty kitchen and thinking I was slovenly, I needed the loo. I looked around the ground floor but there wasn't any obvious sign of a toilet so I *had* to go upstairs. It just so happened that the first room I came to at the top was Ed's bedroom. It was the usual male room with dark blue bed linen but unusual in that it was tidy. All the men I've known live like slobs: clothes strewn everywhere and dirty plates, cups and underwear all over the floor and surfaces. I thought it best to check the toilet wasn't behind one of the doors on the other side of the room so I opened the glass door but it only revealed all his shirts neatly ironed and hung waiting to be worn. His spare uniform was still in its plastic wrapping back from the cleaners. But the best bit was lying neatly folded in the drawer underneath – his boxer shorts. The man obviously likes his designer labels but I was relieved to see the odd pair of M & S Autograph poking out from the pack. Maybe his girlfriend's influence, or sister maybe?

I was just leaving when I spotted some books lying on the floor beside the bed. *'A Buyer's Guide to French Property'* nestled alongside *'Songs of Innocence and Experience'* by William Blake. Blimey! The man's a bit high brow. Where's the fiction? I'm not a complete literary heathen and partial to a good poem but it tends to be in the downstairs cloakroom on the window sill, where my visits are short and sweet, not the last thing I tuck into before I close my eyes. And what's going on with the French property? Is he thinking of moving with girlfriend in tow out there? I suppose he could still fly. Plenty of people in the company live abroad and commute. Still pondering on my discoveries I walked into the room next door. A roll top bath sat neatly in the corner just waiting to be filled with hot, steaming water. I couldn't wait to get my clothes off and balanced on the side whilst I waited for the tub to fill.

There's a particular smell that hits you every time you walk down the finger and onto the aircraft. *Eau de 'Phew'* I call it. It pervades through my clothes, my hair and I can't get rid of it until I've had a hot bath or shower. If I never smell it again I won't be sorry. It's a mixture of sweat, recycled air and *'chicken or beef sir.'*

I'd like to just stand and spray all the passengers with *Eau de 'Something Nice'* intermittently to mask it. So as I wallowed in the bath I indulged myself with all the fragrances I could find. Whilst Ed obviously took his personal grooming seriously it wasn't enough to make me suspicious that he was too vain. I did just wonder at the hair spray in the cabinet though and just hope it had been left by his girlfriend.

I must have been much longer than I thought because as I was walking down the stairs a key turned in the lock in front of me and the door started to open. Thinking it was Ed back and I'd missed his call, I leapt down the last few steps to nearly collide with the petite woman I'd seen in the photo on the mantelpiece.

'Who the hell are you?' she questioned. 'And why are you wearing Ed's bathrobe?' Uh…oh!

Okay, so I can see how it must have looked from her point of view but no wonder she only works for the airline on the ground if that's the way she greets strangers. Even if the stranger is naked underneath her boyfriend's bathrobe. My mind raced – should I come clean and own up to the innocence of it all or play along for a bit?

Hmmm…Drawing myself up to my full 172.5 cms, I towered over Miss Petite and stood my ground. It was a relief that from that angle I could see she was not so perfect as her picture; she really needed to get her roots done.

'Hi, I'm Suzi,' I smiled in my best stewardess way. 'My car broke down and Ed rescued me.' See I'm not all bad. That was adequate. Don't need to explain all the details.

'But why are you dressed like that? Where is Ed?' Her voice was beginning to sound a tad squeaky. Even without my training of recognising the signs for passenger anxiety I could see that she was getting stressed.

'Sorry, you are…?' I answered. Well, if I hadn't seen her photo over the fireplace earlier I wouldn't have a clue who she was. I was only assuming she was his girlfriend because of those puppy dog adoring eyes and the way she clung onto him.

'I'm Candy. Candice Spencer. Ed's girlfriend,' she stated puffing out her tiny chest and folding her arms triumphantly. Candy! What kind of a name was that? Did her parents have a fetish for sweets and hoped she would grow into her name because she certainly wasn't being sweet to me right now. The sound of my mobile ringing made us both turn round. Before I could get past her, Candy walked over to the coffee table where I'd left it, picked it up and looking at the number that flashed up, pressed the receive button and answered the call. Potentially a sticky moment… sticky …Candy…geddit?

'Ed! Ed!' she squeaked down the phone at him. 'What's this woman doing in your house and in your bathrobe?'

It's weird only hearing one side of a row. Poor Ed was obviously getting a grilling for his chivalry. No amount of apparent pleading seemed to calm Candy down as I heard her repeat over and over again that he'd better have a good explanation. Ha! Even the innocent explanation of the real circumstances wouldn't appease this woman. I sat down on the sofa and put my feet up on the coffee table to wait until she finished her rant on *my* phone.

Was Ed just like most of the other men I'd met who fly? Girl in every port so Candy had reason to blow her top, or was she just the over-jealous type who flew off the handle at the slightest hint of anything suspicious? I didn't know Ed well enough to decide whether he liked his women needy and possessive or whether this whole show was a complete turn off for him.

It was just as Candy was mid-flow with choice expletives that my battery went. I forgot to charge it in Antigua, not thinking I would need it much before I got home. Unfortunately I was smiling at the respite I'd inadvertently bought Ed when Candy turned round and caught my expression.

'And what do you think you're smiling at?' she barked at me. Whoa, lady. Calm. I've done nothing wrong. Must be something to do with her height that made her so fiery. Or her name. Time to take charge.

'Look Candy,' I started, getting up from my seat and walking towards the kitchen. 'You're over reacting. I'm going to put the kettle on.' Candy glared at me and opened her mouth to start up again. 'There's no need to have a go at me,' I continued. 'Nor Ed. He was simply being a Good Samaritan and helping me out. I can't go anywhere until I get my car back so why don't I make us a cup of tea and we can wait until he turns up.' Sounded a good plan to me. Candy shrugged her shoulders and seemed to accept the inevitability of the situation.

'Take that bloody robe off,' she said storming past me. 'I'll make the tea.'

Ever spent time wishing you were a thousand miles away? I think, not-so-sweet Candy, must have spat in my tea it tasted so foul. She sat in the kitchen with a face like a bulldog, screwed up and ready to pounce. I retreated upstairs and changed back into my uniform. My suitcase was still in the boot of my car at the airport so I only had the clothes I arrived in. Just as I finished buttoning my blouse, my stockings thrust into my jacket pocket, Ed pulled up outside the house in my Peugeot. I was ready for a frosty reception from him for causing so much mayhem but to my delight it was Candy who got the ice cold treatment. He practically ignored her sitting reading the paper. Well, she was pretending to read but I noticed her glance our way every now and then.

Ed took my arm and after shouting out to Candy that he would see her in half an hour he led me out of the door, up the drive and held open the car door as I got into the driving seat. Good. I like a man who can stand his ground in the face of adversity.

'God, I'm so sorry about that,' he apologised. 'She can blow things so out of proportion sometimes.'

'No, it was my fault,' I explained. Hell. I felt sorry for the guy. The least I could do was try and take some of the blame. 'I had just taken that bath you suggested when she walked in and I was in your bathrobe. It's understandable that she jumped to conclusions.' Ed shut my door and walked around the bonnet to get into the passenger seat beside me. Then he did something so unexpected it made me shiver with excitement. Leaning over he cupped his hand around my face and turned it towards him drawing it close to his.

'It was a real shame I couldn't have been there. I would have liked to see you in my bathrobe.' Then he slowly pulled my head towards his until our lips met and he kissed me.

'Ed!' I giggled lingering slightly before I pulled away. 'She might be watching. Don't you think she's had enough trauma for one day?'

'Okay partner, let's get outta here. Put your foot down.' Trying not to laugh at his pathetic cowboy accent I started the engine and pulled away from the grass verge.

'What was up with the old girl anyway?' I asked keeping my eyes on the road ahead.

'Are you talking about Candy or this old banger?'

I couldn't believe he was being so flippant about her. 'My car of course. That's not a nice way to describe your girlfriend.'

'Well, you could call it lack of combustion, but for you and me it was an empty fuel tank,' he replied ignoring my remark.

I looked at the fuel gauge and saw that it was just off empty. 'Oh my God, 'I'm so sorry. I knew I was low and meant to fill up before the trip but then I was late for check-in and…' I trailed off. 'You must think me a right idiot. All this trouble I've caused you. I'm so sorry.'

'No worries,' he replied smiling. 'It's been an eventful morning. I'll think of a way you can repay me.' Then placing his hand into my jacket pocket he pulled on the thin nylon that must have been hanging half way out.

'Interesting,' he said holding the stocking up to the light and inspecting it. 'This might give me an idea.'

'Stop it!' I laughed as I tried to grab it from him.

'Keep your eyes on the road,' he teased. 'We've had enough excitement for one morning.' And he screwed up my stocking and put it in his top pocket.

'Seriously,' I said trying to concentrate as we came up to a roundabout. 'I must owe you something for Steve and the fuel.'

'No. Steve's a friend and was on his way to a job anyway. He did ask though, if you were blonde.'

'Oh. How typical. Funny you didn't spot I was out of fuel either, Mr First Officer?' I goaded him. 'What did you tell him?'

'I just said no, you were a delicious, brown eyed, long-legged, shoulder length brunette.'

I'm glad he wasn't looking at me at that point because you could have lit a match off my cheeks, Eve.

Love Suzi x

Dear Eve

'Hit it! Hit it… quick. Get your shoe off and hit it!' No it isn't some sort of masochistic game cabin crew play at room parties - just cockroach killing. They sometimes show their heads crawling over the surfaces in the galley on the aeroplane. Someone told me they come in on the trolleys when we stop down-route. I don't care where they get on the plane; I just want to make sure I boot 'em off.

After my encounter with Ed when he kissed me, I drove him back to his car and we said goodbye. I felt sure he would call but after a few days at home - nothing. Ah well, some you win and … I'll just have to put it down to experience. And what a lovely experience. Not only is he fit but makes me laugh like a hyena. Probably not my most attractive feature, head back, mouth wide open and almost snorting with mirth but men like to think they're funny, don't they?

Back at the house things had been progressing for the girls. Remember I told you that Debbie's parents were divorcing and stopping her allowance? Well, this caused her such trauma that after pleading with them and getting no reaction she was at home crying her eyes out at her dilemma when Matt dropped round to bring back some of my things I'd left at his place. He found Debbie awash with grief and stayed to 'comfort her.' Now, I wasn't born yesterday. I've seen Debbie's dramatics. She can really do a major performance when she wants. According to Sarah-Jane, Matt was sucked in like fluff up

91

a cleaner and stayed for the evening. This then led to him calling round the next morning to 'make sure Debbie was alright' and before Sam and SJ realised, the two of them were an item. I didn't get Sam's worried text before I arrived home so it was a bit of a shock to see them ensconced together on the sofa but I'm really happy for them. Really! I think they are ideally suited. I'm so glad Matt was able to get over our relationship so easily. I'd hate to think of him distressed for more than an hour or two before he moved on. They have each now found their soul mate and can do absolutely nothing with their lives and watch endless TV together. I just hope Debbie has enough crisp wrappers and pizza boxes to cover them both.

I stayed out of their way as much as possible whilst I was home, caught up with my folks and friends and am now on my way to Nairobi. Don't worry about me. I've just named the two latest cockroaches I've battered to death with my shoe after the happy couple. I feel soooo much better.

Love Suzi x

16th July - NBO - hotel

Dear Eve

I'm having a bit of a wicker moment. A wicker plate fetish to be precise. I went to the market in Nairobi with Caroline, another stewardess on the flight. Yes, I know I keep throwing names at you, Eve, but that's what it's like. You go to work and have to learn the names of a whole new set of colleagues every time. Most of them I'll never see again in my life, which is really weird as they share the most intimate details of their lives with you because of this reason. Think hairdresser's chair for confessions and quadruple it. The passengers may think we're just polishing the counters when we're in those galleys but really we're divulging our inner most secrets and we've only just been introduced. Caroline's secret is that she's married but has been having an affair with a steward for two years now. I asked her why she didn't just leave her husband but she replied that this way of doing it was much more exciting. See, everyone's at it. It was only the first sector out of Heathrow and I found out her lover is meeting her when we get home from this trip and they're off to Paris for two nights of passion. She's lied to her husband about when her trip finishes and he doesn't bother to check her itinerary.

I don't mind Nairobi. A lot of crew don't like it because the expenses are poor but it's lovely to have a bit of heat coursing through my bones. So, we're at the market and I see all this wicker-work. Like knitwear, I love wicker-work so I bought masses of wicker plates. Ok, I know you're going to ask…what the hell? But I reasoned they would be very useful to put a paper plate on when I have all those summer BBQ's. Feminine logic at its best, eh?

I need to make plans, Eve. One of your strengths. Remember the time we wanted our mums to let us catch the train to London for the first time. You had it all worked out, what we were going to say, with all the answers ready so we could win them round. Well, I could do with your input right now. All this renting is just wasted money and the whole man thing is so unreliable. How do I know I'll ever meet anyone and settle down? Now Matt is off the scene with no sign of a replacement it doesn't look as though I'm going to be able to rely on the 'girl meets prince and live happily ever after' scenario. I don't want it just yet but it would be nice to know it's hovering in the future somewhere. SJ texted to say she's thinking of getting back together with that bastard who dumped her for another not so long ago, Sam's still working on her boss and Debbie, well you know about her. So as I'm going to be the lonely old maid with only my cats for company I'd better make sure I'm the one who lives in comfort. I must save for the future. I like to think I'll have my own place one day and be able to entertain like the Queen. Okay I know she probably doesn't serve the cucumber sarnies at her garden parties on paper plates encased in wicker-work from the market in Nairobi, but I can dream. In the meantime they will be essential for a house warming party. Saving is so boring – it was only twenty plates, not so bad surely? If I have more than 20 guests I'll just ask them to share.

When I got back to the hotel I had to squash and squeeze, eventually sitting on my suitcase, to fit them in – it was just at the moment of trapping my finger in the side of the case whilst questioning my rash decision to buy them in the first place that my phone pinged with a text. Ed! Maybe I won't have to be an old maid after all?

Johannesburg(JNB)

The sector between Nairobi and Johannesburg is pretty laid back. Most of the passengers have already got off and we can't pick up any new ones. We only have to serve breakfast to the remaining few so it's not very taxing. Standing on the tarmac at Nairobi watching the big bird move into its parking spot I was reminded just how enormous these aeroplanes are. I'm always so relieved to see them arrive as they symbolise home and normality. I know on board I will get a real tea bag and catch up with the newspapers. Ok, so it will still smell of *'Eau de Phew'*, have blocked toilets and take its time getting anywhere but beggars can't be choosers. It amazes me that they ever get off the ground in the first place. I never was that bright at science. You were the clever one, Eve. Remember you tried to explain the dynamics of flight using a paper aeroplane we'd made in the science lesson? I still don't understand but am in ignorant awe. I'll never tire of looking out the window at the changing landscape, be it the brown lands of Africa or the white peaks of Greenland; it's all majestic from up there.

Enough starry stuff - down to the more important news. Ed and his text. He wanted to know where I was in the world and when I would be in England. I've left it a while as I don't want to seem too keen but really *'Oooo, love to love you baby'* was running through my mind as I texted back my very casual reply. I asked why he wanted to know but he wouldn't let on, just said *'wait and see.'* Men! They can be so frustrating sometimes. Does this mean he's got something planned? Going to ditch the luscious Candy for me? Or just keeping all his options open in the hope of adding me to his collection for those bored moments?

After the hand over from the previous crew when we got on board, I checked out the passengers and realised we happened to be carrying a hockey team. A male hockey team. Some of the fittest guys I've seen in a long time. Especially the goalie: he had lovely deep brown eyes. Ok, hands up, I admit I didn't just look at his eyes.

Caroline, on the other end of the trolley, was up for a laugh so it didn't take much for the ribaldry to start with the men before we'd even served the first round of drinks. Half-way there we hit some bad turbulence and of course, they made it extremely difficult for us to check everyone was safely strapped in. I did have to make a close inspection of the goalie a few times though, just to be sure of course, that he was snug. Didn't put my hands anywhere they shouldn't be, honest, even when a jolt sent me flying in his direction.

Turbulence doesn't bother me anymore, I only start to think about it when the Captain orders us to be strapped in too, then I know we're in for a roller-coaster ride. This time though I just got the coffee pots chucked down the sink in time. Unfortunately the hockey team were staying quite a way from our hotel and they had a strict schedule, but it's been some time since I laughed my way through a morning's work like that.

Love Suzi x

25th July - Home

Dear Eve

When someone offers you a slice of meat to eat in a restaurant, it seems churlish to refuse. In Nairobi, someone on the crew suggested going for a meal. It seemed a good idea at the time so I put my hand up and went along with the others. There's no point being boring and staying in my room.

The only trouble was I couldn't get the whole leg on my plate. No, really. It wasn't that the waiter had the leg of meat held aloft on a huge skewer as he sliced a piece and put it on my plate that caused me to pause and take a breath. It was the smell that wafted up from the joint put me off placing even the tiniest morsel to my lips. All I could picture as the odour filled my nostrils were soft, brown eyes with those long, long eyelashes staring down at me. After that, how could I eat giraffe?

It was a direct flight home from Jo'burg, so I was exhausted when I got in the front door. The girls were all out. Goodness knows where Debbie was, probably gone to stock up on bumper packets of value crisps, but thankfully the house was quiet. I was too tired to talk to anyone and just wanted to pull that duvet over me whilst I recovered enough to get through the rest of the day.

Sitting on my bed was a parcel. Nothing strange in that but when I opened it I pulled out an exquisitely pale pink, tissue-wrapped package. On further investigation it revealed a pair of very expensive looking stockings, by a make that I wasn't familiar with, but they were in my size. I continued to rummage around for a note and found one tucked in the corner.

'Suzi, - thought you might like these as a replacement for the one I stole from you. Hope to see you in them one day? Ed '

My heart did a small somersault as I held them up against the light to admire. I don't know what Ed's game is, I bet Candy doesn't know about them, but there's no way I'm going to return these.

I decided to send Ed a gift in return as a thank you for rescuing me and for the stockings. Hmmm…what to give a man who possibly has everything and flies around the world so that he can get anything he likes, even if it is fake. A bolt of inspiration then hit me. I remembered seeing the neat pile of boxer shorts in his wardrobe when I'd been in his house.

I had recently been browsing a local 'buy any tat here cheaply' shop (don't ask why) and seen the tackiest, yuckiest pair of Union Jack boxer shorts in really nasty thin material. Result! I couldn't afford to get him anything decent so going way O.T.T. on tat was the best step. I knew where he lived and could put a cheeky note thanking him for his kindness and generosity and add that I hoped never to see him in them. If Candy happened to see the parcel or the note I'm sure it would put the cat among the pigeons but, what the hell? If the man wants to play games he's got to take the consequences.

The next few days were spent catching up with domesticity. I'd like to say that my life is all exotic glamour and if I was telling a stranger I would, but in reality just between the two of us, there is a load of monotonous drudgery involved as well. I could get all my laundry done in the various hotels across the world at a price but as I'm saving that seems just a tad extravagant.

I've decide to start looking to see what kind of property I can afford. I need to stay around this area to make it easy to get to and from the airport but the nicest locations seem few and far between and of course, that's where everyone else wants to live. A cottage a few doors along from Ed is on the market but apart from being way out of my price range, I don't think Candy would be pleased to see me tottering down to put my rubbish out in my PJ's or kindly lend me a bowl of sugar when I run out.

I've got to go to Africa again. See, I told you other crew don't like going there, that's why I got it twice running. Scheduling probably think I won't complain as I'm so new. It's only a quick stop and then I'm off down to Australia. JJ's on that trip. We're due to be away for about a week so I can put up with another Africa in the meantime.

Love, Suzi x

30th July - NBO - Hotel

Eve

It felt a bit like déjà vu flying into Nairobi again. This time though there was a bit of excitement as we were coming into land. I had all the passengers strapped down in my section and the cabin ready, and had just strapped myself into my jump seat when I realised that we had stopped descending and seemed to be levelling off to circle the airport. Continuing to smile as the extremely boring man sitting opposite me tried his best at flirting, I took a quick glance out of the window. There, lined up, were the flashing lights of numerous fire engines with their ambulance companions parked next to them. People standing at the edge of the tarmac were looking up at the plane. Not one to panic immediately, well, not until I hear 'Brace, Brace' from the Captain anyway, I fixed my smile in place and watched as a senior crew member came hurrying up the aisle from the tail end of the aircraft.

'Keep smiling,' she bent down to whisper in my ear. 'We have to circle the airport. We're not sure the landing gear is down. The light for it in the cockpit is playing up. The Captain wants to make sure it's a fault with the switch not the real thing. Hold onto your hat, we may be in for a bumpy one.' And with that she rushed off up the plane to deliver her news to the next crew member.

Love, (a slightly scared) Suzi x

8th August - Home

Dear Eve

All the excitement fizzled out into nothing in the end. After circling the airport once more the Captain obviously decided we had enough wheels to land on and we made our descent. It was a relief to feel the familiar lurch and thud as the wheels made contact with the tarmac, Eve, I can tell you. In true stiff-upper-lip stewardess mode the passengers were none the wiser as my smile was fixed like glue to my face. I must have looked pretty scary – mouth smiling but eyes fixed, wider than usual, as I listened for every sound and waited for any indication that a normal landing wasn't going to happen.

One result from the dramatics with the plane was that no sooner had we checked into the hotel than we received a message to say that after minimal rest we were going to abandon our itinerary and fly the sick bird home. The powers-that-be had decided that something wasn't right with the aircraft. It couldn't be mended satisfactorily in Nairobi so it had to go back to London. Great eh? They wouldn't sanction flying paying passengers but quite happy to risk the crew flying in the wounded machine.

So after just enough time to lay my head down for forty winks I was back in the time machine again and winging my way back to Heathrow. We made ourselves very comfortable in First Class for the journey; didn't stint on the food and put our feet up. I was glad I wasn't working at Upper Deck position as the stewardess still had to wait on the flight crew. An empty 747 is a strange experience but there was no singing and dancing down the aisles this time, I had to behave myself with the others there.

When I arrived back at base there was a message from my line manager asking me to go into the offices and meet with him. This was most odd as after my probationary period I didn't expect to see much of him again. Being summoned could only be bad news.

It turns out it *was* bad news. There had been a complaint about me. He wouldn't tell me who it was from, just that it was a passenger on the flight back from Jamaica a few trips ago. It had been brought to his attention and he had to follow it up. I racked my brains for some misdemeanour I had inadvertently said or done. But nothing sprang to mind. Fortunately my manager was very laid back and said he would dismiss it this time but I came out of his office feeling persecuted. What had I done that was so bad someone would have bothered to write in about me? The flight back from Montego Bay was uneventful as far as I could remember. It was afterwards when my car ran out of fuel in the car park that things got exciting. Alarm bells started to ring in my head.

It was late the next morning as I was mooching around the house trying to get myself going that the door bell rang. The others were all out, so expecting it to be the postman with a delivery and still in my PJ's with my purple fluffy slippers on, I padded to the door. To my surprise, Candy was standing there and boy, was she fuming.

'What the hell do you think you're playing at?' she shouted angrily thrusting an open package straight into my hands. I looked down and recognised my parcel to Ed. The one with the cheeky note and Union Jack boxer shorts in. Stunned that it wasn't what I was expecting, I stood dumbstruck as she continued to rant at me.

'Don't think I don't know what you're up to,' she squeaked. This girl must sort herself out. Not only was she turning a little red and looking flustered but she needed to work on her people skills.

'Oh. Hello, Candy,' I replied calmly. There was no way I was going to let this poisoned misfit get me riled. Shame I wasn't dressed and with my make up on. I always feel better with a bit of lippy on for confidence. She, of course, was in her highest heels and so plastered with foundation I could have scrapped it off with my finger nail. 'I'm just about to put the kettle on, fancy a cup of tea?' No point in being unfriendly.

'No, I bloody don't,' she snapped. 'I told you before, Ed is *my* boyfriend. In fact we're getting engaged. So leave him alone.' She folded her arms and glared at me.

I wish I could say I was intimidated, and I might have been if she had been a bit taller, but I was more angry that she should presume to confront me like this as though we were in the school playground.

'Does Ed know you're here?' I asked innocently.

'No! And what's it got to do with you anyway?'

'Only that I wonder that he might have something to say about you opening his mail.'

'Oh, don't get smart with me,' she replied thrusting out her chest. 'Ed's in America and doesn't even know the parcel arrived.'

'Do you know that opening someone else's mail is a crime?'

'Don't be silly,' she said. Her shoulders slumping slightly in a sign of defeat.

'I'm not being silly. It's against the law if you intended to. Which I think we could conclude, you did.'

'Well, anyway,' Candy said with a toss of her hair.

'Ed's my fiancé and he wouldn't mind.'

'Hmmm… I think I might just ask him if he received my present,' I said mischievously. 'Then we can give him the chance to answer that himself.' Ha! Caught you out, madam. How dare she? I stood leaning against the doorframe as Candy shuffled from one foot to the other.

'Just leave Ed alone,' she threatened. Turning, she started to strut up the path to her car. A thought suddenly crossed my mind.

'Candy!' I called after her. 'Did you write a letter about me to the airline?'

She stopped dead in her tracks for a moment and then carried on. Head low.

'It's also illegal to look through the company files for someone's details. I might just add slander to the list as well.' I don't know how she'd done it but there was no way she could find my ID number for the company, nor my home address, without doing something illegal. I'm sure Ed wouldn't have told her. She may have gone through his belongings but either way, the woman was trouble. She had gone completely over the top when there wasn't any real reason. Okay, so I was being mildly flirtatious but no more than was normal at work. Flight Deck were still off limits to me. There's no way I'd get serious about a pilot. How would I ever be able to trust him if we got married and had a family? Some crew manage to fly and leave their kids at home, but that's not what I want for my children. The more crew and Flight Deck I meet, the more convinced I am that they do not make for stable relationships. I can see myself having a fling or two and then finding someone who doesn't have anything to do with the airline.

I was furious with Candy, Eve. Ed was the one she should have a go at, not me. She had put my job in jeopardy by being crazily jealous. It was so unfair.

I stood watching her as she started the engine and pulled away from the kerb and drove off down the road. Just at that moment Debbie's car came round the corner and pulled up in Candy's recently vacated spot.

'What's happened to you?' she asked, struggling to get a large bag of groceries out of the boot of her car. 'You're all red and you look very angry.'

You know my feelings on Debbie. The fact that she has taken up with Matt hasn't helped but at that moment I needed a friend. I followed her into the kitchen and sat watching her unpack her shopping as I gave her a brief resume of the situation.

'Sounds like you need a stiff drink,' she offered holding up a new bottle of Vodka and unscrewing the top. 'What a bitch.'

I took the shot glass she held out to me and downed it in one.

'What are you going to do?'

'I don't know yet,' I replied. 'But I'll think of something.'

A couple of evenings later Matt came round to see Debbie. I was sitting watching TV after just getting out of the bath. My wet hair was wrapped in a red towel. I was looking forward to just chilling on the sofa for a bit and catching up on a couple of programmes I'd missed. Debbie and Matt plonked themselves down on the sofa opposite and after a while started messing about as if nothing had ever happened between Matt and I. They were obviously not interested in the programme and started kissing. I know I haven't got a leg to stand on, as I was the one to break it all off, but really, you'd think they'd have a bit more sensitivity. I couldn't stand it for long but didn't want to just storm off as though in a huff so I wandered into the kitchen and then disappeared to my room. They probably didn't even notice I'd gone 'till the adverts came on. Debbie loves guessing what product they are advertising in the first few moments. It's the most animated she becomes. It started off being a laugh when we were all watching TV together but when she starts up every time the joke wears a bit thin.

Sarah-Jane was out with her old love and Sam was working late so I decided to hunker down in my bed and watch a movie on my laptop. This whole Candy business has been playing on my mind. Why did she do something as vindictive as sending that complaint in about me? There was nothing going on between me and Ed. Now she knows my address she could instigate any kind of mischief. If she could do something like the complaint what else could she be capable of? I didn't want to lose my job. Did Ed know about this side of his girlfriend? He struck me as a decent type; surely he would be shocked to hear that she could act like that? Should I tell him and if so, should I ring and arrange to meet up or text? Perhaps it would make matters worse if I arranged to meet him. She might find out and it might add fuel to her crazed fire. Oh Eve, I do wish you were here to talk this through. You would look at it all rationally and come up with a plan, I know you would. And it would be a good one to. Do you remember when we caught the bus into town to go shopping and then missed the last one home because we had decided at the last minute to go and see a movie. Our parents went mad but you came up with such a good excuse for our lateness that got us out of being grounded. I could always rely on you.

There's so much to say that it would be about ten texts to tell Ed the whole story and anyway he'd probably think I was just being a tell-tale. I have no evidence. Just the look of guilt on her face, but I can't prove anything.

When I was younger Mum always told me when things got too overwhelming that it was best to sleep on a problem and it would seem better in the morning after a good night's rest. My body clock was all over the place. Seeing Debbie and Matt cuddled up together was just the last straw. I was probably overwrought with jet lag. So I took my mother's advice and switched off the movie half way through and snuggled down under the duvet. I had to go down route next on a long trip east. JJ was on the roster. It would be good to have a ready-made friend to go exploring with. If I got out of England for a while, the Candy business would probably all blow over by the time I got back.

As I drifted off to sleep the words of Scarlet O'Hara from *Gone with the Wind* came into my mind, '*After all, tomorrow is another day.*' Too right and tomorrow I was off to Hong Kong.

Love Suzi x

10th August - Crew Bus - LHR

Dear Eve

It made such a difference walking into the briefing room before the flight to see JJ seated near the front grinning up at me. He blew me a kiss but as usual I was a bit late and flustered so I just smiled in response. The room was already full with crew so I squeezed into the empty seat in the row at the back, trying not to notice the glare coming from the man sitting at the table facing us at the front of the room.

The Senior Cabin member with his two managers flanking him sat looking at us in silence. My heart always started pounding at this point as I anticipated what was to come. It felt like an interview. The first bit of the briefing was usually mundane. A run through of the expected flight ahead including any special details. It only got exciting if at this point he announced that we would be carrying any celebrities. Otherwise it continued in a humdrum manner until we sorted out who was going to work in which position on the plane. The most senior amongst us was allowed to choose first which section they wanted. Usually the first class positions went immediately as folding the doilies for the trays and generally bowing and scraping to just a handful of passengers was highly preferable to dealing with the main sections down the back of the aircraft.

I longed for the day I wasn't the newest member of the crew and therefore the person who had the position that nobody else wanted. Mostly crew couldn't be bothered with the responsibility for the bars as it meant masses of paperwork.

This time round I was assigned to a position at the rear of the aircraft. I didn't mind. It's usually so busy that the flights pass quickly and although it tends to be bumpier on take off and landing at the back, I find it amusing from my crew seat behind the passengers to watch their heads bobbing from side to side with the movements of the plane. Just like the crowd at Wimbledon as they watch the ball rally from end to end of the court, it's as though some unseen hand is sweeping over them forcing them to move as one at its command.

It was the next bit of the briefing that I always got anxious about. Safety questions randomly to the crew. Sometimes the crew member in charge didn't bother but this tyrant was obviously pissed off with the fact that I had crept in late to his meeting. I could feel his eyes boring into me as he fired his question.

'Suzi – if you found a fire in the rear toilets what would you do and where is the nearest extinguisher?'

My heart nearly jumped out of my chest. I could feel my face redden with every hesitant second. I knew the answer, of course I did. I'd only just passed my safety exam. My mind went blank. The silence that filled the room made me cough nervously, 'Hmmm...' I stuttered back.

'Come on girl, the fire will have reached the cock-pit by the time you've decided,' the evil man barked back at me. I felt as though I was in an 'A' level exam with no escape.

'I would tackle the fire whilst calling for assistance from another member of the crew,' I managed to utter.

'Yes, yes,' he said. 'And what about the rest? Somebody help her please.'

I hung my head in shame waiting for someone to rescue me. This wasn't going at all well. My elation at seeing JJ was quashed as I realised I'd have to jump to the commands of our leader or he could make the whole trip a nightmare for me.

After a few more questions fired at other unfortunate victims (but ones who could respond correctly) the meeting was concluded and we all filed out to go and get ready before we got on the bus that would take us airside. I didn't need to go anywhere so just made my way to the rendezvous point to await the others.

Love, Suzi x

Crew rest area - 35,000ft somewhere on the way to Dubai (DXB)

Dear Eve

As we boarded the bus I found myself sitting next to a stewardess, immaculately made up and eager to talk.

'Hi. Suzi, isn't it? I'm Paula. What do you think of the steward working with you, you lucky thing? He looks cute; do you think he's gay?' Blimey she was quick to suss out the talent.

'Who is it?' I said taking the notes from my handbag and scanning the list. But I didn't have to read it as JJ hurriedly piled his things onto the seat in front of us. Reaching over the seat-back towards us he grinned at me pouting his lips for a kiss.

'Suz…Good to see you. How's things?' I leaned forward so that our lips touched. 'Don't worry about that arse,' he said indicating the boss sitting at the front of the bus. 'He's a pussy cat really. Anyway, I'll look after you.'

'Thanks JJ,' I replied ignoring the girl next to me who was obviously waiting for me to include her in our conversation. 'But how do you expect to do that when you're upstairs?'

'Not with it today, are you?' He replied. 'You're going to have to get your arse into gear, my girl. I'm not doing all the work for the both of us.' He stared at me. 'I'm in your galley.' He stared at me waiting for the penny to drop. 'We're working the same trolley!'

I could almost feel the sharpness of claws come flying

109

towards me as Paula sat silent, her face like a rottweiler ready to pounce.

'Hi,' JJ said noticing Paula. 'You alright?'

'Just fine,' Paula replied looking straight ahead. JJ turned round in his seat to sit down but not before he pulled a face at her reply, raising his eyebrows at me.

There are always things to get ready for a flight out of London. The catering needs checking to make sure there are enough meals for all the passengers and although the cleaners will have been, sometimes they are having an off-day and woe betide if there isn't enough toilet roll ready to be sucked into the void. But there's usually enough time for the crew to have a brew-up before we are faced with our glorious public.

As I entered the galley after applying another layer of lippy in readiness for my audience, it was to see JJ flanked by Paula and her trolley partner, Kim. Like bees round a honey pot, one was spooning the sugar into his cup and the other reaching for a biscuit to pass him. I nearly asked Paula if she wanted to chew it for him as well but decided as we had to work together for the next week or so it might not be a good idea to wind her up any further. They obviously weren't keen on me either as I had to pour my own cuppa.

As the flight got underway I realised what fun it could be working with someone like JJ. He was a natural comedian and enjoyed livening things up. The punters soon picked up on his mood and laughed when he tossed me a can of coke which naturally fizzed up and spurted out when I opened it. Luckily I was ready and had most of it covered with a cloth but I still had to wipe a few splashes off my face. I had to stay on my toes for the rest of the meal service for any other practical jokes.

I tried not to look at Paula and Kim working in the aisle on the opposite side of the plane. I could almost feel their jealously spurting from every pore in their bodies. Whenever the four of us were in the galley I always seemed to be manoeuvred as far from JJ as possible.

'Can't you put in a good word for me with the other two,' I hissed at him after Paula had been really awkward when I was trying to stow the trolley back into its position. 'If she was Queen of Narnia, I'd be turned to stone by now.'

'Haven't a clue what you're talking about,' JJ replied putting his arm round my shoulders as Kim came into the galley.

'Stop it!' I remonstrated shaking his arm off. 'Go and put your arm round one of them, or pinch their bum or do whatever stewards do to make them feel wanted. They're driving me mad.'

JJ, annoyingly, just laughed and carried on with his antics. Towards the end of the meal service he managed to persuade me to go down to a passenger by telling me that she had requested more coffee only to find when I got there, pot and tray with milk and sugar in my hands, the poor woman looked at me as though I'd gone nuts. I turned and glared up the aisle only to see JJ's head disappearing into the galley. The other two girls thought it was highly amusing to see me the butt of his jokes. I didn't mind but it did get a bit annoying when I nearly embarrassed a man who obviously wasn't a child stuck in the rear toilet. Luckily I knocked on the door and called out before attempting to open it, an obvious thing to do I thought.

Love, Suzi x

Dear Eve

By the time we got to Dubai I was just about on my knees and my throat was sore. Probably the result of a juicy little bug I'd picked up from the air conditioning. With his antics JJ had just about scuppered any hope of me bonding with Paula and Kim. I had tried to be friendly, offering to help Kim clear the cabin of rubbish when Paula was obviously busy with getting her paperwork finished before landing, but nothing seemed to crack the hostile exterior of the two witches as I had so endearingly named them. So when JJ offered his hotel room for the crew party I decided to leave them to it. The words 'party' and 'pooper' sprung to mind but I didn't care.

I found my room which was next to Paula's and the last thing I heard before my head hit the pillow was her giggling to Kim outside my door that she was going to hit on JJ whether I was there or not.

The next morning after breakfast we arranged to meet up and catch a boat over the Creek to the gold Souq to do some shopping. It was a hot and sunny day or at least it looked hot, but it was difficult to tell in the air conditioned world of the hotel. The moment I stepped out of the massive, sliding glass doors I gasped. I felt as though I'd just been placed in a roasting oven and turned up to full heat to be cooked. Unattractively, I felt sweaty even though I'd just rolled on deodorant. I was relieved to see that Paula was looking as red and shiny as me.

As we made our way onto the shallow, open water taxi

I found a place on the bench seat that ran down the centre next to JJ. With my feet hovering just above the water, there was no rail or side of the boat to stop me falling in. I turned to face the direction we were going in and relish in the warm caressing breeze that fanned my body. JJ was pointing out the collection of dhows unloading their cargo onto the opposite quayside against the sky scraper backdrop behind. I felt someone sit down next to me so closely I felt his thigh press up against mine.

'You smell good enough to eat,' I heard waft along in the breeze close to my ear. I turned my head quickly as I felt fingers squeeze my leg.

'Ed!' I squeaked unable to hide my surprise. I took his hand firmly and placed it back on his own thigh. 'What the hell are you doing here?'

'Hi Suzi,' he laughed leaning so close to kiss my cheek I could smell the faint lemony scent of his aftershave. 'Lovely to see you too.'

'But really,' I continued determined not to be put off by his close proximity. 'What are you doing here?'

'I'm catching the boat over to the Souq, just like you,' he annoyingly replied.

'No. I don't mean now. I didn't even know you were in this part of the world. Where are you going to next?' I insisted.

'Hong Kong.'

'You're not! I'm going to Hong Kong.'

'I am!' he said mocking my voice. 'Looks like I might be flying you there then, my girl.'

My previous encounters with Candy came rushing into my mind and I frowned. How should I broach that subject without making me sound like a real bitch?

'Surely, it's not that bad. I assure you I can fly the thing you know.' Ed said seeing my frown and mistaking the reason for it.

'No. It's not that,' I replied biting my lip in hesitation. 'I've got something to tell you, but now's not the time.' Ed raised an eyebrow and was about to say something else when JJ piped up.

'So Suz, I'm not the only man in your life then.' He held out his hand to Ed.

'Sorry. JJ, this is Ed.' The two men leant across me and shook hands.

'How are things Suzi? Have you missed me?' Ed continued.

'Of course,' I replied as JJ turned to say something to Paula who was sitting on his other side. 'Only just managed to make it through. Missed me?'

'Of course.' Ed mimicked. 'Only just…'

'… I get the idea,' I interjected slapping him playfully on the arm.

'Sorry I haven't been in touch recently,' Ed continued. 'Had a few things to sort out.'

I wanted to ask if Candy was one of the things he'd had to sort out but Ed leaned closer and whispered. 'It is really good to see you Suzi. I was hoping we'd run into each other again. I want to spend more time getting to know you.' I stared Ed straight in the eye to check he wasn't teasing me again. His brown eyes held mine. He linked his arm in mine and held my hand. Whoa! Things were looking even better than I'd hoped. My heart gave a little flutter. Must be the double espresso I'd had for breakfast to wake me up.

The waterfront came up quickly and our boat suddenly bumped into the others as we slid alongside the cluster of empty vessels huddled together at our destination. The only way to reach the quayside was to use them as stepping stones. As I turned to pick up the bag at my feet I caught Paula making a face at Kim and then beckon her head in my direction as she stood up in front blocking our exit.

'And this is Kim and Paula,' I continued motioning towards them. Perhaps if I made a grand gesture and included them they would stop being so unfriendly towards me for the rest of the trip.

Ed could have been reading my mind. He gracefully extended his hand out and helped steady Paula across the bobbing boats until she reached the safety of land. In front of me Kim had pretended to stagger clutching out at JJ who gallantly held her arm until she was safe. It was only as the four of them stood on the side that they remembered me and turned to watch as I struggled, wobbling across the uneven wooden decks towards them.

'Come on Suz…we haven't got all day,' JJ called as they walked off, the two girls slotting nicely into step beside the men.

I followed a pace behind them until we stopped to look at a display of gold jewellery. Kim giggled as she picked up a huge solitaire.

'I'll have this one,' she stated placing it on her wedding ring finger and holding it out to show JJ.

'Hmmm…' JJ grunted. 'Not if I have my way.' By even stopping we had attracted the attention of the stall holder and it was a good few minutes later that we managed to extract ourselves from his insistent protestations of giving us an unmissable bargain offer.

The two girls and JJ continued in front and I found myself walking along with Ed. He casually took my arm in his and turned to me.

'So what was it you had to tell me?'

I hesitated. How could I tell him that he was going out with a real bitch who had tried to get me fired and then come round to my house to berate me?

'Come on Suzi. We're friends aren't we? What is it?'

What should I do? Perhaps if I see how much he

115

already knows. 'Thanks for my stockings. Did you get my present?' I enquired. If he knew about the boxers then he must have seen that the parcel had been opened.

'Oh, so it was you. They were great, thanks,' he replied a little perplexed. 'Not quite my taste though. They were a joke?'

'Of course, didn't the note explain it?'

'What note. There wasn't one, that's why I didn't know they were from you.'

'That's odd. I put a note folded inside the material.'

'Well there was nothing when I took them out. I looked because I wanted to know who had been so generous to send me such a quality present.' He smiled at me.

'How did you get the present?' I enquired further. Candy must have taken out my note and then sealed up the box again.

'Oh, Candy took it in when I was away. The box was a bit battered and half open though. Maybe the note fell out.'

So that's how she'd got away with it, by pretending the parcel had been opened in transit.

'Was that it? What you wanted to tell me?' Ed continued.

We had reached the others who were clustered around another display of jewellery.

'Which one should I choose, Suz?' Ed asked me clearly thinking the subject of the parcel was over.

'Choose for what?' More games. What did he mean now? Were he and Candy getting engaged? I couldn't let him do that. She was deceitful and vindictive. I'm sure he didn't know what she was truly like. He didn't deserve that.

'If I was going to ask someone to marry me?'

Oh, that old chestnut. I looked for the most horrible

ring I could find and pointed at a really garish, ornate monstrosity. 'That one's bound to bring you happiness.' I replied flippantly. 'I'm sure Candy will love it.' I couldn't help it. If he was going through with it then it was only right that she should have something horrid to wear on her finger to match her personality.

'And if I wasn't going to ask Candy?' He looked me straight in the eyes. It was the first time I'd ever seen him so serious.

'Why, have you got a string of girls to propose to?' I answered casually. 'What's she like, this secret love of yours? Give me a clue and I'll make a more informed choice.'

'What if she was someone like you?'

Really Eve, for a moment I didn't know what to say. 'Oh, I want something much more stylish. And much more expensive.' I joked to diffuse the moment, pointing to an exquisite gold ring encrusted with tiny diamonds. 'And that's just for starters. Of course, I'd need earrings and a necklace to go with it.'

'That's the trouble with you women,' JJ commented coming up to us and putting his arm around my shoulders. 'You're never satisfied. Whatever we buy for you, it's not enough. Now, excuse us would you, Ed? I need Suzi for the moment.'

As JJ led me away I looked at Ed standing by the display. He had his hands in his pockets and was obviously displeased. I turned to face him, shrugged my shoulders and opened my hands in a gesture of reluctance. JJ was propelling me towards the doorway of a carpet shop with such force I couldn't resist.

'Thought you needed some help in getting away from his clutches,' JJ confided as soon as we were inside the dark interior. 'He seems a right bore. How do you know him anyway?'

117

My heart sank. I had been quite enjoying Ed's attention again. After his comment on the boat and then the one about the ring I felt as though we were getting somewhere. But it was far easier to be flippant and try to skim over the consequences of his words than question his motive. I stood stroking the soft silk rug hanging on the wall next to me.

'Oh, I met him when I was on a trip to L.A.'

'But he's Flight Deck, Suz. You know, *The Enemy*. You don't want to be fraternising with him.'

'I think he's quite cute,' Kim chipped in emerging from behind a large pile of carpets. 'He could fraternise with me any day.'

When we came out of the shop Ed was nowhere to be seen. As we wandered around the Souq I kept my eyes out for him but he must have gone back to the hotel as he'd completely disappeared. Check-out was later that evening and I spent the rest of the day on my own reading in a quiet corner of the hotel gardens. When I couldn't stand the intense heat anymore I made my way back up to my room to pack.

Love, Suzi x

Crew rest area - 37,000ft - somewhere between DXB and Hong Kong (HKG)

Dear Eve

As the crew gathered in the hotel lobby waiting to depart for the airport, I looked round for Ed. I felt bad about the way I had let myself be led away so easily by JJ and I still wanted to talk to him about Candy. Three men were sitting with their back to me on a white leather sofa across the marble floored lobby. As they stood up I recognised Ed, looking gorgeous in his pilot's uniform. He nodded at me but walked swiftly past as he accompanied the Captain and Engineer onto the crew bus. Maybe JJ was right. I had allowed myself to forget that Flight Deck were Gods. Who was I, a mere mortal, to dare to think he'd seriously be interested in me?

I climbed up the steps onto the bus to see that Paula and Kim had placed themselves in the seats behind Ed and the Captain who were deep in conversation. They were both smirking at the way he ignored me as I walked past his seat.

In the galley on the aeroplane we each went about our duties after taking over from the previous crew. There wasn't a spare seat in my section so I knew that I wouldn't have any time to think about Ed, Candy or what to do next. A mother with two toddlers seemed just about to blow a gasket as her children insisted on running up and down the aisles bumping into some of the other passengers stretching their legs in an attempt to relieve the boredom of the stop.

119

Paula and Kim started off ignoring me but then, inexplicably seemed to have a change of heart and mellowed as the flight went on. Midway through, when we had fed and watered the passengers and had a break from the rush, Kim and I were on our own in the galley. She pulled out a trolley from its stowage and perched on it.

'So what do you know about our luscious First Officer?' she asked conspiratorially. I had my back to her whilst I was straining a tea bag into my cup.

'Oh, not a lot. I met him a few trips ago,' I answered cautiously. This was most unlike her to be so friendly.

'Does he have a girlfriend?' she continued. Ah, so that was it. She was interested in him and thought there might be a slot for her. And I thought Flight Deck were the enemy! Another crazed woman out to catch her pilot. Could be interesting. Maybe another one for Candy to stalk.

'Yes, he does actually. Someone called Candy,' I replied.

'Shame. Never mind that's not to say he can't be tempted away.'

'I'd be careful if I were you, Candy's not to be dismissed that easily.'

'What do you mean?' Kim asked reaching over me for a biscuit from the packet on the shelf above my head.

'Oh, nothing.'

'Come on,' she persuaded. 'You must mean something by that remark. What's she like?'

'I wouldn't take her on.' I threw my tea bag into the bin and poured the milk into the cup. 'She thinks nothing of opening his mail, lying and seeking out her opponent to confront them too, if necessary.' I realised I'd said too much the moment I turned round to see her jaw drop and her mouth open. Just then Paula walked into the galley.

The call-light from a passenger went on. I placed my cup of tea on the side and walked out to answer it, bumping into JJ as he returned from his break.

'Alright?' he asked.

'I'll just answer this,' I said indicating the illuminated light above our heads. 'Then go for my break.'

I hoped the subject would be forgotten by the time I got back.

Love, Suzi x

15th August - HKG - 250ft

Dear Eve

We made good time with a strong wind behind us so there was no time to spare when I came back from my break. Afternoon tea had to be served, including two rounds of teas and coffees, cabin cleared of any rubbish, landing cards given out as necessary and all equipment safely stowed away. I spent a while chasing one of the toddlers round the cabin in a bid to get him secured in his seat for landing and by the time all was ready I had forgotten my information overload to Kim earlier. I was just about to take my seat at the back for landing when one of the pursers came into the galley.

'Suzi,' he commanded. 'Flight Deck have asked if you would like to sit up there for landing. You'd better get your arse straight up there my girl, there's not much time. I'll cover your door.' I looked at him in surprise. 'Don't know what you've done, but the Gods are looking at you kid,' he added with a wink. 'Now hurry up or we'll have landed in Hong Kong already.'

As I made my way past Kim she gave me a look that

121

confirmed, quite conclusively, that I would never be her new best friend.

If I was impressed with Ed before, watching him land the plane into Hong Kong made me almost believe he *was* a God. The two pilots take it in turns to be in charge of a sector. Although of course ultimately the Captain does have overall control, the First Officer uses his turn at being in the driving seat to brush up his skills for when he steps into the main man's shoes. Ed was so completely focused as he conversed with the control tower and manoeuvred the big bird to its graceful descent that I almost didn't recognise him. It was the first time I'd seen him in full work mode. I smiled to myself at all the scathing things I'd previously said about Flight Deck, Eve. There *was* something very attractive about powerful men. Particularly this powerful man.

Flying into Hong Kong was incredible. From my jump-seat at the back of the cockpit I could see directly out of the front window by just peeking over the Captain's shoulder. Seeing the approach straight on instead of the usual view through the side window, often with the wing obscuring everything, made it all seem so much more immediate. Apparently, as the crew informed me later, it was nothing compared to how landing in Hong Kong used to be before they built the new airport. They would descend through the maze of high-rise buildings without being able to see the runway ahead. The island is so built up that as they flew by they were close enough to almost see into the apartment windows as the residents ate their breakfast. The pilot would head the plane for a chequered board strategically positioned on the hillside and once that came into view they would know to turn right. The runway would then be in front of them. How scary was that? Almost flying blind. It must have been nerve racking your first time.

I sat quietly in my seat listening to the conversation between Ed and the control tower until the plane had taxied into place. Once we had stopped I slipped off my safety harness and hurried out of the cockpit door only to be confronted with the upper deck passengers retrieving their belongings from the overhead stowages. When I was able to get down the stairs it took a while until I could gradually make it down the length of the plane and back to my galley as I had to manoeuvre my way through all the passengers. Kim and Paula glared at me as I retrieved my handbag from its locker, placed it on the metal galley counter and waited for the oncoming crew to board. JJ on the other hand was upbeat.

'Who's the golden girl then?' He teased.

'Don't know what you mean,' I replied as I puckered up, squinting into a small hand mirror to refresh my lipstick.

'Lover boy requested your presence, did he? Wanted to show you how brilliant he is?' He continued to jibe.

'No. Nothing like that,' I denied knowing full well that it could only have been Ed who had cleared it with the Captain for me to sit up there for landing.

'Oh yes, we all get to sit in the cockpit,' Paula said snidely coming into the galley as the last passenger leaving the plane passed by. 'I'm booked in for take-off.'

I ignored her remark and smiled at a steward from the on-coming crew who arrived to take over my position. I picked up my bag and walked up the aisle to make my way out of the plane and into the airport building. Our luggage was waiting for us by the time we got to the baggage hall and after clearing customs I waited with JJ for the crew bus that would take us to our hotel. The Flight Deck walked past us and climbed into a smaller bus.

'They stay in a different hotel from us,' JJ informed

123

me. 'Nevermind. You'll just have to make do with me.'

I turned and smiled at him then placed a kiss on his cheek. 'You'll do very nicely,' I offered. I wasn't going to let any of them know how disappointed I felt that Ed had ignored me again. 'Can you ditch your harem though?' I asked looking at Kim and Paula tottering towards us pulling their luggage behind them.

'Maybe. What's it worth?' JJ teased.

'Wait and see?' I joked. For goodness sake. I was in Hong Kong. How amazing was that? I wasn't going to let a couple of jealous girls ruin the excitement of my first time there.

'Now you're talking,' JJ said helping the bus driver to load my suitcase into the rear of the vehicle. 'How about we meet for drinks in my room and then go check out this place?'

As usual when JJ said 'drinks in his room' he always included everyone. He was the most sociable person I'd met. He always offered his room as open house for a party and managed to produce a whole range of alcohol to boost our individual stocks. If I wanted a good time, JJ was the man to supply it. He ended up mixing me such a colourful concoction of a cocktail it went straight to my head on my empty stomach. By the time we moved out of the hotel to find somewhere to eat I was feeling very happy and relaxed. The whole evening passed in a pleasant blur and I was grateful when one of the other stewardesses said she wanted to go back to the hotel so we could share a taxi.

Love, Suzi x

Still in HKG - hotel

Dear Eve

The next morning when I awoke it wasn't only a slight headache I nursed but the desperate need to have a decent breakfast to soak up any residual alcohol. One of the last things I remembered before leaving the restaurant the previous evening was that a few of us had arranged to meet before going out for the day together. I showered and got dressed before catching the lift down to the lobby to await the others. Near the exit doors a man was sitting with his back to me. I walked up to him thinking he was a crew member and he turned around in his seat at the sound of my arrival.

'Just the woman I was waiting for,' Ed said with a smile as he got up, took my arm and led me out through the glass doors.

'But… but I've arranged to go out with the others,' I protested.

'Shame. They're not here though so you'd best come with me,' he grinned not releasing my arm until he'd steered me outside and along the road.

'Now look here,' I exclaimed getting annoyed at his arrogance and shaking my arm free. 'You've done nothing but ignore me recently. You can't just turn up and expect me to do as I'm told. Anyway …' He stopped and faced me, hands casually in his pockets waiting for me to continue. 'I can't just abandon them.'

'Why not? I thought that's what you do. You didn't have much trouble doing it to me in Dubai.'

I felt my cheeks get a little hot. 'Ah…' I stuttered. 'That was different.'

'How Suzi?' Ed questioned. We had stopped beside a bus stop. The yellow double-decker pulled up alongside it and the doors slid open.

'I'm going to Stanley market. Coming?' Ed said turning to look at me as he stepped onto the bus.

I'm so weak and shallow. I know I should have stood my ground, stamped my foot and shouted that he couldn't just click his fingers and I'd come running but I didn't. Ed wasn't even waiting for me. He had boarded the bus and was walking along to the stairs to make his way to the top deck. The bus driver looked at me. He shook his head pressed a button and the doors started to close. I don't know what impelled me but it must have had jet propelled force because I leapt forward, nearly getting my jacket caught as the doors shut behind me. Slowly I made my way upstairs to find Ed sitting in the front seat on the right.

'Sit here Suzi,' he said indicating the seat next to him. 'It's the best way to get to Stanley, you wait.'

I sat down but turned to look at him. He leaned over and put his arm along the back of the seat.

'It's your first time in Hong Kong, isn't it?' I nodded. 'It's an amazing place. There's so much I want to show you.' His eyes were shining. Ed's enthusiasm was infectious. I looked out from our high perch at the street below teeming with life. Everywhere people were bustling along, cars crammed the roads and the bus looked like it would end up trailing bunting made of neon signs they hung out so provocatively. What was I missing out on with the others? The two witches, Paula and Kim, would be there scowling at everything I did and said all day. JJ was the only one I felt bad about. He'd been a real ally and I still had to work the rest of the trip with him.

'The others will be wondering where I am?' I said.

'Just send them a text to say you're not feeling well. That always seems to work.' Ed offered nonchalantly.

'But Ed.' I said. 'What about Candy?' I couldn't just dismiss her. It almost felt as though she was sitting on the seat between us.

'What about Candy? You're here. She's not.' Blimey, his answer was quick and to the point.

'Is that what you think about all your women,' I said rising to the bait, pushing his arm away. 'Out of sight out of mind. Oh, I'll just flirt with this one because she's here.'

'No. You're wrong, Suz. You don't always know what goes on behind closed doors. My relationship with Candy isn't what it seems.'

'Well she obviously thinks it's full on. And you told me when we first met that you were buying a house together. How much more committed does it have to be for you before you consider yourself taken?'

'You know nothing about it. How do you know what Candy thinks?' he said frowning. 'Look Suzi. Forget about Candy. I don't want to argue with you, I just want to spend a nice day exploring this wonderful city. Send your text then let's forget about everyone else. They're not here. It's just you and me.'

I took out my phone. I'd got myself into this the moment I'd stepped on the bus. I could have easily let the driver shut the doors and drive off. I could have walked back to the hotel and met up with the others. Ed and his troubled relationship with Candy were not my concern. There was no reason to think she'd ever know Ed and I had seen each other down-route. Unless she actually worked in scheduling she wouldn't be able to access my roster. There was no harm in spending the day with Ed. Crew always stuck together going sightseeing and

127

shopping. Just because I fancied him, it made no difference. I was being irrational. We could explore Hong Kong together as friends and then walk away. Ed wasn't bothered about Candy so why should I be?

I sent JJ a text. I hated lying but saying I wasn't well did seem the easiest explanation for my absence. Everyone knew I'd had a skinful the previous evening so it would seem feasible. I'd made my choice and there seemed little point being grumpy about it. It was childish to spoil the day because of other people. I sat back to enjoy the ride.

'The first thing we must do is get something to eat though, I'm starving,' I said as my stomach rumbled. Ed reached for a small bag on the floor between his feet that I hadn't seen.

'Here, have these for starters,' he offered handing me a bottle of water and a muesli bar. 'I always have them with me in case I'm starving too. My body clock's often all over the place. Must keep your sugar levels up,' he added with a grin. 'I know a great place to get something proper to eat once we get there.'

Ed was right. The ride on the bus was just like a rollercoaster. The road took its winding route around the side of a hill. At various points of the journey Ed made me lean over him to look out of the side window at the sheer drop to the sea below us. With the cars coming in the opposite direction it seemed sometimes as thought the bus didn't have enough room to safely negotiate the turnings. It was obvious Ed was enjoying the journey as he looked just like a school boy pretending to drive the bus.

'A thrill seeker then?' I questioned as we had just finished navigating an exceptionally narrow turning in the road.

'Yep. Every time. This is the only way to travel, you

don't feel the excitement of being up high when you come in a taxi,' he said.

'Ahh.. Yes, the thrill of being up high. Is that why you learnt to fly?'

'Maybe. But I think it was more my Granddad's influence. He flew in the war and I can just about remember him playing with me when I was a boy. I've always wanted to be able to fly.'

'Got any brothers or sisters?'

'Two sisters.'

That explains it. No wonder he feels so relaxed around women and is so easy to be with. Ed had replaced his arm along the back of the seat as he turned to talk to me and this time I left it there. Eve, I can't remember when I've felt so at ease with someone. Ed was so chatty, telling me anecdotes of his childhood, making me laugh and asking me about my family, interspersed with pointing out places of interest. Before I realised we'd arrived at the market. Along with the other passengers made our way down the stairs and out of the bus. Ed lead me purposefully along an alley lined with stalls to a café and then inside to a table situated at the back. We had just sat down and ordered our food when the door opened and in walked Paula and Kim.

'Glad to see you've made a swift recovery, Suzi,' Kim said sarcastically as they seated themselves a couple of tables away. 'We're meeting JJ in a while. He'll be so pleased to hear you're up and about.'

If I felt any pleasure in the day ahead it was quickly quashed. I tried to ignore them but Ed wasn't stupid. It was obvious how uncomfortable I felt.

'Can we just eat this and get out of here?' I whispered to him. The room was so small it was easy to hear everyone's conversations so I kept my voice low. 'Those two are a bloody nightmare. I don't want them hearing every word I say.'

Nodding his head in agreement, our food didn't take long to come and we finished it quickly. As we paid the bill and walked past Kim's table she couldn't resist having another snipe at me.

'Have a good day you two,' she cried as the door of the café closed behind us.

I sighed when we got outside. Why did I let them get to me? It was nothing to do with them who I spent my time with.

'They're only jealous,' Ed said seeing my relief at getting out.

'Jealous of what?' I teased, picking up his mood as he took my hand and led me towards a stall covered in fake purses, belts and bags.

'That you're with me of course,' he said picking up a Louis Vitton purse and holding it up to ask the stall holder the price. It took a couple of minutes for the two men to agree but Ed smiled as he paid the man.

'Always pays to barter, Suzi. They expect you to.'

'So you're into fake designer purses now, are you?' I teased. Damn Candy. It was probably for her.

'No, just buying it for someone,' he replied casually wandering over to the next stall where shirts were hanging from every possible vantage point. Ed picked a pink one from its perch and held it against him. 'What do you think?' He asked holding it out.

'Totally you,' I replied. 'Shows you're in touch with your feminine side,' I said going behind him and pulling it tight to see whether it would fit. 'Think you need the extra large though,' I added looking at the label.

'Ha Ha. Very funny,' Ed laughed. 'I never bother with their clothes anyway as I always find the sleeves too short for me.' And as if to demonstrate he picked another from its hanger and held the sleeve against his arm. The cuff ended half way along his forearm.

'Would save you rolling them up,' I said, beginning to walk off as the stall holder made his way around to the front where we were standing, ready to pounce with his sales pitch. Ed put the shirt back, shaking his head and waving his hands at the man and quickly followed after me.

'Now Suzi, what would you like? You know you can get pretty much anything here. Fancy this?' he asked holding up the most hideously patterned full length skirt.

'Only as a gift for Can…' I started to say then stopped as I realised it would sound incredibly bitchy. Luckily Ed didn't hear as he had walked into a shop selling paintings at the side of the alley. I followed him in, avoiding the baskets of goods placed down the middle of the floor, as I wandered round admiring the different style of prints and paintings on offer. Some weren't to my taste being too contemporary but I was taken by a couple of small views of Hong Kong harbour; water colour prints, neatly framed in gold.

'Do you like them?' Ed inquired coming up quietly by my side.

'Yes, I do actually. I haven't got many pictures at home and I think it's about time I started buying a few mementos of my travels.'

'For when you're old and grey,' Ed smiled as the owner came over to us.

'Exactly,' I answered reaching into my bag for my purse.

'Suzi,' Ed said taking my hand thus preventing me from getting my purse out. 'Patience. What did I say earlier? You must barter.'

I put my purse back and enjoyed a few moments chatting with the congenial owner over the price of the two paintings. Ed stood behind her smiling

131

encouragement at me when he thought I was on the right track. We eventually agreed on a price and I handed over the cash after the paintings were neatly wrapped. I was secretly glad that I'd managed to bring the price down as I would have handed over the amount marked on the corner of the frame, but Ed's smugness as we walked out of the shop and off down the alley underneath the over-hanging awnings slightly irritated.

'See' he said taking my hand in his. 'It's easy when you try.'

'Ed,' I said pulling my hand out of his grasp and facing him. 'Stop being so smug. I would have got there, just in my own time,' I reasoned. As soon as I said it I wished I hadn't. I had obviously mistaken smugness for something else.

'I was only trying to help,' he said. 'You haven't been here before.'

'I'm a big girl. I can look after myself.'

'So I'm finding out,' he said taking my hand again. 'Only not if it involves filling up the car with fuel.'

This time I ripped my hand from his and playfully hit him across the arm. 'Now who's being funny,' I said as I replaced my hand in his. We were walking along the market looking at all the different stalls when we came to one selling lanterns. Some of them were so low I had to duck to pass under them. It was just as I cleared a large red paper lantern and stood upright again on the other side that I bumped into someone. I recognised JJ's shirt as he bent to pick up the bag that I'd sent flying from his grasp.

'Hello, Suzi,' he said scowling at Ed with obvious displeasure. 'Feeling better?'

'Hi, JJ,' I answered swiftly dropping Ed's hand. 'Yes, thanks. I wasn't as bad as I thought.' Damn. I'd forgotten the girls had said he was in the market as well. It was plain that he was pissed off with me. My snub of his company was clear. We all stood in an awkward silence until Kim came out of a nearby shop.

'Oh, hi again, you two,' she said coming over to us and placing her arm through JJ's. 'Is that for your girlfriend, Ed?' she said seeing the purse tucked underneath his arm. 'Did you help him choose it, Suzi? You probably know what she likes seeing as how you've met her.'

Ed looked from Kim to me, a quizzical look on his face.

'Oh, didn't you know that Candy and Suzi had a bit of a run-in?' Kim said in a conspiratorial manner. 'Oh dear, have I let the cat out of the bag, Suzi? I didn't realise it was a secret when you told me in the galley.' I felt my face flare crimson. Ed looked at me questioningly.

Obviously pleased that her remark had had the desired effect, Kim turned on her heels and, still entwined with JJ, walked off in the opposite direction. 'See you,' she threw at us over her shoulder.

'What the hell did she mean by that?' Ed asked.

'Oh nothing,' I replied starting to walk away towards the end of the market.

'When did you have a run in with Candy? You've only met that once at my place?' Ed caught up with me and grabbed my arm stopping me in my tracks. 'Haven't you? What's going on, Suzi?' he questioned as I stood motionless just staring at him.

I've never been good at hiding my feelings and the way Ed was staring at me only made me feel more guilty. But why? I had nothing to feel guilty about. It was Candy who had caused trouble for me and written that letter of complaint. She was the one who had come round to my place and confronted me. It was all the wrong way round. I could feel my heckles rise at the accusation in his voice.

'If you must know,' I started to explain, careful to keep my voice steady. 'Candy came round to my place before this trip.'

'What!' Ed said, obviously confused. 'Why? And how does she know where you live?'

'Exactly!' I accused. 'I thought you'd say that. If you didn't tell her she must either have looked through your stuff or got it from work. If she got it from work then what she's done is illegal.' I could feel my cheeks going red. I placed my hands on my hips in my I-mean-business-fighting-stance.

'But, I don't understand. Why did she do that? I don't think she would go through my things nor search at work for your address,' he added quickly in her defence. 'Why would she come and see you? You realise that what you are accusing her of is pretty serious stuff.'

He was clearly so enamoured with Candy she could do no wrong in his eyes. Should I shatter his illusions as to the horrible nature of his girlfriend? I looked at Ed as he ran his hand through his hair in bewilderment. A tuft stayed sticking out in a clump at the side of his head.

'You may not want to hear this Ed. And I really didn't want to have to tell you. I thought if I said nothing it would all blow over. But you have one crazily jealous woman for a girlfriend.' I paused to let my words sink in. If he was in love with her it would take a lot of persuading for him to see it from my point of view.

A crowd of school children came jostling into us as we stood in the middle of the stalls blocking their way. I grabbed the material of Ed's sleeve and pulled him out of the centre of the crowd, down between the lantern stall and one selling weird looking sweets wrapped in brightly coloured paper, until we came out beside the water. I leant against the railings putting my paintings down at my feet.

'Okay. I'll start at the beginning,' I said turning to face him. 'After you sent me those replacement stockings, I posted you back the boxers but put a note wrapped up inside them. It didn't say anything risqué but there was no way you would have missed it when you took them out of the package. The next thing I know, Candy is standing on my doorstep, thrusting the boxers into my hands and ranting at me to leave you alone.'

Ed stood looking at me his mouth open in disbelief. 'Okay, she may be a bit jealous but I find it hard to believe she would be aggressive like that.' How dare he question me? My heart started beating furiously as I tried to contain my rising anger.

'So you're calling me a liar now, are you?' I shouted turning on him. I was past caring about how loud my voice had become. 'Why would I make something like this up? You need to put your own house in order before you start accusing me of lying. If Candy's so insanely jealous, she must have a good reason to be.' I threw at him. 'And another thing …,'I paused to catch my breath. 'After you helped me when my car broke down, I got an official complaint from a passenger and was hauled in front of my line manager.' So I might have been exaggerating a bit but my blood was up and I was on a roll. 'Luckily for me he let it drop but when I asked Candy if she had written the letter her silence said it all.'

'You can't just assume someone is guilty because they keep silent,' Ed retorted.'Candy would never do anything so under-handed.'

'Wouldn't she? How well do you really know the woman you're buying a home with?' I questioned. 'Got a key to your house, has she? Ever found things not quite as you left them.' I realised I'd hit the nail on the head as his face changed. He stood staring at me. My anger felt like a balloon starting to deflate. Ed wasn't the one I was angry at. It was Candy. Even thousands of miles away she was making me behave like a wild insane woman. I took some deep breaths and tried to calm down.

'I think it's best if I go back to the hotel now.' I suddenly felt exhausted. I could see a couple of taxis parked over the other side of the road. 'No, don't come with me,' I added as Ed turned to follow me. 'I'll go back on my own.' Damn the expense. I didn't want to sit in silence with him in the back of a car all the way back to the hotel. He had shown where his loyalty lay by his accusations. All the earlier joy of the day had disappeared. I felt tired and drained of all my reasoning powers.

'But Suz,' Ed tried to reason. 'You're wrong about Candy. She's gentle and sweet. She would never do something like that.'

'Ed. I'm not wrong but if you can't see what she's like then so be it. It's your life not mine. I wish you luck.' I left him standing there and walked over to the line of taxis to go back to the hotel.

The winding roads that I'd enjoyed on the way to the market only a short while earlier only annoyed me as I slid from side to side in the back of the slightly spicy smelling cab. My stomach felt awash with its contents and I tried to keep my eyes focused on facing forward as I recognised car sickness taking hold of me. Breathing deeply I prayed for the journey to end so that I could disappear to the comfort of my room. I had been wrong about Ed. Whatever attraction there was between us wasn't based on anything solid. I had kidded myself that he was seriously attracted to me. I had been another flirtation for him. It served me right. I was an idiot. Now that I had burnt my bridges with JJ I would have to entertain myself alone for another day and a half until we left Hong Kong for home the next afternoon. At least I could catch up on my sleep.

I paid the taxi driver and made my way through the empty hotel lobby to the lifts in the corner at the rear. As I pressed the button on the panel to my floor I resolved never to get involved with Flight Deck again. They were nothing but trouble.

Love Suzi x

HGK - Hotel room. *A few hours later*

Dear Eve

The steam from the hot water filled the bathroom as I poured the complimentary bubble bath under the tap from the small container that had been left lined up with a matching shampoo and shower cap on the side of the bath. My earlier encounter with Ed had left me exhausted and I only wanted to sink into the hot water before crashing into bed for an early night with a good book. I decided to order room service and make a night of it! Jeez… did I know how to live or what?

As I sunk down into the bubbles I started to relax and feel better. To hell with men. To hell with them all. I didn't need the likes of Ed nor JJ to enjoy this life. Here I was, travelling the world. A woman of independence and means. I was never going to be like Debbie, only interested in seeing the world from a 14 inch screen. (We had inherited the television from the last tenants. Beggars weren't choosers in our case, it was a free telly). I was due a new roster when I returned. Who knew where it would take me?

I washed my hair, instantly regretting being too lazy to get my own shampoo out of my wash bag as I tried to get

137

a decent lather from the hotel freebie. I wrapped myself up in towels; my hair in a turban. I may have added a few pounds onto my original 126 since starting flying but bloody hell, the towel for my body only just went round enough to tuck in.

I looked at myself in the full length mirror that hung in the corridor by the door. Not only was the towel small length ways, it only just covered my bottom. What a stingy housekeeping service, hotels were usually much more generous than that. I moved up nearer to the glass for a closer inspection. Not my most attractive. My face was like a red shiny apple from the heat of the bathroom. Looking like this I could keep the Kowloon District powered with warmth.

A knock at the main door made me jump. Remembering my adventures in Sydney I looked through the spy hole and, seeing no one outside, cautiously turned the handle. There, sitting in a metal cooler bucket all on it's own outside my door was a bottle of champagne.

I poked my head outside and looked up and down the corridor. No one. Bending at the knees so as not to do an unintentional moony I picked up the note that sat resting against the dark green glass.

'*Sorry*,' was all it read.

Not sure what to do and whether there had been a mistake I picked up the bucket and turned to go back into my room.

'So you forgive me?' A voice said from behind me. The surprise made me jump. At the same time I screamed and let go of the bucket. Quickly grabbing the towel that had come loose from around my body (I wasn't going to do a streak as well) I turned and pulled it tightly across my chest. The glass of the bottle hitting the inside of the metal as the two crashed to the floor, spilling ice across the carpet.

'Ed! You bastard!' I exclaimed as I desperately tried to recover myself and retain my dignity.

'Didn't mean to give you a fright, Suzi, but glad to see you dressed up for me.'

'What the bloody hell are you doing here?' I questioned still standing in the doorway clutching the towel around my naked body desperately hoping nothing was on show that shouldn't be.

'I came to apologise and see if you fancied a drink.'

What could I do? I was standing half naked in the corridor of a hotel, barely covered by skimpy bath towels, my hair swished up in a turban, with a bright red face. A bottle of champagne was at my feet and Ed was looking at me with his gorgeous puppy dog eyes.

I hesitated. It felt like one of those scenes in a movie when you just knew the heroine really shouldn't do what she is about to do, but something makes her throw caution to the wind and she jumps in with both feet. If I was listening to my head, Eve, I would have slammed the door in his face (after I've picked up the champagne bottle, of course) and screamed at him never to come near me again. Good move? Not sure? Listening to my heart was soooo much more exciting.

'You left these behind as well,' Ed continued, reaching down to pick up the watercolours I'd bought from the market from where he had placed them leaning against the wall beside the door.

Head… Heart… Oh, to hell with it. I forced away the resolutions I'd made earlier in the bath. Flight Deck were trouble but why couldn't I have a bit of fun first? I could protect my heart from getting damaged. I knew where I stood. Ed was with Candy and he would return to her once those wheels touched the tarmac at Heathrow. Meanwhile I could have a bit of fun at Candy's expense. I'm not a vindictive person, truly, but Candy wasn't there. Ed was asking to spend some time with me. So be it. Decision made.

I stood back from the door and gestured for him to enter. 'You realise of course that it'll take more than a bottle of champagne to get round me,' I said as I followed him in and shut the door. Ed put the champagne bucket on the wooden cabinet next to the TV and picked up the bottle.

'Well,' he said taking the wrapper off the top and starting to peel the metal cage from the cork. 'How about we start with this and then I take you out for dinner. You didn't have anything planned did you?' He reached into his pocket and brought out two champagne flutes.

'Where did you get them from?' I asked in amazement. Then the penny dropped. 'Don't tell me you borrowed them from First Class.'

'Nooooo. That would be stealing. I always carry a couple of glasses in my luggage. Don't you?' He smiled at me.

'But that means you must have planned this? Or at least hoped you might get lucky.' The scheming bastard. He had this in mind all the time. It must be his usual seduction technique.

'Suzi. You are so sceptical. Why can't I just happen to have champagne glasses with me without any deception in mind? Stop analysing everything.'

'But unless you're here to seduce me, thus adding me to your list of conquests, why are you here?'

Ed finished pouring the champagne into the glasses, stepped towards me and looked me straight in the eye. 'I'm here because I really like you and I don't want our friendship to end on a bad note which it would have done.'

I took the flute from his outstretched hand and gulped a large mouthful. Big mistake. The bubbles from the cold liquid hit the back of my throat and went down the wrong way. I started to choke. In an effort to breathe, the strain of my coughing caused the towel to come off my head leaving my hair tossed around my face in a tangled mass. Ed quickly came to my assistance. He rescued the glass from my hand but in his effort to save me from spilling it everywhere, caught the side of the towel wrapped around my body causing it to slip to the floor. I stood naked, hair like a whirling dervish in front of him, coughing for all I was worth.

'Hmmm… not the usual reaction I get giving a woman champagne,' he laughed as I regained my breath. 'Well, not so quickly anyway. But infinitely preferable.'

I rushed into the bathroom, past caring that I'd left nothing to his imagination.

'Shut up!' I shouted in between breaths as I leant on the side of the bath. After a short while of breathing deeply I'd recovered enough to brush my hair and regain my composure. The bathroom door slowly opened a crack. 'Thought you might want this,' Ed said as he passed me through a large, white, fluffy robe. I put it on and tied the cords tightly around my waist. As I walked back into the room, Ed was refilling the flutes.

'Why don't we start again, Suzi?'

'But what…'

'No buts. I want us to be friends. That's all. Let's forget our argument earlier…' I opened my mouth to protest again. Obviously fed up with trying to rationalise with me Ed took one step closer. Putting his arm around my back and pulling me so close I could smell the champagne on his breath, he held me tightly. Before I could say anything he pressed against me until my head tilted back. He brought his lips down to meet mine. I felt his tongue probing into my mouth. Mmmm… long time since this had happened to me. I'd forgotten how pleasant it was. Sword fighting with tongues we used to call it as kids. Ed was particularly good at it. After what I thought was a keen-but-not-quite-a-pushover amount of time, I pushed him away slightly.

'Not bad,' I said stepping back and appraising him. 'What's that? Stage 1?'

'Suz... you're impossible.' Ed took his champagne and sat down in the chair beside the bed. 'I'm going to ignore that remark and move on. What do you fancy to eat? Chinese? I know a good restaurant just up the road from here. Let's finish this while you get dressed and we can go and see what they've got.'

So, once a First Officer always a First Officer. Thinks he can take control in my hotel room as well as on the plane, does he? Well we're not on that big bird now. I sipped my drink and sat on the bed leaning against the headboard. I wasn't going to do what I was told quite so easily. If he wanted seduction I'd show him who was in charge. I let the robe fall open slightly at the top showing just a hint of my right breast. Probably needless as he'd just seen what I had to offer but I'd watched a movie recently where the woman arranged herself on the bed like that and it worked for her.

'I was going to stay in before you turned up,' I said. 'I am starving though. Does that restaurant do take-away? Seems a shame to gulp this down.' I held up my glass. Overdone a bit maybe? What a harlot I was. I really needed to practise being more subtle. 'What about you go and pick us up something to eat and bring it back here.' Not the best seduction technique but if there was going to be a conquest, it would be on my terms. And anyway I needed to get him out of the way for ten minutes whilst I got myself prepared. Although he'd just seen me naked it wouldn't do for him to look too closely.

Ed looked at me. 'Sometimes I just don't get you Suzi.

You remind me of my sister.' Oh great. Now he thinks of me as a sibling. 'She's a bit barmy as well.' Even better, a mad sibling. 'I now know what her boyfriend puts up with,' he continued. 'But that sounds good. What do you like?'

'Surprise me.' I requested. 'Anything chicken,' I added quickly as he finished his glass and headed for the door. I suddenly had visions of Ed bringing back snakes in batter or something equally yucky just to see my reaction.

'Oh, you'd better take this,' I said handing him the key for the door. Ed leant over and kissed me gently on the cheek. 'I meant what I said, Suz. I do want us to be friends. You're different from the others.' He walked to the door. 'Bonkers, but different. Won't be long.'

As soon as the door slammed I raced off the bed. I reckoned I had about twenty minutes. Gulping down the rest of the glass I refilled it and headed into the bathroom. I ran my hands along my shin. Shit. That would never do. If Ed was going to caress me with his tongue from toe to head it would be in tatters by the time he left my knee. I grabbed the razor from my wash bag and climbed back into the shower. I hadn't de-fuzzed for a couple of days. Well, I reckoned there wasn't much point in doing the whole works if there was no need, only the bits that could be seen.

I swished back the shower curtain and studied myself in the mirror. Okay, the burning bush would have to go. You never know, he might make it as far as there if I didn't blow it beforehand. I hosed myself down and started to squeeze the hair conditioner into my hand. Starting with the black spider hairs on my big left toe (well he's got to start somewhere) I slathered the creamy liquid all over my legs and up over my body until I got to my underarms. In all the movies I'd ever seen, the couple

143

always lay post coital with their hands behind their heads, a bit self satisfied I'd always thought, but best to be prepared for all positions. With the precision of a surgeon I ran the razor over my skin until everywhere was soft and smooth. Impressed that even under pressure I hadn't nicked myself I patted myself dry and reached for a large tub of coconut body butter. Fingers crossed Ed wasn't allergic to coconut, as it was that or baby lotion.

I looked in the mirror again. Nice job. Now I just needed to do something with my hair and face. It didn't take long to select my nicest underwear. Not quite the right ones for a hot night of passion but the best set I could find at short notice. At least they matched and were lacy. At last. I was ready for anything that came my way. My heart pounded as I looked at the clock and realised that twenty minutes had gone by. I switched on the TV and, dressed in a short blue skirt and patterned top that I had plucked from the top of my suitcase, I lay on the bed to await Ed's return.

Damn. My stomach rumbled in protest at being neglected for so long. I leapt off the patterned covers and picked up the remains of the champagne. Tipping the rest into my glass I propped myself up on the pillows and sipping the liquid down, excitedly awaited my night of passion.

Love Suzi x

Hotel coffee shop - HKG

Dear Eve

The shrill sound of the telephone came into my dream just as I was about to drop a large dollop of chocolate sauce all over a man's naked chest. It could have been Ed but, as always in my dreams although vivid, they were usually made up of bits of people I knew who morphed into each other rather than one solid person. I opened one eye and fumbled for the phone on the bedside table and placed it to my ear. An automated voice on the other end announced it was my wake-up call.

Wake up call for what? Where was I and what did I have to wake up for? I opened the other eye and stared at the darkened hotel room. Which hotel was this? I couldn't remember anything. Turning over onto my side I switched on the bedside light. The cover from the bed was spread over me but underneath I was fully dressed in my short blue skirt and patterned top; albeit a little crumpled but the same clothes I'd worn earlier.

Shit... Shit... SHIT... I remembered! I looked at the clock. It read twelve thirty. But was it night or morning? Check-out was at two thirty in the afternoon. But the afternoon of the day after my night of passion!

ED! Where was he and what had happened? I noticed a piece of paper stuck underneath the bottle of champagne. In my rush to get off the bed I got tangled up in the covers and fell on the floor. I clambered to my knees and grabbed the piece of hotel writing paper from underneath the glass.

Suzi, it seems as though you finished this off without me... I read. Picking up the bottle I tipped it up to find only a tiny dribble come from the spout. Bloody hell, I must have downed more than I realised while I was preparing myself. Now Ed would think I was an alcoholic as well as mad.

...so I've taken the food to finish myself. I tried to share it with you but I got no response when I returned. Even when kissing you from head to toe, you only turned over and snored. I usually get a better reaction to my

love-making so decided to leave you to sleep it off and try my luck elsewhere. I have an earlier check out than you as I'm on my way to Oz. Shame it didn't work out between us – maybe next time.

Ed

Ps. The wake up call is just in case you are really dead instead of only comatose in a drunken stupor with jet lag. Wouldn't want you to miss your flight home.

I sat in the chair and stared at the writing. What an idiot I am, Eve! I had completely blown it. So much for all that shaving and perfuming. Now I'd never know if Ed was allergic to coconuts. My seduction technique was so bad it was off the scale. I looked in the mirror at the pillow lines etched into my cheek as though someone had used a pastry cutter to make them. I rubbed the stain of dribble that clung from my lip and down my chin. Perfect. What a picture I made. No wonder Ed had hot-footed it out of the room. Even the promise of sex hadn't tempted him to hang in there and hope I turned into a swan instead of the dribbling duckling.

I licked my finger and scrubbed harder at my face. Christ! I was turning into my mother. Do you remember she used to do that at the school gate to remove the last remains of breakfast before I went into class? It was always so embarrassing but you just used to laugh. Why is it that sleeping deeply always leaves you with such strong imprints on your face you look like the page of a map? I knew I was tired but didn't realise I could be *that* tired.

I switched on the TV only for it to confirm what I suspected. I had slept the whole night and next morning. I had only two hours before I had to check-out. Thank

146

goodness Ed had placed the wake up call for me otherwise it could all have been much worse.

Amazed that I'd cocked up again I threw my clothes into the suitcase. I quickly showered, changed into my uniform and plastered my face in make-up using extra quantities to fill in the grooves down my cheek. If ever there was a time for using a trowel, now was it. I packed up the rest of my things in the room and rang down for the porter to come and collect my bag. I needed a strong coffee and I needed it before I faced those two bitches I was working with.

I decided to walk down the stairs instead of using the hotel lifts in the hope that I could sneak into the coffee shop at the back of the lobby where I would be able to get something to eat and drink. No wonder I was starving, not only had I missed out on the promise of the hottest night of my life, I'd missed a few meals whilst I was doing my impression of Sleeping Beauty.

The coffee shop was empty when I walked in and I found myself a seat in a booth at the side. After ordering myself a nutritious egg and chips, I'd downed two cups of coffee and stood up to go back for a refill when I heard giggling from the entrance. Kim was walking in, arm in arm with JJ.

'Apparently,' she was broadcasting in her loudest voice to the whole of the hotel. 'He arrived only to find her asleep on the bed.' The sound of her high-pitched laughter resounded from wall to wall.

' Our Suzy isn't as irresistible as she likes to make out. Serves her right, if you ask me. Stuck up cow.'

I knew my face was the colour of a beetroot because as I stood there, coffee cup in hand, I saw the look on JJ's face as he saw me and realised I must have heard every word. The only saving grace was that the colour of his face soon matched mine. I wondered what would be the

147

best approach to this conundrum. Should I go up to Kim, slap her around the face, spit in her eye and shout abuse or just pick up the knife lying on the table and stab her? The first option seemed a fair solution; the second would definitely be far more pleasurable but probably end up with me being arrested.

You will be pleased to know, Eve, that I did neither. Taking a deep breath, but with my hand twitching to slap her smirking cheeks, I walked past them and over to the coffee station where I calmly refilled my cup. The two of them obviously thought better of having something from the restaurant because when I returned to my seat they had disappeared as if in a puff of smoke.

I was gutted. It wasn't just Kim I wanted to beat to a pulp, it was Ed. How could he have told anyone what had happened? And how could he have told Kim of all people? Well that was it. I was through with him. I was through with all men. They were nothing but a waste of time and effort. From now on I would be a nun in my approach to all things male. If being an old maid was what it took to survive without all this hassle then, an old maid I would be. But for the moment I had to decide how I was going to dig up the courage to get on that crew bus when Kim would probably have told them all about my non-existent night with Ed. They would probably all burst out laughing as soon as I appeared in the lobby.

Love, Suzi x

Dear Eve

When I'd eked out my time as much as I could, I reluctantly picked up my company issue handbag and left the calm surroundings of the restaurant. It just showed that maybe Kim was right. I obviously thought I was far more important than I was because nobody even registered that I had walked into the lobby. Kim was busy checking out at the reception desk while JJ and a few of the other stewards were seated on the far side of the lobby engrossed in something one of them was showing them on their mobile.

I waited until Kim had finished and paid my bill at the reception desk before taking a seat next to a large pile of tourist flyers detailing day trips. I picked one up and pretended to study it carefully until it was time to get on the crew bus. It's not often I'm defeated but the thought of working a twelve hour flight back to England didn't fill me with glee. Nobody talked to me all the way to the airport and once on board I carried out my pre-flight duties and then joined JJ in our galley.

'How's things, Suzi?' JJ asked. I didn't know if he was trying to be kind or just trying to press his upper hand.

'Oh, so, so,' I answered. If he was being mean I wasn't going to give him the satisfaction of realising just how Kim's words had hurt me.

'I'm sorry you had to hear what Kim said,' JJ continued. 'She's a real bitch sometimes.'

I looked at him. 'But I thought you liked her,' I answered bemused.

'Can't stand the cow,' JJ said frankly.

'But you two seemed so together whenever I saw you.'

149

'I've spent this entire trip trying to avoid her,' he said with a grimace. 'She's worse than a limpet. So boring and so bitchy. If I see her one more time it'll be too soon. Fancy a cuppa?'

I leaned over, placing my hand on JJ's shoulder and kissed him on the cheek. 'You are a nice man,' I commented. 'Thank you for that. It was just what I needed.'

The curtain swished back and Kim came in just as I started to rub my lippy from JJ's cheek. She looked from him to me and then back again, her mouth open in amazement.

'Something the matter?' I asked fortified by JJ's solidarity. JJ smiled at me and walked past Kim to go out of the galley. He turned to face me, put his fingers to his head and waggled them, in a childish fashion behind her back, before laughing and disappearing along the aircraft aisle towards the rear of the plane.

I couldn't resist smiling at his school boy antics.

'You think you're so clever, don't you?' Kim accused slamming the door on the stowage shut. 'Well, you're not. Not every man drops at your feet the moment you pass by.'

I stared at her. She was entitled to her ranting but I'd had enough. 'Anything else you want to say to me Kim? Because if not, just keep your mouth shut before you get yourself into more trouble.'

'What do you mean?' she asked.

'You'll see,' I said walking out of the galley in the same direction as JJ. Boy, was I a credit to the company's *tolerance in all situations*' policy? I didn't have anything on her that she would have to 'wait and see' about but I couldn't resist stirring things a bit. Maybe she would think it had something to do with Ed being Flight Deck. If I could frighten her into shutting up for the

150

journey home it would be worth it.

The rest of the flight passed far more pleasantly than I'd expected. JJ was on top form again and we had a laugh at the passengers' expense. We managed to have a heart to heart at one point and it made me realise he was one of the good guys. If we meet again on another trip, I know that we will be able to go out and explore around the world as good friends.

Love, Suzi x

20th August - Home

Dear Eve

I felt exhausted as I put my key in the lock of the front door at home. It was early afternoon and I had been awake for so long my eyes were stinging. No wonder I'd slept so long in Hong Kong. I was abusing my body and it had obviously decided when it tasted the champagne I was slugging that it was a good time to call it at day and protest at my actions. All I wanted to do was sink my head into the pillows on my bed. If I slept for a couple of hours I would then be able to get up and maybe go out for the evening. I found it was always better to try and get straight onto local time, however skanky I felt. I would just have to man-up and cope.

A squeal greeted me as I dragged my suitcase behind me into the narrow hallway. Sarah-Jane and Sam came skipping along to greet me. SJ grabbed my arm, placed hers around it and led me into the lounge, patting my wrist with her hand. Sam looked as though she would wet her pants she was so agitated.

'What the hell is the matter with you two? Can't it

wait, I'm tired.'

'No it can't wait,' SJ said sternly. 'Sam, pour Suzi a large shot of this,' and she held out a bottle of vodka. 'We've got some news and I'm not sure how you'll take it.'

'Bloody hell. Vodka in the afternoon. Who's died?' I asked looking from one to the other. Sam handed me the glass and I put it to my lips.

'No one's died. We needed to make sure you heard it from us and not on the grapevine. We've been waiting for your car to draw up for ages.'

'Okay, so I'm here now. What is it?'

'Debbie and Matt have got engaged.'

I spat the vodka out all over SJ and down my uniform. 'What!' I shrieked. 'They've only been going out for five minutes! When the bloody hell did that happen? Tell me everything. NOW!' I demanded, taking the bottle of vodka from Sam's hand and pouring myself another large shot. I carefully placed the near empty bottle on the small wooden coffee table that stood alongside one wall and plonked myself down in the centre of the shabby, rust-coloured sofa opposite. SJ, who was busy wiping the spit marks from her top with a tissue, looked up and smiled at me.

'You okay? Thought that might cause a reaction,' she said coming over and squeezing in next to me. 'Maybe not quite that one.' She took a small cushion from the floor beside her, lifted her leg and placed the cushion underneath it over the coiled spring that poked out of the worn material. 'Bloody sofa,' she cursed softly. 'You should see the mess it made of my leg last week. I've still got the scab.'

'I'll have another go at ringing the landlord,' Sam observed. She came over and sat on my other side, half turning her body to fit in. We sat in a row like the three wise monkeys.

'Bloody hell, you two!' I exclaimed. 'As much as I'm sorry to hear about your injuries SJ. That's not the hot topic. When did they get engaged? Where is Debbie now?' My head went from side to side as I questioned first one girl then the other.

'Well,' Sam answered, drawing in her breath as though about to make an announcement. 'The first we heard of it was when we saw Debbie wearing a ring on her engagement finger while she was making toast yesterday morning.' She looked past me at SJ.

'She tried to deny that it was an engagement ring. It's supposed to be a secret but I could see she was just itching to tell someone,' SJ finished.

I squeezed myself out of my position between the two girls, using them as leverage to get up. Grabbing a wooden dining chair, I turned it round the wrong way and sat down facing them as though mounting a horse. I leant my arms along the back of the chair, placed my chin on top and looked straight at them. 'That's better; I can look at you both at the same time now. Go on.'

Before either girl had time to reply, an evil thought crossed my mind. I stared at them. 'It's not a smallish solitaire is it? Came in a dark blue velvet box?'

'Yes,' they both shrieked.

I saw a look cross Sam's face as though a light bulb had just been switched on. 'It was never yours, was it?' she asked.

'Sounds just the same,' I answered finishing my vodka and placing the empty glass on the floor by my feet. Sam's cheeks were going slightly pink and her fringe stuck up from where she had rested her head on her hand. She uncrossed her legs and leant forward.

It was all so weird and almost too much in my jet-lagged state. I started to recap. 'So Matt, who only asked me to marry him a short while ago, has now asked Debbie instead, using my ring. Well, I'll give him credit for economising.' The two girls giggled. SJ pulled her trouser covered legs up to her body and hugged her knees. Another thought crossed my mind. 'Does she know he asked me?'

'Only rumours. We've only heard rumours about you and Matt,' SJ answered. Letting go of her knees and folding her legs underneath her. 'Nobody was sure. You know after Katie and Ash's wedding? We all saw him go down on one knee but neither of you said any more after that, so nobody knew for certain.'

'Except me,' piped up Sam. SJ straightened out her legs, turned and looked at her. I smiled. Both of them were so jittery and wound up, neither could keep still.

'You knew all the time that Matt had asked Suzi and you never told me?'

'Now girls, that's not the issue.' I intervened quickly to get Sam off the hook. 'I asked Sam not to say anything. What we have to establish is whether Debbie suspects.'

'Whether Debbie suspects what?' a voice came from the doorway. With my back to the door I had to turn my head to follow the gaze of the two girls on the sofa as they sat, mouths open staring at Debbie framed by the door.

'Hi, Debbie,' I oozed. Getting up quickly I nearly knocked over the chair in my rush to give her a hug. 'Congratulations. The girls have just been filling me in on your news.' Thank God for my training. I had obviously paid far more attention than I realised. Lesson 1 – *How to deal with the unexpected – distraction.*

'Let's see the ring?' I demanded, grabbing her hand and holding it to the light. 'It's beautiful,' I murmured. I was such a bitch. Eve. A two-faced bitch. How could I look at the same ring that had been offered to me and not feel anything? Worse still, I was making such a fuss about it, she was bound to suspect. I usually only grunted at Debbie when I passed her in the hallway.

'So you're not angry with me?' Debbie asked in a quiet voice.

'Angry?' I questioned. Why would I be? Goodness, what was going on in her mind?

'I just thought you might still fancy Matt and be upset at our news,' she said.

Now I got it. I had the upper hand. Debbie did have a conscience. She had been worrying that their engagement might upset me. He must have failed to tell her that it was me who had ended our relationship. Typically male! Save face, make out that he'd done the dirty rather than admit he'd been dumped. It obviously hadn't crossed her mind that Matt might have asked her on the re-bound. I stared at each girl in turn. To be honest I wasn't sure how I felt. It certainly wasn't anger. No. Nor sadness that it wasn't me. In fact I think it was relief. I wanted to laugh. If Matt could transfer his affections so quickly from me to Debbie, thank goodness I had stood my ground and turned him down. The fact that he used the same ring only convinced me what a cheapskate he was and that he wasn't the person I thought. It was the best thing possible that I was shot of him.

'No,' I reassured her. 'That's all water under the bridge now. I'm really pleased for you both. What are your plans? Are your parents pleased?'

My reaction seemed to galvanise Sam and SJ out of their stupors. They had been sitting like an audience watching the climax of a play. Sam jumped up and motioned for Debbie to take her seat while she took another chair and placed it next to mine so that we could face Debbie and give her our full attention. We both sat down again at the same time.

'I know,' SJ said pulling herself up out of her seat. Really, these two were acting like puppets being pulled by strings they were so fidgety. 'Suzi's finished off the vodka.' Debbie looked at me and raised an eyebrow. 'So I'll put the kettle on and we can hear all your news, Debbie, over a cup of tea instead.'

Now it was Debbie's turn to get up. Blimey. Perhaps it was something in the water? None of them could keep still for a second. 'No, wait a moment, I've got something to show you... and ...' she said taking her car keys out of her pocket. 'In answer to your question, Suzi, yes, my parents are pleased. They've bought me an engagement present. I'll just go and get it from the car.' She walked to the door and went out into the hallway. We heard the front door shut behind her.

'Jeez,' Sam said, grinning from ear to ear. 'You saved us then. I nearly peed myself when she walked in just as we were talking about her. Talk about distraction. You should get a bloody Bafta for that performance, Suz.'

'You realise that he's doing this on the re-bound,' SJ whispered, glancing nervously at the half open door, expecting Debbie to walk in again.

A wave of exhaustion swept over me. I nodded in agreement.

'At least her parents are pleased,' Sam offered.

'Yes, probably because they can shift the responsibility of her,' SJ giggled. 'If she does end up marrying Matt, he'll have to look after her.'

'Do you think she'll move in with him soon? God, can you imagine the state of their place? They won't need any duvets they can just stick all her sweet and crisp wrappers together and sleep on the sofa under that. Then they wouldn't have to move to watch the telly,' Sam said.

'What do you think they've bought her? A *How to*

Keep House manual?' SJ continued.

'No. *What To Do If You Have No Skills Whatsoever* - the complete works,' Sam concluded sitting back and folding her arms.

'Sh… stop bitching you two,' I whispered as we heard movement coming from the hallway. A second later Debbie waked into the living room carrying a large box.

It turned out that Debbie's box contained nothing more exciting than a coffee machine. I had at least been expecting something as useless as a puppy. Her parents for all their procrastinating that Debbie had to get a job and that they weren't going to fund her anymore, still seemed to give her everything her heart desired. I wondered if they had paid Matt. How cynical was that? Matt was messing up his own life. And Debbie's. Or maybe they were meant to mess up each other? Far be it for me to judge.

Apparently in a moment of rationality her parents felt the coffee machine would make a suitable engagement present to start off Debbie's bottom drawer, ready for when she got her own home. I must admit I could think of far better things for her bottom drawer – cookery or housekeeping lessons or even a double duvet, but I mustn't bitch. Who was I to have an opinion?

I pleaded jet lag and the need for my bed and left the three of them in the kitchen, studying the manual and working out how to set the machine up. I carried my suitcase up the stairs to my room. If I wasn't tired enough when I got home I was now exhausted by all the emotion of Debbie's revelation. I opened my bedroom door and laid my suitcase on the floor, unclasping the lock. Taking my wash bag from the top, I pulled out the eye make-up remover, doused a cotton wool pad that had been tucked into the side pocket of the bag and started to wipe away all the traces of my kohl eyes. I looked into the small mirror that hung on the wall next to a framed Hockney print. One of my favourite painters and my last birthday present from Matt. My eyes started to water until a large fat tear coursed its way down my cheek. I had moved onto spreading the cleansing milk over my cheeks in a sloppy, creamy lather before I realised that they were real tears and not just because I'd poked myself in the eye earlier getting the last traces of the blackness from my lashes. What was the matter with me? I really didn't care about Matt. Or did I? It wasn't as though I wanted to marry him. I had had my chance. In the words of Elizabeth Bennett from the film *Pride and Prejudice*, I wouldn't have accepted him if, '*...he were the last man in the world I could ever be prevailed upon to marry.*' So why the tears? I washed my face with water from the tap of the small basin in the corner of the room. My reflection showed it was now a clean, shiny pink. Slapping on some moisturiser (something my mother said I should never miss out on if I didn't want my neck to resemble a turkey's in later life) I stripped off and slipped into my pyjamas, jumped into bed and snuggled down. I was over-tired. That was the only reason for my tears. It would all be alright after a good sleep and bloody hell, did I need another of those.

Love Suzi x

25th August - Home

Dear Eve

My mum was right about the restorative qualities of sleep, as well as turkey necks. (But they always are, aren't they?) It's amazing how much better everything seemed after a good solid sleep. I didn't stir for the next four hours and when I woke up life, Debbie and Matt in particular, didn't seem that bad. Everyone was out when I went downstairs so I just pottered around making myself a cup of tea and some beans on toast.

The next day I decided to go and see my Dad. Since my parents' divorce he'd moved out of London and now lived alone. He'd chosen to set up a small-holding in a village about an hour south west of London. I'd come to the opinion that, rather than put up with the clucking of my Mum or another woman he'd much rather try his luck with a few geese, ducks and a couple of pigs, Clarence and Clarissa. Can't say I blame him. Life for my Dad had turned from wading through the shit of corporate life to wading through the shit of his animals.

I'm not a country girl, having spent most of my upbringing in suburbia, but I thought I knew about animals. As a townie I had been drip fed that sheep go baa, horses go neigh and cows go moo. Now I am not so convinced – after visiting my dad in his rural idyll, I'm convinced that when cows hear that click of the latch on the gate in their field, thirty collective heads look up from their chewing, 'fun time guys,' the boss mutters. 'Daisy, you take the left flank, and I'll bring up the rear. Slowly does it and when she's in the middle of the field, move in and surround her.' I love cows; it's just the sight of a field of them in my path that gives me palpitations. Like driving around Trafalgar Square, you find you're approached at every angle with no obvious way out.

Mind you, if cows are the heavies, they are nothing to a field of horses. When I say field, it only has to be one to make me want to turn back. Horses are just so inquisitive. Hasn't anyone told them it's rude to stare? Eager to see if you're carrying any titbits, they boldly walk after you then, just when you're about to bolt, they act all cool, hang back and start chewing again. Like adolescents at the swings – just testing to see how scared you are.

Each time I visited there seemed to be a new addition to my Dad's menagerie and I'd taken to naming each and every one of them. So it was no surprise when I got out of the car, leaving the engine running, to open the gate to the entrance of his drive that Mabel the goose should come clucking along to greet me. She reminded me of an overweight version of Kim. All messy blonde hair, rotund and waddling to busybody her way into everyone's lives whether invited or not. I shooed her away and drove up to the house.

But before I could return to lock the gate behind me to prevent any inmates escaping, my favourite resident came bounding around the corner of the small white timber clad farmhouse leaping the front flower bed to try and butt me in the bum. Gruff is a Saanens goat, completely mad but friendly and believes he is a member of Steve McQueen's team from the '*Great Escape*' movie. He refuses to stay in his field and would have been a real asset in the prisoner of war camp as his ears are constantly pricked forward straining for any sound. I tickled him under the chin and grabbed his tether leading him down to the gate where I fixed the bar into place securing the compound.

I led my motley assortment of goat, geese and chickens who had all come to see what the commotion was about, along the gravel drive and around to the back of the house. The one acre plot stretched right around the building and was divided neatly into compartments. The allotment ran the length of one side with the fruit cages, like fishing nets spread out to dry, protecting the raspberries from the birds that sat waiting on the fence for the opportune moment to dart through the door to feast on the forbidden fruit. The ducks enjoyed their own private

160

pool in the far corner where they paraded their cleanliness to Clarence and Clarissa. I always thought it was cruel to put the pigs next to the ducks who spent most of their time preening themselves. I'm sure they only did it to impose their superiority on their two mud-wallowing neighbours.

Dad was bent over his potatoes. Think, Pop Larkin from *The Darling Buds of May* and you will have summed up my dad. Not the flirty bit but the fun-loving, relaxed and caring man with a twinkle in his eye. I made my way over to the goat enclosure beside him. Just as I finished tying Gruff to his fence my mobile phone vibrated in the pocket of my jeans.

I took it out and pressed the screen. The word '*BITCH*' showed up clearly against the grey background. I shoved my phone back in my pocket hoping that the shock hadn't registered on my face.

'Hello darling,' Dad greeted me. 'This is a surprise. What brings you here?'

'Come to check up on you,' I smiled, embracing him with a long hug. I let him go and stepped back to survey his appearance. 'Looking hot, Dad,' I laughed. He looked down at his corduroys, torn at the knee and picked at the loose wool of his knitted jumper with its holey elbows.

'No point in messing up good clothes,' he said bending down and picking a tomato for me from the plant beside him. 'Try this. They're a new variety I'm trying out.' I popped the red ball into my mouth. The flavour burst out with the juice as I bit into it.

'Have you still got my skiing things in the attic?' I asked. 'Only I'm off to Alaska next and thought I might try and get out on the slopes.'

'Come inside and I'll put the kettle on,' he replied leading the way along the path between the rows of produce and waiting for me to step through the small wooden gate before he shut it securely.

'Not today you don't,' he hollered at Gruff who was watching his every move like a hawk.

'Little bugger got in last week when the catch slipped. Had a good snack of my carrots before I realised and chased him out. Your skiing things should still be here somewhere. I'll have a look.'

As I followed Dad across the lawn and into the house I took my mobile from my pocket and brought up the message again. The word BITCH still screamed at me from the screen. I flicked through to find the sender's number but it was unavailable. Who on earth could be sending me something like that? I was careful who had my mobile number. It must have been a random caller. Not meant for me. I tried to dismiss it and caught Dad up as he went through the back door and into the kitchen.

If the kitchen is the heart of a house, this one was coal black and definitely not pumping. Although Dad was precise in arranging and organising his garden, when it came to the house it was completely different. I did love him, but how on earth he could live in this mess was beyond me. The dark, once terracotta, tiles on the floor looked as though even if scrubbed with a toothbrush and bleach, they would never be shiny and proud but always be miserable wearing a grimy brown coat. The glass at the small-framed wooden windows screamed to be treated to a cataract removal operation and the animal feed demanded to be treated like a cordon bleu ingredient in the larder not chucked higgledy-piggledy in a heap on the floor. The whole place needed cleaning up before e-coli took hold. I took two cups out of the oak cupboard above the draining board and was about to put a tea bag into them when I saw what looked like something moving in the bottom of one of the cups.

'Dad!' I exclaimed shoving it under his nose. 'When

162

did you last wash this up?' He peered in as a small spider scrambled to avoid the finger that he thrust inside the china to remove it.

'Only a bit of dust,' he smiled nonchalantly. But that was enough for me. Running the hot tap and pouring in loads of washing up liquid, I filled the sink and plunged in all the plates, cups and cutlery that I could get my hands on. All my practising, night after night for my Brownie housekeeping badge, leapt to the forefront. I was on a mission and I was not going to stop until I could see the gleam of a TV advert sparkle on the place.

Dad left me to it. I probably reminded him of the reason why he left Mum in the first place. Too bossy for his liking I'm sure. After about twenty minutes when I had just finished obliterating some stubborn brown marks from the paintwork surrounding the doorway to the garden, (I didn't want to think what they were from and how they'd got there; no match for Marigolds, bleach and elbow grease though), Dad reappeared carrying my blue and white checked ski jacket and black trousers.

'Now, are you staying for dinner?'

I ended up spending the night at Dad's. By the time we'd opened a bottle of wine and he'd cooked his speciality, ratatouille with fresh produce from the garden, it was far too late (and anyway I would have had to admit to a policeman of being a little bit drunky-wunky if stopped in the car). As the evening wore on the wine did a dirty on me and I found myself spilling out to dad about Matt and Ed. It was as I was recounting the effect that the engagement announcement had on me that my phone vibrated again. I looked at the screen. The same message as earlier leapt out at me. Dad looked at me and raised an eyebrow. I shook my head and got up from the kitchen table. He didn't need to know about that.

'Isn't it about time you fed the animals?' I asked.

'Christ!' he exclaimed jumping up and knocking his chair to the floor. 'I forgot. Grab your coat and come and help me,' he demanded. He handed me the torch that sat on the ledge by the back door and like two intrepid explorers we embarked on his nightly feeding round.

Love Suzi x

30th August - Anchorage, (ANC) Alaska - 120ft

Dear Eve

If ever I've wanted an ejector button for a passenger it was the man in 35C on the flight to Anchorage. Sitting in an aisle seat he stared at me every time I walked past him. Okay, so a stewardess's job is a bit like being on stage. I expect everyone to be watching because often the flight is so long and there is nothing much else to do. Watching I don't mind but touching is definitely out. It was during the drinks round that I was aware of what he was doing. As I backed the trolley down the aisle towards him he 'accidentally' had his arm leaning over the side of his armrest. Just as I bent down to retrieve a bottle from the bottom drawer he moved his arm back into position but not before his hand made contact and swept over my bum cheek. Not in a glancing, '*Oh dear, I'm sorry*', sort of way but in a '*firm pressure, feel every curve*' manoeuvre. So, unsure if it was intended or not and to give him the benefit of the doubt, I let it pass.

While I was serving the hot meal I realised it was no accident. He was doing it for his own gratification. The trolley was positioned just in front of him and I had been dealing with a particularly awkward customer who had complained about everything already and then didn't like the way the vegetables with his chicken dish were a little bit dry at the edges. I wanted to say *'you're bloody lucky mate, you should see the rest of the dried up mush we've got for the guys coming next,'* but I didn't. I smiled sweetly, apologised, saying that if he could wait until I'd finished the service I would see if there was anything else I could replace it with. (Sometimes if you're feeling kind, you can go up to first class and blag some left overs to placate the punters. Obviously this has to be done discreetly otherwise the whole plane will riot over their food. Can you blame them? Alternatively, if there are any better looking veggies left in the galley you can swap them to keep the peace.)

So there I was, squatting to retrieve a meal from the bottom tray when the groper accidentally dropped something onto the floor of the aisle just beside me. The next thing I felt was his hand sweep down round my bum, until he was almost giving me an internal examination. I jumped up and turned to him. I felt like punching him right between his monobrow to remove the leering grin from his face.

'Have you lost something, sir?' I enquired fixing him with my most fearsome stare. 'Because I'm quite sure you won't find it there.' To hell with the customers always being right. This guy was a pervert and he needed to be told. Turning my back on him I carried on with passing out the meals.

I didn't have any further problems with 35C. He must have been a chancer. One of those men that try and get away with touching you up but if you confront them they deny it and stop. I'm not one to let opportunities pass though and later in the flight when we were clearing the cabin for landing I made use of a bit of turbulence to 'accidentally' spill the remains of his coffee cup into his lap. It wasn't hot but it did leave a nasty stain right on his crotch. Dumping a few napkins on top to soak up any residue I apologised sweetly and walked back to the galley, warning the steward I was working with what I'd done.

After we had landed and the passengers were disembarking, the woman who had been sitting in 35B, next to the groper, stopped as she walked past and leaned close to speak to me.

'Well done,' she whispered. 'He tried it earlier with me. Just wish that coffee had been hot,' and winking at me she stepped out of the plane. Result! Job satisfaction comes in many different forms.

I walked past the stuffed polar bear standing upright, his claws ready to pounce, in a glass cabinet at the airport at Anchorage when my mobile vibrated again. This time the message from my anonymous sender was more explicit. Not only was I apparently still a *BITCH* but a fucking one at that!

Over the next two days I got six more anonymous messages on my mobile, ranging from mildly abusive to downright disgustingly abusive. I could have changed my number but I didn't want to. It would feel like giving in to who ever it was that was sick in the head. I racked my brains for who could be doing it. I didn't think it was a guy. It just didn't seem to be something men would do. Far more likely to be a woman. And a disgruntled one at that. It wasn't rocket science to put Candy's name on the top of my list of suspects. She was the most vindictive, disgruntled woman I'd come across recently. This cyber attack was taking it a bit too far though. She had no reason to know about Ed's champagne visit to my hotel room in Hong Kong. I wish I hadn't messed up our date. Candy would have least have had something to send me abusive texts for if I had tasted the delights of Ed's fabulously fit body. His six pack had a six pack on it and

I could just imagine our bodies entwined, rolling among the sheets. I would have been as smooth as silk to the touch (after all that wasted preening I did, shaving every stray dark hair and slathering myself in coconut body cream) and he would have been completely enamoured with me, whispering undying love. Okay, Mills and Boons time again but fantasising is the nearest I've got to having sex for ages.

Every time I thought about how I messed up that night I cursed myself. I hadn't contacted Ed since he left me sleeping. Partly because I was so embarrassed at my behaviour but mostly because I was so pissed off with him for telling Kim what had happened. How could he have let it slip to her, of all people, that I had passed up the opportunity of a hot night of rampant sex with him to sleep off the effects of the jet lag and champagne combo I'd indulged in? If it was Candy sending the texts, I would need some hard evidence to convince him. And what if it wasn't Candy? I would find myself in a huge heap of the smelly stuff if I accused her and it was proved to be unfounded. Best to just leave it and see what happened.

Meanwhile I'd bonded pretty quickly with four of the crew on this trip. They were all up for a laugh and had plans to go skiing. Dave, the only male in our group, who it seems had been a steward since time immemorial, had been to Alaska before and knew how to get to the skiing resort at Alyeska. We girls took it upon ourselves to encourage him by just giggling and looking suitably glamorous. He took charge and hired us a car. We'd all come prepared. Except after all that effort of getting my gear from Dad's, I'd only gone and forgotten my ski gloves. It wasn't until we were flying over Greenland that I realised. I happened to be getting the meals out of the oven at the time – strange how the aircraft oven gloves

167

jumped into my bag at that point. Ever resourceful I decided that I could forgo style for comfort. (Don't mention the 'thief' word to my employers, I only borrowed them and intended to put them back on the next aircraft.)

When Mum and Dad split up, Dad took it upon himself to teach my sister, Mia, and me how to ski. Every February half term he would pack us into his old camper van and we would make the long journey to the Alps. Not the most glamorous way to encounter the whole ski scene. The word après ski didn't enter my vocabulary until I grew up and went skiing with friends. I didn't realise that not everybody returned to their vehicle at the end of a hard day's skiing to light the gas stove and hang out their snow-soaked salopettes over a rope carefully strung between one hook attached to the rear window curtain and another to the windscreen. Whilst it was cramped, with my sister's toe poked in my ear most nights as we shared a bed over the fold-away table, it was fun to wake up trying to convince her that I was secretly smoking as the air froze inside the van.

Early the next morning saw the five of us squeezed into the red hire car and snaking our way along the snow covered roads to the mountain resort of Alyaska. The unknown pistes didn't faze me. Although not a world class skier, I could get down most slopes even if in a sitting-on-the-toilet position when it turned a bit steep. Which is more than could be said for Cathy, stewardess extraordinaire and complete beginner.

The rest of us had the joy of introducing her to the wonders of the ski boot, the incongruity of the snow plough skiing position, holding her hand as she negotiated the chair lift and watching as she wobbled and slid her way from top to bottom of the first piste. It was as she came flying towards me, screaming for all she was worth that I realised that the day could get dangerous. Luckily her rapid descent was curtailed when a ski instructor, in his yellow jacket, skied expertly alongside her until he could safely bring her to a controlled stop.

Gareth turned out to be a bit of a bonus. Tall and wiry, he was about the same age as my dad and from the moment he met us he proved to be just as caring. Not only did he have deep brown eyes and a face that was as wrinkled as a pug from all his exposure to the elements (should have used more moisturiser I couldn't help noticing) but when we explained who we were, he insisted on showing us around and taking charge of Cathy. Dave had long since got fed up with his lack of popularity and disappeared to ski alone saying he'd meet us back at the car. Surrounded by his posse of women, Gareth took the lead and directed us, whilst controlling Cathy, to a small log cabin that served hot drinks.

Being the first to arrive, I was just bending to unclip my boots after stacking my skis into the rack when I felt my phone vibrate in the pocket of my shirt underneath all my layers. Scrambling to reach it, I managed to unzip my outer jacket and feel my way to undo the zip of my fleece when the cell phone stopped. I left it and carried on undoing my boots so that I could walk more easily into the cabin. The girls and Gareth meanwhile, were busy finding seats and looking at the menu.

I plonked myself down on the only empty chair and searched again for my phone. Gareth, sitting opposite, was passing round a hip flask for everyone to have a taste. I swiped the screen of my phone and looked at the name of the missed call. Gareth was staring at me as I looked up.

'Trouble, Suzi?' he enquired handing me the hipflask.

I stared at him. 'Why do you say that?'

'Because your expression changed as soon as you

looked at your phone and you frowned.'

I smiled at him. He held out the small metal container. 'That would be most welcome,' I said taking it from his outstretched hand and pouring a large swig down my throat.

'Hey, save some for us,' Cathy moaned. 'You're supposed to just add a little to your coffee. It'll all be gone before the coffee's even arrived.' She took the flask from my hand and put it firmly down in the middle of the table. I waited while the waitress came up and took our order and they all continued to chat.

'You don't happen to have a bottle of that stashed away anywhere, do you?' I asked Gareth as he stretched out his legs under the table jolting mine as he did so.

'Ahh…Boyfriend trouble, eh?' he enquired astutely, gesturing towards the phone in my hand.

I grimaced, shrugged my shoulders and looked at the screen again. The missed call was from Ed, but a text message was displayed. *Ring me as soon as you can*, the message read. Well, I sure as hell wasn't going to ring him from a mountain café in the middle of Alaska. Whatever he wanted couldn't be that urgent. He would just have to wait.

Love Suzi x

Dear Eve

'What have you been saying to Candy?' Ed demanded down the phone. After the day's skiing I had gone back to our hotel with the others. A hot bath with plenty of bubbles was necessary to warm my bones and it was only then, with a glass of something alcoholic in my hand to warm my insides as well, that I decided I was brave enough to ring Ed back after his earlier message.

'What do you mean?' I replied. Bloody hell, this wasn't what I was expecting. I was hoping for something more romantic and perhaps flirtatious from him. Something that was going to move our relationship forward. Something along the lines of *'Suzi, I've not been able to sleep or think of anything else but you. I must see you. NOW!'* Not bloody Candy. What had she done now? In my head, he was supposed to be ringing to tell me he'd ditched her for me.

'I haven't been saying a word. In fact I've had nothing to do with her since the last time she contacted me,' I defended myself.

'How come she knows about Hong Kong?'

'Knows what about Hong Kong?' There was no way she'd learnt anything to do with that from me. 'Nothing happened if you remember,' I reminded him. Jeez, here was I getting it in the neck from him when he was the one who had blabbed about it.

'I know that, but she seems to think we planned the trip and spent the whole time together.' Now I understood. He was in the shit with Candy and he wanted to blame me.

'I haven't a clue about how Candy found out anything.' I wasn't going to let him get away with laying

171

it at my door. 'And talking about finding out about things. How come Candy has my mobile number?' I know I said I wasn't going to mention it in case it wasn't her sending me the messages but I couldn't resist it. It was the wine's fault. My cheeks were hot and my blood was up.

'I don't know,' Ed replied defensively. 'Certainly not from me.' Good. At least that got a change of tone in his voice.

'Well, someone has been sending me abusive texts and she's the only one that I can think might feel she has a reason to. Maybe she didn't only intercept my parcel, but searched through your phone too!'

There was a long pause on the other end of the line.

'Anyway, I've got a bone to pick with you.' I said not wanting to lose the upper hand. I walked over to the window and stared out at the frozen landscape. 'How dare you tell Kim what happened between us in my room.'

'Kim? Kim who?' So he was going to deny it was him?

'Oh, don't play the innocent with me.' I retaliated. 'Kim! That bitch on our crew who told everyone (a little elaboration never hurt anyone) that you'd left me sleeping in my room.' I knew my voice was getting a bit squeaky at this point. It's always been one of my problems. Ever since I honed the art of arguing over toys with Mia in the playroom, I've always been relied upon to reach an ear shattering squeak quicker than most of my friends when distressed. Attractive I know, but in the heat of the moment, out of my control. You always used to tease me about it, Eve, by mimicking me - but it immediately lowered my tone an octave. Another pause from the end of the line.

'Suzi.' Ed said in a steady voice. 'Where are you?'

'What?'

'Where in the world are you?'

'Anchorage,' I uttered, my voice returned its normal level.

'Good,' he continued. 'Shall we start again? We seem to be talking at cross purposes here. There are a few misunderstandings we need to clear up.' I stopped in my tracks and took a deep breath. I smiled. His random question had completely defused my tension. All my huffiness had been deflated. I felt my shoulders detach themselves from my ears and relax back to their rightful position, giving me a swan-like neck. Well, I like to think it's swan-like, probably more Jemima Puddle Duck. Oh well done, Mr Captain-in-the-making. Taken charge of the situation, calmed down the hysterical little woman whilst concentrating on resolving the conflict. How well you have studied your *How-to-Cope-With-Tricky-Situations* manual.

'Well, if it's going to be a long conversation,' I said sitting down in the seat beside the window, leaning back and stretching out my legs so that my crossed ankles rested on the sill. 'You earn much more than me. Do you want to ring me back?' I took another swig of my wine but the mouthful came straight back as my feet slipped off the window sill, jolting me upright again. I coughed and spluttered. A deep laugh came down the line.

'No problem, skinflint,' Ed replied. 'Stay put and try not to choke. By the way, when do you get back to England?'

'In about nine days. Japan next, then round the top of the world, via Hong Kong, Mumbai, then home.'

'Make sure you go to the Japanese gardens when you're in Kyoto.'

'What! Are you turning into a tour guide again?' I questioned. I wiped myself down and regained my composure. 'Do it on your own phone. Get off the line and ring me back.'

I ended the call and stared out of the window. I couldn't be cross with him for long. He had some serious issues to deal with. Namely Candy. What on earth had she said this time to make him cross with me? The sooner he realised what a screwed up, malicious woman he was going out with the better. And how on earth did she find out about Hong Kong? Even Kim didn't have the capacity to gossip that far back to England.

I looked out of the window as I waited for Ed to ring back. A woman with a small dog slipped over on the frozen footpath outside when the lively spaniel pulled a bit too hard in its bid for escape. A tall man in a black, Michelin-tyre style, padded coat came running over to her aid and helped her up. The dog meanwhile was casually squirting wee up a snow covered lamppost, leaving a trail of yellow behind him.

Why was Ed taking so long to call? I'd be going grey by the time it took him to redial. I looked at my watch then picked up my book from the table and started to read. A few of us had arranged to meet up for a meal in the hotel restaurant. It was too cold to venture out without multiple layers of clothes on and none of us could be bothered to get dressed up again. I read two chapters and then looked at my watch. It had been twenty minutes since Ed had promised to call back. I checked my phone to make sure I still had a signal. Something must have happened to delay him. Well, it was too late now. I threw the book on the bed, grabbed my room key and went downstairs to the restaurant to join the others.

Love, Suzi x

1st September - On the way from ANC to Japan (KIX) - 36,000ft - crew rest area

Dear Eve

The man in seat 30B was sitting in between two women in a row of three. Both women were blonde, middle aged with doll like features and it was clear that they were twins. It turned out that one was his wife. I had seen the three of them chatting together but it was during the drinks round when I asked the woman in the window seat what she wanted that the man in the middle butted in before she had a chance to answer.

'A gin and tonic here,' he indicated to the table she had pulled down in readiness. 'I'll have a Scotch and another gin and tonic here.' He pointed to the woman sitting in the aisle seat.

'Would you like ice and lemon with that?' I asked the blonde in the window seat.

'No. Neither,' came the gruff reply from the man in the middle.

I ignored his rudeness and prepared the drinks. I tried to hand the over the coaster and napkin to the window seat woman but the man took them and placed them on his table.

'What's with the three in row 30?' I asked Cathy, who was working the other end of the trolley with me, as we finished the drinks round and pushed the cart back to the galley.

'Why?' she inquired and I filled her in on what had happened. 'Perhaps they're mute?' she suggested.' Or can't speak English?'

I laughed. 'I heard them chatting, in English, as I served the row in front. He called one darling and the other by her name. It began with an M but I didn't hear it properly. They are neither of those things and he is just a downright rude bugger.'

'It must be you then,' she laughed. 'He doesn't like you.'

'Or he's their personal speaker. Like having a personal food taster, or back scratcher.'

'Or arse wiper?' Cathy suggested.

'Too much detail, it doesn't bear thinking about what the three of them get up to.'

'Bit kinky though, don't you think. Having a wife and sister-in law that look the same. Do you think they have threesomes?'

I smiled. 'Go and have a closer look at him, Cathy. He's lucky he got a onesome. Tell me whether you'd want a threesome with him?'

'Ahh… but it's not about me is it? Beauty is in the eye of the beholder. Maybe he's got hidden talents we don't know about?'

I playfully hit her arm as she disappeared around the corner of the galley with a plastic bin liner ready to clear the cabin of empties.

Love, Suzi x

3rd September - KIX to HKG - 34,000ft - crew rest area

Dear Eve

Arriving in Japan was like landing on another planet. The airport at Kansai was magnificent. It stretched out over the water like a flag attached to the mainland by a long thin pole. After getting over the fact that we hadn't landed in Osaka Bay the landing looked so tricky, the airport building itself was a revelation. It was a vast metal structure, curved in an arch on one side. Incredible architecturally, it reminded me of the ceiling of a cathedral - unlike anything I'd seen before that didn't have Michelangelo stamped all over it.

I followed the rest of the crew as we made our way through the airport and to the transport linking the airport and the mainland. Not for the first time, I was relieved to have the comfort of being in a group when arriving in a foreign land. I like to think I'm a great explorer but really I'm a cowardly-custard who relishes the fact that there are at least fourteen other people going to the same place as me and odds on one of them will have been there before and know what to do.

Our intrepid skiing group of five decided that we would take a train to visit the gardens at Kyoto the next morning. Arriving at the station I was completely out of my depth and felt like holding the hand of our designated leader, Dave. He took charge of his women and led us through the station to the right platform. I followed the pack with my mouth open. There was nothing that I could read on any of the signs! Usually when abroad there is

177

something I can understand, but although I tried to find it, nothing looked vaguely familiar.

It was obviously commuter time as waves of people rushed in every direction through the large warren of tunnels leading to the platforms. Commuter hustle and bustle was something I was familiar with but what was most bizarre was that every now and again amongst all the young people in western clothes, an older woman in traditional dress would shuffle along like a rare eastern jewel. Then I realised it was the way that they walked that made them look so special. Everyone was intent on getting to their destination as quickly as possible but dressed in their long kimonos, the women were restricted in the size of their stride making them slow down, glide and seem calm amongst the chaos.

When the train arrived we squashed in, ignoring the fact that we were the only westerners in the carriage. The gardens at Kyoto exceeded my expectations. The Japanese have such a precise way with shape and pattern with their landscaping and planting. Wandering around the serene gardens had a calming effect. Every rock and stone had its place in the bigger picture and the ground was swept and raked into intricate designs. Ed was right, there was no way you could miss out a visit to these gardens.

I was standing on an arched, wooden bridge overlooking a small pool. The water rippled across the surface as it splashed over some boulders on its way through the plants. What was Ed up to? When he'd rung I'd forgotten to ask him where in the world he was. It was a shame he hadn't called back. I was sure he didn't mean anything by it. If he was on the other side of the world, even with today's modern technology there were often line cuts and interference. I thought I'd wait until we got to Hong Kong before I tried reaching him again. I had to find the right balance. Ed was obviously still involved with Candy and I didn't want him to think I was just waiting on the sideline for him to click his fingers and I would jump. I would have done, of course. He was beginning to get to me. Not cool at all. I realised I had been left behind and ran to catch up with the others who had wandered ahead. It wouldn't do to be left alone without the rest of the group. It would be a case of *'Suzi in Wonderland'* with no White Rabbit to guide me.

Later that day I nipped down to have a look at the local market a few streets away from the hotel. When I say market, I mean a few tables with produce on. Nothing fancy or extensive just the usual mixture of fruit and vegetables, (some I recognised). At the end of the row I came across an old woman selling bonsai trees. Her face was as gnarled and wizened as the stems of some of the trees on her stall. A pink, cherry blossom tree sitting on the top plank of the make-shift stall caught my eye. I've always fancied one of these ever since I saw them in a magazine as a child. They are so exquisite and I reckoned this one must be at least fifty years old.

'Do you speak English?' I enquired of the woman. She just looked at me, smiled revealing dirty brown teeth and shook her head.

'Konnichiwa,' I continued. The woman's reaction took me by surprise. Holding her large belly she doubled up in laughter and beckoned for her fellow stall holders to join in the joke, rattling off something at nineteen to the dozen to which they all stared at me and laughed too. As far as I knew this meant 'hello.' Not knowing what joke I'd inadvertently made, I just kept smiling as she shook her head at me, her mouth open wide as she held her sides. I picked up the pink bonsai I'd taken a fancy to.

'How much?' I enquired. She continued to laugh at my joke. One of her friend's came over from where he'd stood watching us. I took my purse from my bag. He said something to her and they laughed again. I hoped it wasn't the equivalent of *'why don't you fleece this western woman for all she's worth and give us all a laugh.'* She held up her fingers and pointed to the notes I held out. I did a rough calculation. What she was asking was only going to work out to be a few pounds in sterling. I thought of Ed. Perhaps it wasn't a good time to try and barter. I smiled back at her and handed over the money. Even if I'd just given her a fortune I could afford the bonsai at that price. She pocketed the money and kept smiling at me.

'Sayonara,' I said as walking off towards the hotel to pack my things for departure. The woman bent over again with laughter and repeated my goodbye as she waved to me. If only it was that easy to keep everyone happy.

I don't have a clue if I can take the bonsai into Hong Kong or indeed back into Britain. More importantly if ever I was inventive with plastic bags, soil and packaging, now was the time. All those years of watching *Blue Peter* would have to come into play. I had to get my bonsai into my luggage without: a) killing it, not ideal when it's managed to survive fifty years under its own steam only to be cut down in the prime of its life by an amateur; b) not cover all my clothes in soil and c) not be detected and thrown out of a country or arrested at customs for smuggling.

Love, Suzi x

6th September - on route from HKG to India (BOM) - 34,000ft - crew rest area

Dear Eve

It was as we landed into Hong Kong and I saw huge signs saying that all plant life must be declared that I started to panic. Up until now I was planning on just breezing through customs in my usual way; innocent smile at anyone who looked at me. But knowing that I was about to do something illegal caused my insides to quiver. My palms began to get sweaty, face coloured up and heart beat raced with each step I took nearer to Customs. I'd be bloody useless as a getaway driver, spy or drugs trafficker. My hands would drip so much they'd slip off the wheel and we'd be caught mid heist, or the enemy would hear my rasping breath from 100 metres and walk over to the cupboard door where I was hiding and be able to go 'Boo'.

I decided I couldn't take the pressure of walking through Customs without giving myself away. I would confess before they bought out the cuffs. Well, for once I was glad that I did come clean. If the ripple of panic I caused by declaring the bonsai was anything to go by, the major trauma that would have occurred had I not owed up could only be imagined. Anyone would think I'd attempted to smuggle in a stash of cocaine the amount of activity that ensued. At first they wanted to take the tree off me. But I wasn't having that. I hadn't wrestled with my new purchase to get it into my bag without damage for nothing. I eventually negotiated with them that I would leave the bonsai in quarantine and pick it up on my way out the next day.

Talk about paperwork. I don't think the guys had ever heard of their carbon footprint as it was leaving giant-size steps behind each and every one of them. By the time I'd finished filling in every detail apart from my bra size, the rest of the crew were through the airport and sitting in the bus waiting for me to go to the hotel. As you can imagine I wasn't the most popular girl on that vehicle, but I just smiled at all the grumpy faces. I just hoped my bonsai would be alright and not feel abandoned. It was only tiny and all on its own in a foreign land.

Although we were in the same hotel as last time, I had a different room configuration so was able to shut out memories of Ed and our romantic, sexual near- miss. I decided to keep my head down and catch up on sleep by resting and watching movies. I knew the way to the coffee shop in the hotel after my last experience with Kim. Once ensconced in my room I only ventured out of the hotel one time to wander the local night market to make sure there wasn't a fake handbag with my name on it.

We left late the next day and, after arriving at the airport, I began to make enquiries as to how to retrieve my bonsai. I dread to think if I'd left anything of value or that breathed behind, as no one in the quarantine department was around. I stood tapping my toe at the empty desk and watching the minutes tick by on the large clock behind on the wall. The plane was due to take off in forty-five minutes. The passengers would be loading in fifteen minutes and I would be bollocked if I wasn't there to smile at their arrival. I wasn't even sure being this late to board the plane wouldn't get me court-marshalled.

A small Chinese man eventually turned up. I thrust my receipt in his face and asked if he would mind hurrying as the plane was about to leave. Nothing. Not even an expression of acknowledgment or recognition crossed his face. He took the piece of paper and nonchalantly sauntered off through the door in the corner of the room. I waited. The clock ticked by. Blimey at this rate I would have to abandon my bonsai to its fate and run like the wind: probably down the runway doing my Indiana Jones impression. I would give him two more minutes and that was it. Goodbye bonsai. The official would be able to take it home to the missus or flog it. A minute ticked by. I'd run out of time to do my pre-flight checks. Hopefully my partner would cover for me. I bent down to pick up my bag and run when the door at the back of the room opened and in walked the man carrying my tree. Like a puppy reunited with its owner I leapt at the plant and grabbed it (resisted licking it all over) spilling some soil out on the pristine floor as I turned and ran.

Why is the departure gate always the furthest away when you're late? Through the sheer glass windows I could see the colours on the tail of the 747 as it stood parked on its stand waiting for departure, right at the end of the airport building about a million miles from me. If only I'd taken my fitness more seriously and taken up rowing or at least jogging, my chest wouldn't have been screaming at me to stop as it tried to get enough oxygen down to power my legs. I gasped. I strained. I mustered every ounce of my being into charging through the airport building. If I hadn't been in uniform I would have been screaming at people to get out of my way as I hurled myself at them.

The ground staff looked at me with disbelief as I pushed past all the passengers waiting in their neat queue to board the plane. I tore down the ramp and entered the aircraft door at the front, bags flying wildly about me, but clutching my prize. The first class steward looked up from preparing his doily encased canapés and raised an eyebrow as I rushed past and down the aisle to my station in the back galley. Throwing my bags onto the seat beside the door as I stripped off my jacket, I bent over and took a deep breath in an effort to gain control and not pass out from the exertion.

'Bloody hell, Suzi, you cut it a bit fine,' Cathy said as she kindly poured me a cup of tea. 'The chief was down here a few minutes ago asking where you were.' I quickly looked up. 'Don't panic. I covered for you. I've also done all your checks. Get a grip, the punters are coming. You owe me at least an extra rubbish sack round or two for this.' She walked over to her position by the door to greet the first passengers.

I quickly changed into my flat cabin shoes and thrust my baggage into the overhead stowage.

'Bloody bonsai,' I moaned, grabbing a slurp of tea, smoothing down my wayward hair and salvaging any remains of lipstick I had left by rubbing my lips together furiously, just as the first passenger entered the cabin. 'Don't care how old it is. It's not worth this much agro.'

Same flight on route from HKG to India (BOM),
39,000ft - had more time to write this than I thought.

The passengers on this sector are extremely demanding, just like kids on a school trip. Each one seems to want their own personal assistant to pander to their needs and give them attention. I would have liked to stand at the front of the cabin and just yell 'SHUT UP!' but didn't think it would do my prospects of promotion any good. It's a slow old process up to the top of the ladder for cabin crew. I will have to clock up years of lowly service before being considered suitable enough to be first class trained. Then another few years before I am deemed worthy enough to move to the next rank in the pecking order. I will be well wrinkly before I make it that far. I think it is a quicker process on short haul, but where's the excitement in just going round Europe and back, usually not even always staying over night? Hush my mouth. I've probably just infuriated all the short haul crews that love their jobs. There always is a bit of rivalry between the two fleets. Us long-haulers no doubt thinking we are far superior. Which of course, we are. Ha ha!

It was during that time of the flight when the passengers had been fed and watered and settled down to watch the movies and I had just finished getting a particularly awkward man at the rear of the cabin his third cup of coffee (the second time forgetting the sugar, so I had to walk the whole of the aisle yet again to have the pleasure of smiling sweetly at him and saying 'why didn't you bloody tell me before I went back up last time - not') when I noticed a young mother travelling with her two children. They were seated in a row of three; a girl of about four sat in the seat next to the window crayoning quietly, her colours laid out all over the table top. The baby, about six months, was refusing to drink its milk from the bottle and the woman was getting more and more flustered as the baby started to cry.

'Are you ok?' I enquired, leaning over to catch the bottle as the baby hit it away with its hand.

'I think so,' the woman replied, but I could see when she tried to smile up at me that her eyes were welling up. 'He just won't seem to settle,' she confided. 'He's normally so good. It's this one,' she moved her head towards the angelic little girl, 'who can play up.'

'It's probably all the distractions and different noises,' I offered, leaning on her seat back. Bloody hell, where did that pearl of wisdom come from? I know nothing about babies except that they cry and poo. The baby continued to cry, the volume increasing with each breath.

'Would you hold Rex for me for a moment?' she asked offering me the little demon. 'I'm desperate for the toilet.' I hesitated for a moment. Babies and I just don't get along. Apart from Matt's sister's, I'd had no contact with them. Anyway he would probably scream even more being passed to a stranger. I remembered my training. I was there to serve.

'Of course,' I replied. 'Here, you go. Rex, did you say?' Blimey, no wonder he was crying with a name like that. Jeeez. Not the most attractive name. Poor bugger. My friend had a dog named Rex. Sounded just the kind of name for getting the piss taken out of you at school. I gingerly took the screaming monster and clutched him to my side. I balanced him on my right hip like I'd seen mothers do. His face went from pink to purple and he reached a crescendo as he watched his mother walk away along the aisle and disappear into the toilets at the back of the plane.

'What's your name then?' I asked the little girl who hadn't even looked up from her colouring as I tried to ignore the time bomb stuck to my hip.

'Lucy,' she answered selecting a dark blue from the packet of crayons and quickly obliterated the drawing of a clown on the page of the colouring book.

'Do you like it?' she asked holding it up for me to view.

'Lovely,' I lied in my most enthusiastic voice. Is it best to tell the truth to kids? Or am I likely to scar her for life if I tell her that it was really awful?

She finished scribbling and held it up to me. 'You can have it if you like,' she offered.

'Fantastic!' Okay, so maybe I'd overdone the deceit but I knew which bin it was going straight in. 'Here, Lucy,' I said raising my voice to be heard over the clamour her brother was making right next to my ear. 'What do you do to make Rex stop crying?'

'Blow up his nose,' she said choosing a yellow crayon and starting to obliterate the next picture of a teddy.

'Sorry?' Surely I didn't hear her correctly?

'Blow up his nose,' she repeated. 'That's what I do. It makes him stop.'

I looked at her in amazement. Could I possibly trust this girl? I knew all about sibling rivalry. I had once shut Mia in a cupboard and then emphatically denied it when Mum questioned where she was. Well, she had nicked my Barbie Teresa doll; it was my absolute favourite and slept beside me on my pillow at night. And you Eve, look how you pinched your younger brother so he cried just because you didn't want him to follow us. What if I did blow up Rex's nose and he keeled over? There would be loads of witnesses and I could be had up for manslaughter. Rex was still a deep shade of purple, snot now dribbling from his nose as he squirmed in my arms. His screaming was so loud that I felt myself going deaf at the extreme sound issuing forth from his lungs. Jeez, how could such a small thing make so much noise? My ears would be ringing soon from his rock concert-like decibels?

I looked towards the rear of the aircraft but there was no sign of his mother returning. She'd probably decided to sit it out for a while in the relative peace of the toilet cubicle. Can't say I blamed her. I jiggled Rex up and down. I made soothing noises. I wiped his nose but he only shook his head from side to side in protest so that I spread it even further across his cheeks. I paced up and down doing what looked like a weird style of hip hop dance. Nothing. Bugger. With a swift look to make sure the passengers immediately surrounding us were concentrating on the screens in front of them I slipped into his mother's seat. Ignoring the biscuit crumbs, half empty bottles and damp muslin, I turned Rex around so he was facing me and, waiting for his next inhalation, took a large breath and blew directly up his nostrils with enough force to stoke up a fire. Well, there was no point in just wafting it past him gently. I reckoned I only had one chance at this so I might as well mean it.

It worked! It only bloody worked. Rex's eyes widened as though he'd been caught in the headlights, he gasped at the flood of oxygen forcing its way up his nostrils and the shock of my gust of breath made him stop in his tracks mid wail. Result!

'I told you,' commented Lucy holding out her finished teddy masterpiece. I smiled at her and nodded my head. Rex continued to look at me in amazement as though I'd just zapped him with a bolt of electricity. Then, as though from the depths of his boots, he let out the biggest burp I've ever heard in a man, let alone a small baby. 'That was what was bothering him,' his mum said from behind me as Rex smiled up at her in recognition. 'Well done. You're a natural. I'd been rubbing his back for ages to wind him but it must have got stuck somewhere. Whatever you did worked.'

I glanced sideways at Lucy who was still colouring. This time it was a box full of toys spilling out over the paper.

'You really are good at that, Lucy,' I said quietly leaning over to admire her work. 'That's my favourite. Could I have that one as well?' I had to give the kid some credit. If she hadn't told me the secret of making Rex stop crying, it would all still be a disaster zone. I could just about see the image of some toys underneath the thick lines of crayon, maybe she was improving. No harm in giving her a bit of praise.

'Would you like me to take Rex for a walk round the

cabin?' I offered. Okay, so I was chuffed with myself but I saw this as an opportunity for some good PR. 'It's a while until the next service round. That way you could get a bit of a break yourself.'

'Could I come too?' Lucy chirped up from her seat.

'If it's no trouble that would be lovely,' her mum replied. I handed Rex back to her as I got out of her seat. Helping Lucy pick up her crayons and replace them in the box, we struggled out into the aisle where I took Rex back in my arms and led Lucy to the galley.

'What's this?' asked Cathy. 'Pied Piper time?'

'This is Lucy,' I said, introducing the little girl at my side. 'And her brother, Rex. They're going to stay with us for a bit while their mummy has a break.'

Cathy raised an eyebrow and then pulled out a trolley from its stowage, placing a cloth over the top. 'Right, Lucy,' she said kindly. 'Would you like to be an honorary stewardess and help me fold these?' She bent down, picked up Lucy and sat her on top of the trolley so that she was at galley level. A napkin lay next to her.

'I like colouring,' said Lucy.

'I tell you what, help me fold this napkin into a boat and then we can colour it,' Cathy persuaded.

So while Rex and I watched, the origami class got underway. I looked at Rex, now quietly contentedly perched on my hip concentrating on his sister. He turned to look at me and put one of his chubby hands up to my mouth. He smiled as I blew a raspberry on it and placed it near my lips for another. Maybe this baby business wasn't so bad after all. We're all entitled to have our moments. It just so happens that babies can't explain that they've got trapped wind and need a good belch. This baby was quite cute. If it was my baby it would be even cuter and I would like it even more. But if it was Ed's and my baby, I would just adore it. I wonder what Ed's baby

189

would look like? Probably dark haired like him and it was bound to have his brown eyes. Suzi McEwan. Mrs Suzi McEwan. It sounded nice. We could have a wedding in an old abbey or ... I sniffed. Something disgusting was wafting up underneath my nose. I sniffed again. It smelt like an open sewer.

'Cathy, can you smell something?' I asked as she was helping Lucy fold a tricky part of the boat.

'Yes!' she answered emphatically. 'It's your new charge. He's shit his pants.'

'Cathy!' I exclaimed. 'Little ears.' I motioned towards Lucy who looked up at us and smiled sweetly. 'Oh don't worry. Mummy says it all the time and then says sorry after.'

I grinned at Cathy and looked down at Rex, his eyes had glazed over and he had a fixed expression on his face. His cheeks had a slight flush to them as he concentrated on filling his nappy a bit more.

'Think I'd better hand him back,' I said turning to go.

'Check your skirt,' Cathy advised, laughing. 'Just in case of leakage.'

Grimacing at her I held Rex away from my body and took him back to his mother who was reading a magazine.

'Sorry it wasn't for long,' I apologised. 'But I think he's done something in his nappy that only a mother would love.'

She smiled at me and started to gather fresh nappies and wipes in readiness for changing him.

'Is Lucy alright?'

'Lucy's fine and helping fold napkins. Can I take her crayons though?'

With only a few interruptions from the other passengers for drinks, the next thirty minutes passed pleasantly with all three of us in the galley, colouring.

Cathy showed Lucy how to keep her crayon scribbles in-between the lines of her picture and we found some sticky tape to plaster the cupboard doors with her art work. When it was time to serve the meal round I took Lucy back to her seat. Rex was fast asleep cradled in his mum's lap and she was snoring slightly as well. I lifted the little girl over the sleeping pair and into her seat by the window and went back to make the tea and coffee in the galley.

Love Suzi x

8th September - BOM, 46ft - hotel

Dear Eve

The journey from Mumbai airport to the hotel was an education. I had never before seen people sleeping in their make-shift shacks, not only along the sides of the road but on the dry dust in the middle as well. It was poverty with a capital P. We'd already had a hell of a ride where the bus had to weave in and out of the green or yellow topped rickshaws to avoid crashing with the maddest drivers I'd ever seen. The rest of the crew didn't seem to notice, Eve. I suppose complacency is an attitude that sneaks up on you after seeing the same sights over years of visiting India. But for me it was a major eye-opener. The walk through the airport had been interesting enough. I couldn't believe how many huge bundles of bags were strapped precariously, tied with bits of old string to a set of trolley wheels, and dragged along behind passengers hoping to travel. If the Far East had been a culture shock it was nothing compared to India.

Arriving at the hotel (which looked as though it was

still held in a time warp of the British Raj) we were greeted by a doorman dressed in full Indian national dress, complete with multi-coloured turban. The gold buttons on his long coat jacket gleaming, buttoned up stiffly to its Nehru collar. After checking in I made my way to my room for a long hot bath before meeting up with Cathy to do a bit of exploring. The room smelt musty so I opened the window to get some fresh air in and lighten the austere dark décor. Pulling back the bed covers (I've got into a habit of always checking out the mattress on arrival to gauge what kind of sleep I am likely to have. You'd be amazed at the difference in hotel mattresses. Luckily I've never encountered anything scurrying to escape my scrutiny –yet). My heart sank as the white cotton sheets felt damp to the touch. My mobile buzzed with an incoming message. I searched through my pocket to retrieve it, swiped the screen and read. *'Suz, when do you land in England?' Ed.* Ah…so he hadn't forgotten me.

Cathy had been to Mumbai many times and insisted that we went to the hotel beauty salon for a massage and bikini wax; apparently they were not only fabulous but extremely cheap. Not one to miss an opportunity for a bit of plucking and pampering, I agreed. We made our appointments and although I had once had a massage from Carrie, a friend practising for her Hair and Beauty exams, I had no idea what to expect of a massage in India.

The room I was led into was very dark and as far as I could make out had nothing in it except the couch, a chair and a small table which held a few items. A little light glimmered from a single lit candle. This was nothing like my experience with Carrie. Then it had all been about soft relaxing music and perfumed candles creating an aromatic paradise. I had been left to get changed in this perfumed haven down to my underwear. Lying on the couch I was wrapped in soft towels which smelt of sunshine while Carrie performed what felt like a towel dance as she carefully manoeuvred the towels around me making sure that not one bit of extra flesh was on show that shouldn't be.

'Take your clothes off,' the older woman who had followed me into the room barked, whilst motioning me towards the couch.

'What! All of them?' I squeaked. My voice had risen an octave to panic mode. Okay. I'm not a prude but I'm not used to getting my kit off on demand.

She wobbled her head from side to side in that Indian way and held out a bit of string which looked as though it had an old bit of bunting attached to it. I held it up over my groin. No. There was no way it would even cover half a bum cheek let alone two full on cheeks and the front, much-more-in-need-of-covering area. It was difficult to tell just how large she was under all her layers of colourful material but she must have felt that westerners are only slight things and so only justified minimal coverage. She looked at me, shrugged her shoulders and walked out of the room, waggling her head as she went. I think that meant the ball was in my court. I undressed and placed my clothes neatly on the chair and fixed the piece of bunting around my lower body, deciding that the triangle was best attempting to cover my triangle.

Clambering up onto the couch and lying on my back, I found that I had choice - boobs bare and legs covered or décolletage safely concealed and thighs exposed. The towel was only big enough for one. I chose the latter and wriggled until I had the towel covering maximum flesh. I could hear laughter coming from outside. My masseuse was probably regaling her colleagues with how the shy westerner in her room was complaining about taking her clothes off. Did she expect to have a massage fully clothed? I lay and waited. Shortly after, with no gentle knock to make sure I was ready, the door opened and the woman walked in, the light from the outside shining so brightly behind her, like the spotlight of an interrogator. Perhaps it wasn't supposed to be a relaxing massage but the precursor to a torture session. The woman hummed softly to herself as she fiddled with the things on the table behind my head. Then turning to me, her hands covered in oil, she unceremoniously pulled up the towel from my lower body and proceeded to slather me until I felt like a turkey, well basted and ready for the oven.

To give her her due, the long soothing movements as her hands rhythmical slid up and down my legs soon began to lull me into a false sense of relaxation. False, because as she moved from my calves to my thighs and began kneading the muscles at the top of my hips, I tensed as she paused in her actions. I held my breath and waited for her to proceed to my arms or ask me to turn over so she could massage my back when she suddenly lifted the towel from my chest. Recoating her hands in more oil she swung into action massaging first my right boob, then my left. Whoa! Not what I was expecting. Jumping up and shrieking didn't seem an option. I lay frozen with shock. Should I lay still and just let her get on with? The longer I lay debating with myself, letting the woman cup each boob in turn in her hands and gently massage them in a rotational movement, the longer it seemed futile to make a fuss when she had probably nearly finished anyway. Perhaps it would help make them bigger? I'd always felt a bit on the small side in that area – needing the extra-full-thrust-and-lift bras to make the most of my assets. I could do with a little help in an extra cup size that didn't cost me a packet and involve anything silicone.

Moving onto my abdomen she continued to make firm, circular movements, her finger tips pressing firmly into my flesh almost as though she was trying to knead dough into a mould. I tried to shift my bottom to the side to subtly tell her I'd had enough. Her fingers kept kneading just near my left hip. Round and round her hands probed. I felt her pressing against a hardened lump in my intestines. Ouch! This woman had overstepped the mark. If she wanted to practise her bread making technique on her unsuspecting clients, this one was going to stand up to her torturous ways.

I felt something stir deep within my bowels. Whoa! I clenched my bum cheeks together. What the hell had she done? I felt my intestines gurgle and belch as something moved along. This woman was a walking bowel plumber. How did she know I was having an internal blockage problem? Whatever she'd done it had shifted something along its path. I tightened my pelvic floor muscles in an attempt to ensure that nothing escaped from down below that shouldn't.

'Turn over, Madam,' she demanded. With no towel to hold over me to retain my dignity I clumsily wriggled around until I was lying on my tummy – the triangle of the material strung around my waist having been dislodged in the move so that it hung from my hip over the side of the couch like a flag at half mast. Clearly this material was only a gesture to reassure me as she proceeded to untie it from my waist and discard it onto the chair, leaving me lying naked, my two cherry shaped bum cheeks fully exposed.

It's a strange feeling having your buttocks massaged. If I thought my boobs felt weird, buttocks definitely topped it. With a pressure crossed between pleasurable and masochistic, there were times I wanted to hit her as she delved so deeply into my muscles that it felt like she

195

was reaching inside and arranging the knots into long straight rows, one by one.

'Very tense,' she proclaimed as she spent what I considered to be an inordinate amount of time on the same spot on my lower back. 'You must relax more.'

Nothing I didn't know, I wanted to answer. It's pushing those damn trolleys up hill on ascent, but at the time my teeth were gritted so firmly together to deal with the excruciating pain, I would have only been able to spit at her in reply. Finishing her treatment with massaging my neck and head, the woman left me lying completely spaced out on her couch. Dazed, I slowly got up, dressed, and walked outside into the salon reception area.

'Blimey. You look good,' Cathy offered sarcastically, looking up from her magazine. I caught sight of myself in the mirror on the wall opposite. My hair was greased up and hanging in clumps and my face as scarlet as though I'd just done two hours on the treadmill.

'Hmmm…' I replied.

'You probably need a shower before you go for your wax.'

'I'm going back to my room,' I said opening my purse to pay at the till. 'You have your wax, I'll meet you after.' A girl can only take so much torture in one day.

Sashaying down to the hotel lobby after my shower I found the masseuse had turned me into a six foot model. I felt inches taller as my back was as straight as if I'd had a pole inserted up my arse and stapled to my spine. Bit of a miracle I know, as I'm usually only five foot eight but with all the knots, lumps and bumps smoothed out from my muscles I felt that instead of being bent like a dowager with a humped back, I could look anyone right in the eye.

Cathy was waiting for me after her waxing session and we decided to venture out into the city. We only had a one night stay and I wanted to see as much as I could. Well, it wouldn't have mattered how many times I re-read *Shantaram* (epic book about the experiences of Gregory David Roberts in India) or watched re-runs of the film, *Slumdog Millionaire*, nothing would have prepared me for the 'Indian Experience.' I felt as though I had wandered into the Indian equivalent of a sweet shop; with so much to stimulate the senses I was on a sugar-fix high overload.

The moment we left the relative safety of the hotel grounds it seemed we might as well have had a huge neon sign over our heads to point us out to the locals. No going incognito here. Straight away we were surrounded by people trying to sell us things. Shoving them in our face and offering *'veryyy good price, madam.'* I was taken aback at how readily my personal space was invaded without a care. I fingered the flimsy fabric of the T- shirt a man was holding up for me to inspect and then shook my head. He just smiled at me revealing a gap in his front teeth. Big mistake. I should have remembered my London night-street-walking strategy and kept my head down, avoiding eye contact, and walked on. Now it felt like he was my new best friend, he was so attentive.

'Vvvery good quality, madam, no price for looooking.' He scurried after me, repeating his sales pitch. Cathy grabbed my arm and hurried me on but he continued to follow us saying, *'You want aliii babas, no price for looooking, madam.'* I started to laugh. It was just so absurd. Cathy was walking so quickly I almost broke into a trot to keep up with her. The heat was making me start to sweat buckets. Fat lot of use having a shower just before I left. I put my hand up to smooth my hair down. Even without a mirror to confirm it, I just knew I would have a barnet like a frizzy afro by the time I got back to the hotel; my hair and the humidity not a great combo.

Our new friend pursued us along the street, matching our hurried steps until he finally lost interest in his sale, dropped off and hung back. We turned a corner to be confronted by a cow plodding down the street. No one else seemed a bit bothered and everyone just steered around it as though it was nothing unusual. Cathy deftly skirted around the animal just missing being caught by its tail as it swished the flies away. Like a woman possessed, she zoomed along, head down, determined not to be delayed again, as though a pack of wolves were at her heels.

I slowed up and dropped behind her. This place was the best entertainment value I'd ever come across and I didn't want to miss it. I watched a woman in a brightly coloured, orange and red sari swaying gracefully as she sashayed along in front of me. She stopped to talk to another woman also clothed in the most exquisite, dazzling fabric. The two of them looking like bright jewels. Between them they had more bling than a night on the red carpet at the Oscars: but it wasn't distasteful, it enhanced their gracefulness and beauty. A small nose ring piercing and strong dark kohl eye make-up made them appear so exotic.

A skinny, mangy dog passed close by and sniffed at the bag one of them was carrying. The woman took no notice and carried on chatting gaily to her friend. The contrast between here and England stood out like a beacon. How many times had I seen commuters scurry across London in their dull, grey clothes, head down in their own cocoon of moroseness? Okay, so the weather had something to do with it. It's hard to feel jolly when the rain is lashing down and the evenings get dark at four o'clock in the winter, but even with such poverty these Indians gave the appearance of being far happier.

'What're thinking about?' Cathy asked as she grabbed

my arm to stop me walking past a small shop door. 'You were frowning.'

'Oh, just the difference between here and England. Grey verses colour.'

'Well, don't think too hard... we're back there tomorrow. Now, down to business. Here's a good place if you want to buy any souvenirs.'

Love Suzi x

9th September - Crew bus - LHR

Dear Eve

We left Mumbai the next day. I had smuggled my bonsai into India and smuggled it out again. There was none of the dramatics of the Chinese in Hong Kong. I don't really think Indian customs gave a toss what the crews were bringing in or out of the country. They seemed to have their hands full stopping their own people bringing in half the western world's consumer items.

The flight to Heathrow seemed to go on for ever. I was knackered. I had been round the world in such a short space of time, coping with time changes and belligerent passengers and I decided it was time I got a tad belligerent myself. I'd had enough of customs and their rules. The bonsai was in my suitcase and if they wanted to take it off me and clap me in irons, I couldn't give a damn. Arriving in England, I filled in my customs declaration, being rebellious and omitted to mention the bonsai. Silly move. I should have known I couldn't do anything illegal no matter how hard I wanted to buck the system. It was just as the crew bus was approaching the customs area that the Purser, sitting at the front of the bus turned to us.

'Don't want to cause alarm guys, but rumour has it we may be rummaged.'

There was a collective groan from the rest of the crew. Cathy's face turned pale. Bloody hell. No point in reconsidering my decision to rebel. I'd signed my customs form and had to take the consequences. I quickly thought about the state of the clothes in my suitcase and what else I'd hidden amongst my knickers that I hadn't declared.

Being 'rummaged' is the term given to an inbound crew having the contents of their luggage dissected by customs as closely as if it were a frog, pinned, spread-eagled on a laboratory slab and every orifice inspected. There was nothing that customs wouldn't look through if they so desired. 'Rumour control' was always sending shock waves of tales of 'this' crew having their underwear spread out for inspection or 'that' crew who had their trainers ripped apart as someone was suspected of smuggling drugs. And if they didn't have any reason to suspect a crew of wrongdoing, customs choose at random to perform a rummage just to keep the rest of us on our toes.

If they were brave enough to tackle my dirty underwear after being away for just over week then they were welcome to it. Even my washing machine groaned after I returned from some of my trips as it struggled to cope with the quantities it had to deal with. I stayed in my seat on the bus and decide to act cool. Surely a bonsai wasn't going to cause that much interest? Maybe I should have declared it? The bloody thing was turning out to be so much trouble; it was going to have to blossom all year round and not just spring to pay me back for the aggro. Note to self: try not to act on the spur of the moment and get carried away buying pretty things. I thought of the bags, bracelets and sequinned slippers I'd purchased in the shop with Cathy. Was I over the limit? I was always pretty blazé about how much I'd actually spent. We had an allotted amount before we were charged, but I took no notice of that.

The bus stopped and we sat for half an hour outside customs while two senior crew members went in to negotiate. Perhaps it was just them who were being rummaged? I thought the Purser looked a bit dodgy the moment I saw him in the briefing room. Shifty smugglers eyes I reckoned. He hadn't said much to me all trip except to moan that the cabin needed tidying. Definitely guilty. They probably had a whole dossier on him and had been waiting for him to try re-enter the country again so they could pounce.

Suddenly the two men reappeared, boarded the bus and the engine started up again as we passed through the checkpoint post that marked the airside boundary. No one said anything but fourteen collective shoulders relaxed and smiles broke out. So I wasn't the only one with a guilty secret.

'They always do that,' Cathy confided, the colour returning to her cheeks as she swung round in her seat to look at me, her face pushed between the dip in the seat backs.

'Do what?'

'Put the fear of God into you for no reason.'

'What have you got to hide?'

'Oh. Only a bit of booze off the aircraft and some souvenirs,' she replied winking at me as though I was in some great conspiracy. They must be dodgy souvenirs to have caused the look of panic on her face earlier.

Love, Suzi x

9th September - waiting for the taxi near Chichester

Dear Eve

When the coach drew up outside the crew building that serves as our base, the driver unloaded the suitcases and placed them on the pavement in a row. Just as I was about to grab the handle of my suitcase I heard someone shout my name. I looked up. There walking towards me was Ed. He was dressed in jeans and a tight blue T- shirt under a brown leather jacket. Obviously not working then. I'd forgotten just how fit he looked. He'd caught the sun since I last saw him which made his brown eyes stand out even more. He smiled at me and I noticed a slight dimple in his left cheek that I must have missed before.

'Ed. What on earth are you doing here?'

'Waiting for you.'

'Bloody hell. For what do I deserve this honour?'

'I thought it was about time we put things right between us and as we're not often in the country at the same time, I needed to catch you when I knew you would be here.'

My phone vibrated in my pocket. I automatically searched it out and swept my finger across the screen to open the text that had arrived.

'YOU FUCKING BITCH. DON'T THINK YOU'VE WON.'

My face froze. The last abusive text I'd received had been a few days ago and I'd hoped that it had all stopped.

'Suz? What is it?'

'You tell me?' I replied thrusting my phone up to his

202

face. 'Your bloody precious Candy, I reckon.'

He took the phone from me and read the message.

'What the…?'

'It's not the first,' I explained. 'I've been receiving them for quite a while now. Candy is top of my list of suspects. Did you know she came round to my house and warned me off you?' To hell with it. It may not be the most appropriate place for him to learn about his poisonous girlfriend but I was tired and I'd had enough.

The rest of the crew, after selecting their suitcases, had gone into the building leaving just the two of us standing outside; my suitcase on the pavement between us.

'God, Suz. Why didn't you tell me earlier?'

'Oh yes. Like you'd have believed me if I'd said, - 'Oh and by the way Ed, your girlfriend is stalking me and sending me abusive texts?'

'Maybe not then but now…' he started to explain.

My phone rang as he held it in his hand.

'If that's Candy, you'd better go away as you might not want to hear what I've got to say to her,' I exploded.

'No. It's not Candy,' Ed said handing me the phone. 'It's someone called Mia?'

'My sister?' I said surprised as I grabbed the phone from his outstretched hand and placed it to my ear. Mia never phoned me, not knowing if I was abroad or not. She always texted and I would ring her back.

'Suzi?' her voice was strangely high pitched. 'Where are you?

'Just got back into Heathrow. Why? What's the matter, you sound odd?'

'Suz. Don't panic, but it's Dad.'

I stared at Ed. I couldn't take in what Mia was saying to me. Ed was looking at me questioningly.

'Is he alright?' I shouted down the phone. 'Where is he?' There was no reply. I repeated my questions.

Louder. I looked at the phone. The signal had gone.

'Suz? What is it?' Ed asked concerned.

'It's…it's my Dad.'

My phone rang again. I could feel the tears welling up in my eyes. I stood still, the phone continuing to ring.

'Suz. The phone?' I didn't move. It hung in my hand getting quite a few bars through its Coldplay ringtone. Ed took it from me and answered.

'Hello, yes this is Suzi's phone. I'm Ed, her friend. How is her father? Where is he?...Yes. Okay… I'll bring her down straight away.'

He ended the call and picked up my suitcase.

'Suzi. Come on,' he said firmly. 'Your father is in a hospital near Chichester. He collapsed. They think it's a heart attack. I'm going to drive you down there now. He's going to be alright.'

I continued to stare at him. My mind had gone blank. I couldn't think what to do. Me - who believes she is so cocksure of everything. Well, not with the men in my life but general day to day stuff I can cope with. Remember? I had that 'dead' passenger on my first flight. But this was my Dad, Eve. My mind whizzed back to that last phone call with you on that sunny morning. There had been nothing in your voice to warn me of what was about to come. It had all happened so suddenly out of the blue then. Surely it couldn't be happening twice? 'No it's okay,' I muttered and, after what seemed like the flicking of a switch, I regained the use of my brain. 'You don't need to bother. I'll be alright.'

'Like bloody hell you will,' he replied taking my arm and leading me along the road to the crew car park. 'You're in shock. Look at the state of you. You're in no fit state to drive anywhere. We'll leave your car here, it'll be safe enough. I can drive you there. Suz?' He stopped walking and looked at me. 'When did you last sleep?'

Thoughts came tumbling back into my head. 'Hmmm… not sure. Yesterday I think… in Mumbai.' Hmmm…maybe not all my thoughts. My brain seemed to be clogged with something thick and sticky. I couldn't rationalise. One thought kept coming back. My dad had had a heart attack. My dad. 'Do you think he's going to be okay?' Ed put down my suitcase and came over to me. He put his arms around me and drew me close, encircling me. I could smell his deodorant. It was a mixture of lemons and 'Eau de Ed.' Deliciously warm, sweet and comforting. Or maybe that was just how it felt to be in his arms at such a moment.

'Mia said that it happened whilst he was feeding the animals and he managed to phone for the ambulance. They're doing tests. Best if we get you there as quickly as possible, then you can find out more.' He gently released me and, taking my hand in his as though I was a child, picked up the handle of my case so that he could wheel it along behind us. We reached Ed's blue BMW which was parked in a convenient space in the carpark near to the exit. He opened the boot and swung my luggage inside. I climbed into the leather passenger seat after clearing some newspapers and a tube of mints out of my way, leaning over and placing them on the seats behind.

'Sorry, about that,' Ed said getting into the driver's seat. 'I wasn't expecting to have a passenger. Now, I know how to get to Chichester but I'm not sure exactly where the hospital is.'

I nodded. 'I wonder if Dad had finished feeding all the animals before he collapsed?' I mused aloud. OHMYGOD! What kind of heartless daughter was I? How can I be thinking of the animals at a time like this? I should only be thinking of Dad!

'What kind of animals does he have?' Ed asked as he started the engine and drove out of the car park and onto the airport perimeter road.

'Oh, just a few livestock. Nothing too large, but they do take a bit of looking after. He lives on his own. I'm not sure what's going to happen to them now he's in hospital.'

I stared out of the window. Actually it helped to take my mind off whether Dad was going to die if I thought about something else. Ed seemed to realise this and carried on the conversation.

'Does your dad live far from Chichester?'

'No, only about twenty minutes the other side.'

'Why don't I drop you at the hospital then? You give me his address and I can go and check on the animals while you see how he's doing? At least I could be doing something useful.'

He momentarily took his eyes from the road ahead and looked at me. I smiled at him. He placed his left hand over mine briefly and gave it a quick squeeze.

'It'll all be alright. Trust me. It'll take us an hour or so to get there depending on the traffic. Why don't you try and get your head down. You look exhausted. You must be jet-lagged.'

'Is that your way of saying I look rough?'

'In the nicest possible way, of course,' he smiled.

I continued to stare out of the window watching the houses pass by. There was no way I'd be able to sleep. But I took off my jacket and folded it into a make-shift pillow, placing it against the window. Dad was only sixty-five. Far too young to have a heart attack. Far too young to die. I rested my head on my jacket. I mustn't think like that. Positive thoughts only. I looked out of the window fixing my gaze until the houses blurred into one long picture. The warmth from the heated seat beneath me started to seep into my lower back and I could hear Ed quietly whistling my ring tone under his breath.

The next thing I knew Ed was gently shaking my arm and calling my name.

'Suzi, wake up! We're at the hospital.'

I sat upright and looked out at the sombre brick building in front of us. A few lights were shinning through, but the windows were mainly blackened out.

'I thought you didn't know where it was?' I questioned.

'Your sister told me the name on the phone and well...' he looked sheepish. 'It wasn't that difficult to find once we got nearby.'

'Of course.' I ran my fingers through my hair and pulled down the sun visor to look in the mirror to check for any unsightly dribbles or bogeys that might have sneaked out whilst I was asleep. Just a few crease marks from my jacket were etched into my cheek. I rubbed vigorously to restore smooth skin. 'I was forgetting you are a pilot. If you can navigate your way onto the runway at Hong Kong, finding a district hospital must be a breeze.'

Ed smiled and reached into the pocket of the driver's door.

'Now, what's your dad's address?' He picked up a sat nav and plugged it into the cigarette lighter socket. The penny clicked. 'You bloody cheat!' I accused. 'You didn't find the hospital just by being clever. You used that, didn't you?'

Ed laughed and started pressing buttons on the machine. 'Had you going though didn't I? You thought I did it using my brilliant navigational skills?' He looked out at the sky. 'Oh, yes. The moon is just rising so it must be second star to the right and straight on 'til morning.'

I playfully hit him on the thigh and reeled off my dad's address while he tapped it into the sat nav. 'You must make sure you shut the gate when you arrive,' I ordered. 'Otherwise Mabel will escape and... watch out for Gruff. He's friendly but you have to be strict with him and show him who's boss. All the animal feed will be in the store room off the kitchen but make sure Jemima and Puddle don't get in because they'll eat everything.'

Ed looked at me. 'That's fine. It's only a few animals, Suzi. I'm sure I can cope. Oh, and if we're playing at who's boss, have you got enough sterling, in case you need anything?' I picked up my handbag and looked through my purse. I only had a few American dollars and some Indian rupees. Ed reached into his pocket and took a £50 note out of his wallet. 'Take this.' I shook my head. 'It's only a loan, not a gift.' I started to gather my things and put my hand on the car door handle. 'You've forgotten something though,' Ed said staring patiently at me.

'Thank you?' I answered gingerly.

'No, you idiot. A key or something. How do I get into the house?'

'Oh, that's easy. Go round the side of the house until you get to Gruff's pen. There's a spare key just inside his shed on the right under a stone. Dad reckoned that a Gruff was the best protection against burglars.'

'And Gruff is…?'

'A goat of course. Don't you know your fairy stories?'

'Of course, silly me,' Ed laughed. 'Obviously! Who thought of these names? No, don't answer that. That's obvious too.'

I got out of the car and looked towards the entrance. Somewhere inside the building my dad could be dying. I took a deep breath and made to shut the door.

'Suz,' Ed leaned over the passenger seat and looked up at me. 'It'll all be alright. Ring me when you're done and I'll come and get you.' As I stood and watched Ed drive off along the road my heart sank a little. Part of me wanted to call him back so I could get straight back into that car and drive off with him. Then I wouldn't have to face what was waiting for me in the hospital. I gave myself a swift mental kick up the arse. Man up, Suzi. It's Dad you're talking about. Time to grow up and get a grip.

The automatic doors swished open as soon as I approached them. After checking the information board in the entrance, I followed the coloured pathway line drawn on the floor until I reached the first floor ward. I don't like hospitals - after the time I had to go and have my chin stitched when I fell off the boy next door's bike.

I entered the main men's ward and looked round the first four-bedded section, searching the beds for my dad. The bed nearest the door was occupied by an old man, lying propped up on his stack of pillows, fast asleep with his mouth open. His skin was almost translucent with thin, blue veins criss-crossing over the gnarled hand that lay on top of the pale sheet. Well, he certainly wasn't Dad. He looked as old as Methuselah and as dead as him too.

I glanced at the old boy laying in the bed next to him. No. Not dad either. He was as fat as a barrel and had the audacity to wink at me. He was obviously in the wrong place if he could still do that. Really! Just because he was poorly and in his PJ's he thinks it gives him license to flirt at will. Oh my god. The bedcovers weren't over him properly. I resisted having a second glance to see if it was what I thought it was, peeping through his PJ bottoms. Oh I wouldn't be a nurse for anything in the world. At least if the punters get a bit frisky on the flight I can 'accidentally' pour something on them. Here you'd be arrested for mistreatment if you did something like that to an old boy who could always plead dementia. Most nurses had seen it all before anyway, surely? And don't they say that once you've seen one, you've seen them all?

I walked along the corridor to the next room. It was nearly empty except for two occupants (not peak time for being ill, obviously). A curtain was drawn across the bed in the corner, next to the window on the far side. I crept softly up and peeped round the patterned material.

Bingo! Dad was asleep lying flat on his back. I walked up to him and stood looking at him trying to decide whether to disturb him or not. His cheeks were pale and his hair askew but apart from that he looked the same. I sat down quietly on the large chair next to the bed, trying not to make a sound. But I must have been noisier than I thought as Dad's eyes flickered open.

'Hello, darling,' he said trying to wake and prop himself up all at the same time. 'I suppose Mia rang you. I didn't want her to bother you,' he apologised squirming to get the pillows in order.

'Dad!' I exclaimed, jumping up to help him arrange the pillows with the skill of Florence Nightingale so that he was comfortable. 'It's no bother. You're ill. I would have killed her if she hadn't let me know. How are you feeling?'

'Okay. But I think I've been a bit of a fraud. They've done some tests and it appears that rather than having a heart attack, I may just have an irregular heartbeat and that's what caused the pain and made me faint.'

'Are you sure?' Relief flooded over me. It felt a bit like when the Tree Ents released Saruman's dam in the closing stages of Tolkien's, *Lord of the Rings* (I loved those movies, couldn't plough through the books but once had a 'Frodo' saturation weekend when Matt and I watched the trilogy straight off).

Dad nodded his head and took hold of my hand.

'Really, I feel fine. A bit tired, but that's all the excitement. They keep sticking needles into me and taking blood for tests. I'm going to stay in for a couple of nights just to make sure. Really Suzi, you mustn't worry.'

I pulled my chair up close to his side and snuggled in for a cuddle. The whole day had been emotionally exhaustive. I had steeled myself to hear the worst. I reckoned if I was prepared, it wouldn't come as such a shock. But my dad wasn't going to die. Well, he was one day, but not today. Or tomorrow. Or the next. He would soon be out there again scattering chicken feed and being followed by Mabel. Thinking of Mabel I chuckled.

'I'm pleased you're pleased,' Dad said. 'But I didn't expect you to be laughing about it.'

'I wasn't laughing at you. I was just thinking about Ed. He's gone on to your house to feed the animals.'

Dad lifted my head from its position tucked under his arm and looked me straight in the eye. 'This isn't the Ed you told me about before? The one you like but who has girlfriend and you don't know how he feels about you?'

I nodded.

'Seems like you've got your answer, my girl. If he's driven you down here and volunteered to be butted by Gruff and snapped at by Mabel, he must like you. Has he had much experience of farm animals?' Dad asked.

'I've no idea.' We both grinned.

'Well, it'll be a baptism of fire then.'

Visiting time had only just begun when I arrived so I stayed with Dad for a couple of hours until his eyes drooped wearily. Mia had visited earlier and Mum was going to pop in later in the evening to check all was okay. Half way through my visit I realised I was starving, so ventured down to the hospital shop and selected a panini, crisps and hot chocolate which I took up to munch while Dad filled me in on all that happened in the last twenty-four hours.

By the time it came to say goodbye, he was looking tired but much brighter. Although I felt relieved by his

211

news, I was completely knackered. I decided to use Ed's money and get a taxi to Dad's house.

Love, Suzi x

10th September - Dad's House near Chichester

Dear Eve

When I opened the door on the cottage a short while later, it was a surprise to find it all quiet. Ed, was sprawled out asleep on the sofa in the small sitting room. Mabel was also comatose at his feet and five chickens were dotted comfortably around the room on anything soft they could find to sit on. A gentle snore rose from the inert form on the sofa and the quiet clucking of the hens as they shifted position made quite the country scene. I left him sleeping and walked back into the kitchen to fill the kettle. Realising I'd left the back door ajar I went to kick it shut with my foot. Suddenly all hell broke loose. Gruff came bounding through the doorway from the garden, butting it back with such force that it smashed against the wall, tore straight past me and headed for the sitting room. All I could hear was the clamour of clucking and a loud groan and a shout as the sleeping party were rudely woken up.

'How the bloody hell did you get in again?' came angrily from the room. 'Argh... bloody animal!'

I smiled as I poked my head round the doorframe to see Gruff standing over Ed who had been knocked onto the floor. Ed's hands were up trying to fend off Gruff's attentions.

'Having trouble with your new friend?' I asked laughing at the scene.

'Bloody hell, Suzi. Get the beast off me.' I went over

and took Gruff by the collar. Heaving him away from Ed I walked him firmly out of the room and back to his pen, where I released him and made sure the gate was secured once again.

When I returned to the kitchen Ed was brushing himself down.

'You could have warned me?' he reproached straightening up. 'He's been a nightmare ever since I got here. It took me half an hour to get past him so that I could get the front door key. Every time I went to enter the pen, he'd put his head down ready to attack me. Eventually I went and got some mints from the car. I threw them into the furthest corner and the greedy pig was so busy trying to find them that I managed to sneak in and get it. He caught me on the way out though.' Ed turned round to reveal the torn pocket of his jeans. 'I obviously didn't secure the gate properly in my desperation to get out of his way 'cos the next thing I knew he was following me into the house.'

Ed stood with an expression like a four year old waiting for someone to praise him for trying his best. 'Jeez, your dad was right when he placed the key in his pen. No burglar in his right mind would come within an inch of the place with that bloody goat around.'

I picked up the kettle and started to fill it. I wasn't going to say, I did warn you but you were so bloody sure of yourself with the, 'it's only a few animals' line.

'Stop smiling,' Ed ordered. 'It's not funny.'

'Yes, it is,' I answered. 'Gruff's harmless really. You just have to be firm with him.'

'If you can get near the damn thing, without him going for you.'

'You seem to have charmed Mabel,' I observed looking at the goose standing quietly beside his legs. 'I thought she would be the one to give you trouble.'

213

'Ah...' Ed answered wisely. 'She's like most females. Give them something nice to eat and tickle their tummies and they're putty in your hands.'

I raised my eyebrows and got the mugs out of the cupboard.

'How's your dad?' Ed asked changing the subject.

While I made the tea I filled him in with Dad's progress. We went and sat in the sitting room. Mabel followed us and the chickens settled down again after realising there was nothing to scavenge from the floor.

'This feels like an episode of '*Escape to the Country*,' I mused as Ed finished lighting a fire in the wood burner. 'I don't watch it but I imagine it must involve fires, animals and ...'

'...being terrorised by the animals you mean.' Ed continued. 'Are you hungry? I stopped off at that supermarket in the village on my way down. Thought we'd have chicken curry.'

'Shhhhhh...'I said gesturing towards a chicken asleep on his discarded jumper that was laying on the chair by the window. 'Have you no heart. It could be her relative.'

Ed laughed and began rounding up the chickens and shooing them out of the door and through to the kitchen. 'We'll just have to hope that they've had a family row and they don't get on with each other anymore.' I picked up the tea cups and followed him through to the kitchen chasing Mabel in front of me in the process.

'So you're going to stay then?' I asked as I placed the mugs in the dishwasher which looked as though it hadn't been used for ages.

'Thought I would. If that's ok?' Ed said looking at me. 'I wasn't sure how your dad would be so thought you might need company.'

'But you were the one telling me all the time it would be alright?'

'That's because I can hardly say what you were thinking, can I? - Oh, by the way Suzi. Start worrying because it sounds as though you're dad is going to peg it. Not the most comforting of approaches, is it?'

I shrugged my shoulders. 'I suppose not, but at least a watered down version would have been more honest.'

'I never do watered down,' he replied emphatically. 'First rule in the pilot's training manual. If the plane is going down and you're all going to die. Blatantly lie.'

I laughed. 'Yeah, right. I heard that when that flight back in the 80's sucked in all that volcanic dust into its engines over Jakarta, everyone started praying and crying. What did the Captain say then? Don't worry everything's going to be fine?'

'No. In fact it's well known that he delivered a master class in understatement.' Ed put on his tannoy announcing voice.

"Ladies and gentlemen, this is your captain speaking. We have a small problem. All four engines have stopped. We are doing our damnedest to get them going again. I trust you are not in too much distress."

'What?' Ed jumped back as I playfully hit his arm. 'They used it as an example in my training. The plane was nick-named the glider.'

'It must have been only too obvious there was a major problem. With all four engines stopped. It would have been so quiet up there without their roar. I can't imagine what that must have been like.'

'Nope. Nor do I want to dwell on it. Thank God they kept on trying to start the engines. So if I'm staying..?' he looked at me questioning. I nodded my head. It would be good to have some company. I'd never stayed at Dad's place on my own. It got pretty dark in the country without any street lights. Besides it was getting late and who knew what might happen? Maybe I could make up for the

215

disaster in Hong Kong. The question was... should I make up the spare bed? It was a large single. Ed might want to be chivalrous and sleep there. Or should I just be slutty and change the sheets on Dad's double? On the other hand. Noooooo. The thought of having sex in Dad's bed made me shudder. It was almost as bad as thinking of my parents at it. No, the large single would have to do. Or...I could change all the sheets on both beds, that way if necessary, I could sleep on my own in the double and Ed could have the single. Maybe it wouldn't look as though I was planning anything... and... if I did get lucky, we could both just about squeeze into the single. Blimey! The whole issue was doing my head in.

'Suzi?' Ed questioned. 'What is it? You've gone all quiet and you're frowning. I don't have to stay.'

I rubbed the crease away from my forehead and forced a smile. Best not to tell him what was bothering me...yet.

'No. It was nothing. Stay. Please.' Did that sound a bit too desperate? 'But perhaps we ought to go and check on the animals one last time and make sure everything's ok before we get cooking. It gets very dark here.'

Ed reached into a carrier bag that was placed on the floor beside the kitchen cupboard. 'Surely we've got a while before that happens? Try this? I bought it with you in mind.' He pulled out a bottle of champagne and proceeded to unravel the gold paper at the top. 'This time I'd quite like my share though.'

'Ha, ha. Funny man,' I jibed turning to fetch a couple of glasses from the cupboard. So he had remembered Hong Kong. Good, perhaps it would be the large single bed after all. 'But Ed.' I looked him straight in the eye as he popped the cork and proceeded to fill my glass. 'What about Candy?'

'Always one to spoil a beautiful moment, aren't you Suz? I tried to tell you earlier.' I took a gulp of the golden liquid in my glass. 'Candy and I have spilt up.'

I took a breath. The fizz from the bubbles went straight up my nose causing me to cough, splutter and keel over as I tried desperately to catch my breath.

Ed put his glass down on the worktop and patted me on the back. 'What is it with you and champagne?' he questioned. 'Can't you drink it without choking?'

I spat the remaining liquid into the sink and heaved some oxygen into my lungs. Taking a few moments to recover, I turned to face Ed.

'It's not the bloody champagne, you idiot. It's you dropping a bombshell at the wrong time. When? What happened?'

Ed grinned. 'I knew you'd want the whole story.' He topped up my half empty glass and started to unload the contents of the grocery bag, laying a pack of chicken fillets and a jar of bhuna curry sauce on the worktop. 'After you told me about Candy and what you thought she'd done,' he saw me raise my eyebrows again and held his hand up in protest. 'Let me tell it my way. I brought up the conversation with Candy when I was home last and yes, it turns out she was the one sending you the texts.'

'And wrote that letter complaining about me?'

'Well, she didn't admit or deny that one.'

'What made you think I was right?'

'I found your note. The one you sent with those hideous pants.'

It was my turn to grin. 'You have no taste. Nothing wrong with them. How did you find it?'

'Accidentally. She asked me to get her purse out of her handbag one evening when we were going out and it fell out on the floor.'

I folded my arms smugly and looked at him. 'Go on,' I encouraged.

217

'That's about it really.'

'What do you mean, that's about it? That's not about anything. It tells me nothing about what happened. How did she take it?'

'It was all a bit messy really, but I realised when she started getting hysterical that you were right.'

'In what way?'

'That I really didn't know her. She started turning into a person I didn't recognise. It all escalated into a huge row so I suggested we take a break from each other.' He hesitated.

'What?'

'Before I knew it she was slagging you off and revealing all kinds of things I didn't know. It seems she had been monitoring my emails as well as my phone calls.'

'How on earth…'

'Whenever I left my computer on or the phone lying around the house apparently. In an attempt to calm her down I went into the kitchen to get her a drink, when I came back to ask her what she wanted she hastily dropped my phone back on the sofa. Seems she was just checking you hadn't called.'

I stood silently. I didn't approve of spying on someone else but had I been unfair to Candy? Perhaps it wasn't just me that was the problem? Why was she so suspicious of Ed's behaviour that she had to check up on him?

'What?' Ed asked. 'You're doing it again?'

'Doing what again?'

'Thinking. Your face goes all serious and you frown.'

I never realised that I gave myself away so explicitly. 'Although I don't agree with what she's done, I was wondering why she felt the need to spy on you. Have you played away from home before?' It was time for a few home truths. I needed him to be honest with me.

'Suzi! Is that what you think of me?'

'Well, you are Flight Deck and you did bring a bottle of champagne to my room in Hong Kong when you were still going out with her.'

'That's unfair. For one, don't tar me with the Flight Deck label and two, I haven't done it before.' He looked hurt. 'You don't get it, do you? You're special, Suz.'

If I was a weaker woman or a character in a romantic movie I would have succumbed to Ed's puppy dog eyes at this point and rushed into his arms to nestle against his hairy chest. But I was made of sterner stuff. I would need far more convincing than his sweet talk. Oh, why did relationships have to be so difficult? I wanted nothing more than to believe his every word but I just couldn't. I took another sip of my drink and stood there. What now? The way the conversation was going I'd have a choice of both the double and the single beds to myself tonight.

'Candy has a few issues,' Ed said diplomatically. 'I'm not going to tell you anymore as I don't want to break her confidence but I just didn't realise that she wasn't coping with them very well.'

'What like she's a stalker and psychotic?'

'No, but she did apply to be crew and never made it.'

'So that makes it alright for her to take out her revenge on me, just because I did make it?' My voice was becoming high pitched and a little hysterical now. Candy's psychosis was catching. I took a deep breath. What ever sympathy I felt towards Candy had gone. 'Where is she now?'

'She's moved the few things she had out of my house and gone back to her place. We've agreed not to contact each other for a while.'

'Has she agreed not to contact me too? She has my mobile number and knows where I live.'

'I've told her not to. I think she just needs some time

to realise what she's done is wrong.'

'And you think that's enough? I wouldn't trust her inch. Her boyfriend has just dumped her and she blames me for it. She's bonkers, anything could happen. I wouldn't be surprised if she came and attacked us with a knife.'

'Really Suzi, I think you're over reacting.' I stared at him defiantly. 'It's over as far as I'm concerned but I don't want to hurt her anymore than necessary.'

'So what now?' I had to ask. I hadn't a clue what our relationship was anymore. If it was just a quick shag and then goodbye while on a break from Candy then he could forget it. I wasn't going to be treated like that. Especially not by him. I was beginning to care more for Ed McEwan than I wanted to admit. Best to keep my feelings buttoned until I knew what he was feeling if I didn't want to be hurt.

'I think, Suzi,' Ed said as he walked over to me and took the glass from my hand, placing it down beside us on the table. 'If you're willing to give us time, we could just see where it leads.' Ed was so close his face was directly in front of mine. 'Perhaps this might give you an idea of how I feel about you.' He put his arms around my waist and pulled me firmly against him, fixing me in his embrace so that I couldn't move. Searching out my mouth he placed his lips on mine and kissed me hard, forcing my lips apart to put his tongue in my mouth passionately. I couldn't resist. I could taste sweetness on his breath and smell the scent of the alcohol intoxicatingly seeping up my nose. I leaned into his body and let the experience envelop me. Ed pressed his body harder against mine so that I could feel every inch of him. Matt had never been this passionate. Even in the beginning of our relationship he'd been half-hearted in his approach. I felt a tingle shoot from my lips straight

220

down through my body to my toes. If I was still in that romantic movie I would be lifting up my leg behind me inadvertently. Instead, I pulled away slightly and came up for air. Bloody Hell! Why had I thought of Matt in the middle of Ed's embrace? What was wrong with me? I should have been all consumed with stars and hearts circling my head like a halo if Ed was the one. Ed sensed my resistance and relaxed his hold a little.

'Not to your liking?'

I was in serious danger of messing this up again. Shove off Matt. I moved back into Ed's arms fixing his hands together around my back. Bringing his head gently down towards me again with my hand, I found his lips and kissed him hard. He responded and I felt him move his hand down to my bum and press me against him. No doubt my kiss was having a reaction. Pulling away slightly, Ed lowered his head and started kissing my neck. I caressed his back and followed the line of his shoulder, never relaxing the pressure. Time to show the man that I meant business. He stepped back moving us apart so that he could slowly undo the buttons on my blouse. One at a time as he kissed the skin on my throat and then lower and lower as the flesh was revealed.

Blimey. This might be it. Here in Dad's kitchen. At last Ed and I might be getting it together. Not quite what I'd envisaged, but beggars can't be choosers. I helped him release me from the sleeves of my cotton shirt and stood before him in my uniform skirt and lace bra. His breath was coming quicker. He pushed me back against the table and lifted me up onto it, easing my legs apart as he stood in between them. I could feel a ridge of the wooden surface scratching my skin through my stockings as I leaned back on both arms and let my head drop back. My hair cascaded down my back and over my shoulders.

'You are special, Suz. I knew it from that first moment

in LA when I saw you. You are unlike anyone I've ever met,' he murmured as he licked my right ear lobe.

My heart skipped a beat. Where was my resolve now? I was in danger of succumbing to his sweet talk. All that sensible advice I'd given myself earlier was about to go right out of the window. Bloody pheromones. They had a lot to answer for. If he wasn't so gorgeous I would've been able to resist him, but this is what I'd been wanting for ages now. But I still didn't know if it was an act and his usual seduction technique. I had to make a decision and stop analyzing his every move. Either I went through with it or stopped it now before it went too far.

He moved to cup my face with both hands and started gently kissing my eyelids, all the while stroking my skin as though I was something fragile. Decision made. Any man that held me that tenderly was worth a go. This was going to be too good to miss. I leaned back and surrendered myself to him. I felt his tongue trace a line from my face down my neck and linger, teasingly on my skin, just above my breast.

Suddenly the kitchen door was flung open. A woman's outline was silhouetted in the frame. I leapt off the table. Bringing my knee up at the same time as Ed leapt backwards, I just caught him in the balls as I turned my head in panic to see who was standing there.

'Mia!' I exclaimed, grabbing my blouse off the chair where it had been discarded and holding it up in front of me in an attempt to cover myself up. The relief that swept over me was as intense as when I'd been allowed to leave the assembly hall to go for a pee when I was in primary school. 'What the hell are you doing here?'

'Jeez, Suz,' Ed groaned as he moved away from me clutching his groin.

'Ohmygod. Ed. I'm so sorry,' I exclaimed leaving my sister for the moment and going over to where he was bent double.' Are you alright?'

'I'll survive,' he said trying to straighten up. 'But I don't know whether my future children will.'

'Sorry Suz, didn't realise you'd be having a shag in Dad's kitchen. I came down to make sure the animals were okay. You seem to have got here first,' Mia said as she dumped her rucksack on the floor and walked over to Ed. Holding out her hand she introduced herself. 'Hi, I'm Mia. Suzi's more attractive but equally charming sister.'

'Ed.' Bent double, he grinned and took her out stretched hand.

'We spoke on the phone, earlier, didn't we?' Mia said turning to where I was standing behind her. 'You kept him quiet Suz. Not surprising though,' she added glancing back at him. 'I'll give you two a couple of moments to get your clothes on, shall I?' And with that she walked out of the door and we heard her feet clatter on the wooden floor as she went upstairs.

'I'm so sorry, Ed,' I apologised walking over and putting my hand on his arm.

'Come here,' he said as he grabbed me, holding me tight as he bent his head to kiss me again. 'Looks like we may have to put everything on hold… again.' He added ruefully. 'Don't know how you manage it Suz. But if I wasn't the persistent kind, I'd think you planned this just to avoid me.'

'Oh, and my behaviour just then was all avoidance tactics was it?' I asked, putting on my shirt and buttoning it up.

'Maybe not,' Ed agreed. 'Just wished we'd got a bit further than the last time.'

'Last time,' I reminded him. 'I was naked before we started.'

Ed grinned and kissed me again. 'And a very nice sight it was too.'

I smiled as I tucked my shirt into my skirt and finished straightening my appearance just as Mia came back into the room.

'So how long have you two been an item?'

'Mia, there's no need for the full inquisition now. How long are you planning to stay?'

'Bit blunt aren't you? I can go if you like. Although I'm not sure when the next bus is.'

I realised how mean that must have sounded and started to back track. 'No I didn't mean that. It's just…'

'…it's just that we're about to cook dinner and Suzi wasn't sure if you were staying to eat with us.' Ed finished for me. I gave him a quick look of thanks.

'Didn't look like dinner to me, unless you were on the menu, Suz,' Mia said. 'Depends what you're having. I only intended to stay overnight and then go in the morning. But I can go now if you like and leave you two alone.' She made to pick up her bag.

'Mia.' Ed said walking over and taking it out of her hand. 'Stay. You just caught us at an awkward moment.'

'Tell me about it. Although it looked as though you were on to a winner there, Ed,' Mia said smiling at me. 'Bit of a catch, our Suzi.'

Ed put his arm round her shoulder and whispered in her ear. The two of them laughed and looked at me.

'What?' Ed asked as I glared at him. How dare he conspire with my baby sister who he'd only just met? I could see how he did it. No wonder Candy felt the need to spy on him. This man was a nightmare, turning on his charm like a tap. Mia came over and stood next to me.

'You could be twins,' Ed said reaching into the cupboard and taking another glass that he filled with champagne and gave to Mia.

'Funny you should say that,' she responded. 'It's been remarked on before, but I'm in much better nick than this old lady.'

'I'm only three years older,' I reminded her.

'Now Ed what are you cooking for us then? I'm starving,' Mia asked ignoring my remark.

I sat down at the kitchen table and proceeded to watch as my sister flirted with Ed who was preparing the meal. She giggled. She leaned provocatively on the worktop, leg pushed out in front while she twisted a strand of brunette hair around her finger. She hung on his every word as he proceeded to tell her about his job as a pilot. Her teeth flashed white as she threw back her head and laughed at one of his anecdotes. Ed smiled, winked at me and tried to bring me into the conversation.

'I didn't realise you had such an interesting younger sister, Suz.'

'Always was the more popular one,' Mia piped up. 'Suzi's dreadfully competitive though. Have you noticed? Always gets riled over the smallest thing. Couldn't bear to have her arse whipped at any game, especially Monopoly when we were kids. Can't take the competition, can you Suz?' Mia goaded playfully.

There was no point retaliating to her comments. I'd learnt years ago that Mia was one of those annoying people who always has to have the last world, no matter what argument you come back with. I sipped my drink determined to remain calm and not let her have the upper hand.

'What do you do, Mia?' Ed asked.

'I'm at Uni, studying History of Art,' she answered grandly, followed by a toss of the hair and a flutter of her eyes. I'd had enough of this. It was bad enough having to decide whether Ed was for real but having to watch my little sister make eyes at him was too much.

'How's Max?' I enquired. I decide that the only way to shut my sister up was to bring her back to earth. She had been stringing, her boyfriend along for a couple of years now. Whatever she did Max always came running back for more. It was time to make his presence known to present company.

'He's fine. Gone away with the boys this weekend thankfully. Far too clingy.' she confided to Ed. 'Can't stand men that are like that.' She turned away from me towards Ed, excluding me from the conversation as she proceeded to inform him on what she liked about her men. I smiled. She obviously still couldn't take her drink. Verbal diarrhoea always did come tumbling out of her mouth, even when we were younger. She was working it far too hard. I could see Ed nodding politely with the practised air of a pro. He looked like he'd been caught by an extremely demanding passenger who was refusing to let him get back to the cockpit.

With the curry bubbling away on the stove and the light from outside beginning to dim, I reckoned it was about time for someone to do the last check on the animals. So, leaving them to it, I carefully slipped my feet into Dad's rubber boots standing in the porch, picked up the pig feed and slipped outside.

The chickens were wandering close to their hen house and Gruff was chewing quietly on the other side of his pen when I entered the garden. I wandered over to Clarence and Clarissa, lifting the latch on their gate. The two pigs ignored me and continued to snuffle and push up the earth with their snouts looking for food. I went over to their trough and poured in the bucket of slops.

'Blimey, can that girl talk,' Ed said as he came over to join me, standing just outside the pen, his smart brown shoes just missing squelching in a muddy patch of ground.

'She gets it from our mum,' I offered as a way of explanation. 'I'm more like Dad.' I finished feeding the pigs. Taking the empty bucket I wandered over to the chickens and shooed the last one up the ramp of the hen house, closing the door behind it.

'Bit of a country girl at heart, are you?' Ed asked leaning on the wooden rail of the pig sty and watching me.

'I suppose so. Definitely more than Mia. She couldn't survive without a Starbucks or McDonalds. It's peaceful here. I like being with this lot.' I gestured towards the animals all now safely locked up for the night. 'They're uncomplicated.'

'What made you start flying then?'

'It's a long story,' I answered joining him. Now was not the time to tell him about Matt. Ed took the bucket from my hand but as he did so lost his balance and slipped on the soft mud. With no grip on his soles his legs went from underneath and in one swift movement they flew up in the air leaving him lying flat on his backside in the mud.

'Perhaps I'll tell you another time,' I laughed as I helped him to his feet. He hadn't hurt himself. The only bruising being to his ego. As he turned round the whole of his back was covered in thick, oozing brown mud. 'Not a country boy then?'

Ed wiped his backside with his hand and twisted round to see the extent of the damage. 'Seems I'll have to get my kit off after all,' he said.

'Watch it,' I warned. 'The sight of your rippling muscles might send Mia into overload.'

'What about you, Suzi? Will they send you into overload?'

'I'm there already,' I joked as we walked back to the house.

Mia, who had been laying the table, looked up when we walked in.

227

'He's fine,' I said seeing her concerned look at the state of Ed. 'Nothing a shower and washing machine can't fix. Go and take your clothes off, Ed. Dad's probably got something you could borrow for the time being while I wash your stuff.' Ed walked out of the room and we heard his footsteps on the stairs, then the rattle of the pipes as he turned on the shower.

'Good job, Mia,' I said sarcastically. 'Thanks for the master class in seduction techniques. Shame it wasn't successful. Is no man safe from you?' Even now she could wind me up. I thought we'd left our rivalry behind. No wonder we didn't meet up very often. Mia shrugged her shoulders and continued with what she was doing. 'Thought it was worth a try,' she said leaning over and placing the knives down. 'Have you been to see Dad?' she asked.

'Yes, I called in at the hospital earlier. Seems he's much better. Thank God. I had such a fright when you rang earlier.' I pulled a chair out and sat down at the table watching her. She wiped the strand of hair that had fallen across her face but before I looked away I was sure I could see something wet glistening on her cheek. Seems my tough baby sister had had as much of a scare as me.

'He seemed so much better than I thought,' I assured her. 'Reckons he'll be out in a day or two.' Mia nodded her head and picked up a wooden spoon to stir the mixture bubbling in the pan. 'We'll just have to work out how to cope with this lot until then.'

By the time Ed had showered, the curry was ready. He came downstairs dressed in some joggers and an old T-shirt of Dad's. I put his dirty clothes in the washing machine along with some of my dark coloured laundry from my suitcase. At least I knew what Mia was all about, I reasoned as I poured the powder into the slot and pressed the start button. She pretended to be strong and put up a good show of being independent and care free but there was a vulnerability about her. By the time we'd finished the meal and polished off two bottles of wine, Mia had switched back to her old head-strong self and was reminiscing about our childhood escapades. I meanwhile, tried to stop her revealing too much detail. I started to yawn. It had been a long time since I'd had a good night's sleep. The mixture of food and drink had left me feeling mellow. 'Probably time to turn in,' I said looking at Ed to gauge his reaction.

'Good idea. Shall I take the single bed and you two the double?' Ed suggested grinning at me. I smiled back at him. He was making it easy for me. He must have had a quick look round upstairs while changing earlier. There was no way I could sleep with him for the first time with my sister next door listening to my every moan. That's always supposing Ed was good enough to make me moan.

'I'll get the sheets,' Mia organised. 'Come on Ed, come and help me make the beds. We can leave this till the morning,' she commanded piling the dirty plates up on the draining board. 'It's been a hell of a day.'

So it was only fifteen minutes later that I found myself slipping into my Dad's double bed with my sister on the other side. Not quite the scenario I'd hoped for but I was so exhausted, for once I didn't care. I looked at Mia lying with her back to me, as she fiddled with the duvet. She always had been demanding as a child. My parents had split up when she was thirteen: just as she was at her most vulnerable. It was no wonder her need for attention had continued into adulthood. I gently stroked her back. 'I'm glad you're here,' I said as a wave of sentimentality swept over me.

She turned over and looked at me, her dark hair fanning out across the pillow. 'Me too. Sorry I

229

interrupted your evening. He's nice, isn't he?'

'I think so,' I answered. But nice wasn't good enough. Loads of men were nice. What I wanted to know, Eve, was he worth it?

Love Suzi x

17th September - Home

Dear Eve

When I awoke the next morning, it took a while to work out where I was. I've got used to waking up in strange beds (hotels', not men's) but, depending on my level of jet-lag, it often feels as though I'm walking through a sticky fog as I wait for all my faculties to engage. I lay quietly for a while, listening. Mia's side of the bed was empty and I could hear singing coming from the shower. Padding down to the kitchen in my PJ's, I found Ed sitting at the table naked from the waist up, draped in a towel. His hair was still wet from his shower. Result! This guy has no problem with getting his kit off and boy, did he look good enough to eat.

'Morning,' he said brightly, getting up to pour me a cup of tea from the pot he'd made. 'Sleep alright?'

'I should be asking you that. Yes, I feel much better, didn't realise quite how knackered I was.'

I sat down at the table as he handed me a mug. I sipped my tea. 'Any plans for today?' Ed enquired.

'I thought I might ring the hospital and see how Dad is before I decide what to do. I'll have to do it from the corner of Gruff's pen though?'

Ed raised one eye brow as though questioning my sanity.

'Only place I can get a signal in this outback,' I explained. 'What about you? Do you have to be anywhere?'

'No, not particularly. Thought I might stay around, if it's okay with you. You could teach me how to tame Gruff,' he grinned knowingly.

'When's your next trip?' I asked.

'Oh, I've got a few days off now. There are a few things I need to do, but nothing that can't wait. Do you think my clothes will be dry by now?' Bugger. I forgot that was the reason he was in the towel. I'd jumped to the wrong conclusion. I got up and went over to the tumble dryer. I reached inside to pull the jumble of clothes out just as there was a knock on the back door. We both looked round as a middle-aged woman, wearing Wellington's and a thick blue, fleece jacket, opened the door and backed into the kitchen as she struggled to lever one boot off against the step.

'Morning, Ken,' she called out. 'I'm back.' She bent down to remove the remaining boot from her foot and turned round.

The three of us stood looking at each other.

'Oh, sorry,' the woman apologised as she noted Ed's nakedness and my PJ's. 'If I didn't know better I'd think I was in the wrong house.'

Mia walked into the kitchen, her hair wrapped in a towel like a turban on her head and an even smaller one wrapped around her body just reaching down past her bottom. The woman at the doorway froze, her hand still clutching the door handle.

'Shower's free, Suz. Oh, hello,' Mia said to the woman whose mouth had dropped wide open. 'I'm Mia and this is my sister Suzi. Oh, and he's Ed,' she gestured towards Ed who was leaning against the worktop. 'Excuse our appearance but we were wondering whether a nudist colony would take off in the village and are doing some research.'

I got up and went over to the woman who had bent down to collect her boots again to retreat. 'Hi, I'm Ken's daughter. Perhaps you'd better sit down and I'll explain what's going on.' I manoeuvred her towards a chair. 'Cup of tea?' I offered as Ed, taking my cue, started pouring her one. 'Ken… Dad, was taken into hospital yesterday. It was a suspected heart attack but it seems it's not that now.'

Her face went pale and her hand went up to cover her mouth as she dropped her boots. 'He's fine,' I reassured. 'Both Mia…' I gestured towards my sister, '…and I went to visit him yesterday. In fact I'm just about to ring the hospital and get the latest on him. Are you a neighbour?'

Sitting clutching a mug of tea, the woman looked flustered with all this information.

'Yes,' she said her voice quiet as she took it all in. 'I'm Marion. I live two doors along.' So this was Dad's bit of tottie, eh? Sly old fox, he'd never mentioned her before. Quizzed me about my love life but not a hint about his. She was an attractive woman with short blond hair flecked with grey that framed her heart shaped face. Dressed in jeans and a flowery blouse underneath her jacket, she wouldn't have seemed out of place strolling around town except for her green wellies. I had to give it to Dad; he hadn't lost his taste in women. A soft line of brown kohl eyeliner outlined her hazel eyes highlighting their almond shape as she looked up at me; they were turning slightly red with a watery tinge. 'I've just been up North for a few days visiting my son. Ken, your dad, and I always get together for walks and things. I just thought I'd pop in and let him know I was back,' she continued.

It didn't take long before Ed and I had put Marion at ease. We found out that she usually looked after the animals for Dad whenever he was away. Bonus. Keen to help out once she knew the extent of his ailments, she willingly agreed to come in regularly and look after the menagerie until Dad came out of hospital. After another cup of tea, we had bonded so much that we had agreed on the best moisturiser for really dry skin, how useless men were at multi-tasking (Dad included) and exchanged mobile numbers. Marion promised to phone me if she had a problem. We waved her off home and proceeded to get dressed and make plans. Ed was going to take Mia to the nearest train station while I sorted out the animals, rang the hospital and packed everything up ready for Marion to take over her duties that evening. We were then going to call in and visit Dad before Ed drove me home.

I was sorry to say goodbye to my sister. Since she'd gone to university we hardly spent anytime together and the recent few hours made me realise maybe I'd been a bit unfair to her. She was good company.

'Make sure you hang on to this one,' she shouted out of the car window as it pulled out of the drive. 'He's useful.' I waved at her and went inside to collect all I needed to do the feed round.

Ed was soon back. We had a while before visiting time so I suggested a trip to the beach at West Wittering. The sky was blue and it was a surprisingly warm day for so late in the year although there was a sharp wind that swirled about now and again unexpectedly. The tide was out and we walked along the wide stretch of sand. There are some advantages to having a suitcase full of clothes, even if half of them were dirty, as I had garments for all weather conditions. I took off my ankle boots and sunk my toes into the slightly damp sand. Ed took my hand and we walked along the shoreline watching a couple of children throwing a ball for their collie which bounded into the waves to retrieve it. The breeze caught my hair and I pulled my jacket closer around me for warmth. Leading the way Ed pulled me up towards the pebbles at the back of the beach where a few tuffs of long grass and brightly coloured beach huts gave more shelter.

'Ed?' I asked. 'When I was at your house that time, I noticed a book about moving to France. Is that something you and Candy were going to do?'

'Not snooping were you, Suz?'

I shook my head and bent down to pick up a handful of moist sand, squeezed it into a ball and threw it at him. Before I could stoop for another he charged at me and, in a rugby tackle, wrestled me to the ground pinning me down with his body weight. I could feel the dampness of the sand seeping into my back as he pressed me firmly underneath him.

'You are the most infuriating woman I know,' he proclaimed. His face inches from mine. He kissed me gently.

'I thought I was the most wonderful woman last night when you were about to have sex with me on my Dad's kitchen table,' I teased. 'I was only asking?'

'You have to spoil a lovely moment by bringing my ex into the conversation.'

Good. He was still referring to Candy as his ex, so that must mean the separation was likely to be permanent on his side. I stared into his brown eyes. 'Are you thinking of moving to France then?' I persisted.

Ed rolled off me. I sat up awkwardly wiping the sand from my back. He helped brush me down. He lay on his back, propped up on his elbows, looking at the sea. I sat down beside him.

'Just an idea. Maybe. I don't want to fly for the airline all my life. Anyway it was always a sticking point for Candy and me. She couldn't see herself leaving the area.'

'Not so adventurous then.'

'No. In fact I wasn't surprised that she didn't get in as cabin crew. She really doesn't like travel.'

'Then why did she apply?'

'I think it was a status thing. She needed to prove that she was as good as the girls I work with. Looking back now, I always thought she was jealous of my lifestyle but I never thought she would take it to the extremes she did.'

I sat and reflected for a moment. This was all good news. Another thing that wasn't working out between him and Candy.

'So what now?' I questioned. 'Don't you want to stay in the airline until you make it to captain, with all the benefits that go with that?'

'Not really. I've seen the other pilots. They get sucked into the lifestyle and then before they know it they may have travelled the world but they've missed out on so many other things because they've been away from their families. I love flying but I'd much rather work for myself. I just haven't worked out how to do it. France was just an escape route really. I thought if I talked enough about it she would come round to the idea in the end but we weren't getting anywhere really. But what about you, Suz? What do you really want for the future?'

'Oh, the usual,' I said. Damn. It might be too early in the relationship for this kind of revelation but it seemed as good a time as any. If I was about to blow it then so be it. 'After a while of frivolity, husband and kids.'

Ed looked out away from me across the shoreline. He was silent. Damn. Damn. Damn. I had blown it. Should have kept that one quiet for a bit longer. 'Plus a country house, cocktails and a cleaner,' I added in an effort to make him think I was joking. It had always made us laugh, Eve, whenever we approached that vast 'what do we want when we grow up' question. Ed smiled and turned his gaze back to me. 'It's okay, Suzi. I want kids too. Eventually. But you said you'd tell me about Matt.'

'I never said I'd tell you about him.' Oh help. This man knew how to churn my emotions up. 'I just said it was a long story.'

Ed grabbed me and started tickling so hard that I had to hold him off while laughing. He let go and sat up looking out to sea. I sat beside him and put my head on his shoulder.

How could I tell him everything about Matt? It was far too long a story and anyway, the rule is that there's nothing more off putting than talking about your ex. I changed the subject. 'I'm getting cold but more importantly, I'm starving. Let's go and get lunch at a pub I know on the way to the hospital.' I didn't give him any option as I got up, picked up my boots and started walking off along the sand back to the car.

Dad was sitting up in bed and looked as right as rain when we called in. Ed and he sat discussing football and Formula One while I gazed out of the window. I reassured Dad that Marion was going to take care of everything and that I would be down again in a couple of days when he was due to be discharged so that I could take him home.

The journey back to London was a sombre affair. I'd got used to Ed's company and the thought of not knowing when I would see him again was depressing. It seemed to take ages to get back to the car park at Heathrow. Both of us were wrapped in our own thoughts.

'Suz,' Ed said as he lifted my luggage out of his boot and into mine. 'I'm away tomorrow for a while on my next trip. I'll text you but... could we do this again when I get back?'

'What about Candy?'

'Candy and I are over. I've just got to make her realise

it too?'

Yessssss! The lingering kiss I gave him was his answer. I climbed into my car and started the engine.

Sam was the only one in when I arrived home. She seemed surprised to see me and hastily took my arm, making me dump my suitcase in the hallway before she marched me up to my bedroom where she told me to sit down on the bed.

'What?' I questioned. 'I always get scared whenever you do this. It's turning into a habit.'

'Suzi. Debbie is pregnant and they've brought the wedding forward. It's in two weeks time.'

Love Suzi x

20th September - Home

Dear Eve

It's not often that I'm hit by a tornado but for the next few days it felt like it. I can't lie. I'm not easily taken aback by anything and I didn't know what I felt. Betrayed – not fair, as I was the one to finish the relationship with Matt. Hurt – again not fair, as I was the one … you get the idea. I tried to rationalise the situation in 101 different ways. Ultimately, I concluded, I felt relieved. If he could switch from one girl to the next so easily then I was so much better off without him. It was only a short while ago that he had proposed to me and wanted my babies. How easily this man could change his incubator! What if I'd given in and gone along the path he had so clearly mapped out in his mind? I could be pregnant and chained to a lifetime of Matt Murphy? Phew! What a lucky escape.

I have to admit my ego has taken a bit of bashing though. I didn't realise that I could be so easily forgotten. It's a bitter pill to swallow. All those years together. All those times I cleared up his vomit from a drunken night out, sat and watched boring footie matches with him, or listened to him saying how much he loved me. What a fool I was. Well, I sure as hell wasn't going to make those mistakes again. Any relationship would have to be on my terms, I wasn't going to be just someone's egg supply.

Debbie didn't appear again at the house, thank God. Sam said she is spending the time at her parent's home preparing for the big day. She didn't want to walk down the aisle with a large bump showing so they had determined to get the whole thing done and dusted before she started to look as though she was up the duff. It did cross my mind that maybe she had planned this all along. At least this way she wouldn't have to get a job. Her parents were desperate for grandchildren. If Debbie played her cards right she could still spend her days on the sofa watching soaps while her mum did all the childcare and Matt brought in the money. How cynical of me? But I was glad she wasn't around. I'd find it difficult to speak to her. And of course, if she was around, Matt would be too.

I had enough on my plate as it was. My turnaround at home in between trips was packed to the limit with Dad being in hospital and all my usual chores to catch up on. It felt like no sooner had my feet touched the ground than I was hot footing it back to the airport to take off again. I had ensconced Dad into the care of Marion, who was just bursting to play nurse to his dying swan. I could tell she was the right woman for the job the moment Dad and I stepped back into his cottage. The whole place gleamed, something bubbled on the hob and it looked as though she had all the animals lined up for inspection, after washing and dusting them, *and* their pens.

I heard from Sam that I was to be invited to the wedding which was going to be with just a small number of guests in an old manor. I wasn't sure if I was pleased or not that I would get home from my next trip in time to attend provided nothing changed. I reckoned I would just leave it to fate. If the trip went wrong and I missed the wedding, so be it; if not I'd go and use it as a kind of closure (thank you, America, for that idea). Secretly I wanted to look Matt in the eye and force him to admit what a rat he was. I also wanted to know what kind of outfit Debbie would wear. To meringue or not to meringue? Quite honestly she didn't have a lot of choice. Even without a bump she was a big girl; harsh but true. A slinky, close fitting little number would have been too risky. Full meringue with cream on the top was bound to be the order of the day. Knowing her, she'd have the whole shebang.

Love Suzi x

26th September - LHR - Bangkok(BKK)

Dear Eve

I kept myself ultra busy on my days off so I wouldn't think about the wedding. All too soon I was making my way back to the airport. Karl was in the briefing room before the flight; a real bonus. (Remember, he was JJ's friend on my first trip to Australia.) Having a ready-made friend on the crew changed the whole feeling of the trip. Although I'd had the roster with all the crew's names on, it is always subject to change. I was never sure just who was going to be in that room until I walked in and squinted round. Karl grinned up at me on my arrival, patted the chair beside him and I just knew he would make it fun.

The flight out East was full. I've got used to the constant demands of the passengers and can now switch into automatic mode. Whenever I walk down that walkway or climb the steps to the aircraft my face sets into a smile as I scrutinise the passengers on entering. It's always good to check them out, to get an idea of what lies ahead; also you never know when a nutter might pop up to disrupt the flight. Karl and I weren't working the same trolley but we were in the same galley so there was plenty of time to catch up with news and gossip in between the feeding and watering rounds.

The trip was taking us to Sydney with a stop at Bangkok. Not having been to Thailand before I was looking forward to discovering a new city. Karl was eager to be my guide and, like a circus ringmaster, promised me sights that I'd never witnessed before. It was late when we arrived in Bangkok but Karl and some of the others were keen to get out so five of us took a taxi to a bar that they knew.

The taxi pulled up outside a small doorway in a narrow street that was sandwiched between a clothes shop and a stall selling various dodgy looking electronic goods. We were hustled inside by the doorman and I found myself in a large room with what seemed like an arena in the centre with spectator seats placed around the sides. It was dark inside, but I could see that the tiers of seats went back for a few rows just like around a boxing ring. We made our way around to the opposite side of the arena. Karl sat down in a red velvet chair in the front row. A waitress came up and sat on his lap, her back to me.

Her hand slid around his shoulders and she played with his hair. I sat down next to him but I might as well have been invisible because she paid me no attention but continued to caress Karl. Two other girls came and sat on the laps of the other male stewards who had joined us. Karl grinned at me behind her back.

'What do you want to drink, Suzi?' he asked. The waitress threw me a look over her shoulder as though I was a piece of turd clinging to her shoe.

'A beer would be fine,' I smiled at her and placed a hand on what was left of Karl's thigh in the hope that she would think he was my boyfriend and push off. It made no difference, I was still a piece of turd. Karl continued to talk to her.

Suddenly she muttered something under her breath, got up and walked off.

'She's pissed off that we only wanted beers,' Karl explained. 'They try and persuade you to have something more expensive.'

I only just heard him as my attention had been taken by what was happening in the ring. A young woman scantily clad in bikini top and pelmet skirt had gracefully walked to one corner and was holding up some table tennis balls. Then, without further ado she squatted down. I couldn't quite see properly but I could make out enough in the dim light to realise she was deftly inserting them up her vagina.

You know I mentioned earlier that I wasn't easily taken aback by anything; well I'd just like to retract that statement. She leaned back on the rope surround of the arena, like a boxer taking a breather. The next moment the ping pong balls came flying through the air in an arc towards us as she ejected them.

I continued to stare at the spectacle before me. That woman had pelvic floor muscles to die for! Even a quick bounce on my friend's trampoline sent me running to the loo squealing, yet here she was projecting ping pong ball after ping pong ball right across the room as though firing a gun at the soft toys in a fairground. What a party trick that was, although I couldn't think of many scenarios where I would be able to use such a feat. Still, a skill to have up your sleeve (or in your knickers) if ever you were caught on the hop and asked to perform something entertaining. Hmmm… not sure how well it would go down with the oldies at Dad's village fete. Couldn't imagine the vicar appreciating the skill involved and hours dedicated to the art. And it wasn't just balls that were coming out of her nether regions. My mouth gaped open as her act progressed and she dazzled us with an array of items from within her depths; like Hermione's beaded bag that could hold everything Harry and Ron needed on their quest to hunt down Voldemort's horcruxes in JK Rowling's books. I almost expected a tent to pop out at any moment. At one point she swivelled round so that a ball flew high into the air and landed on Karl's lap. He just laughed and threw it back at her.

'Ewww,' I shouted in his ear as the noise from the accompanying music drowned out conversation. Karl laughed and handed me a drink.

'It's all just part of the act,' he shouted back close to my ear. 'You wait for the next bit.'

Just as he said it another woman walked onto the stage carrying a birthday cake, complete with lighted candles. She placed it down in front of the performing woman and walked away. Taking out a straw, the woman squatting down, placed it in her vagina and proceeded to blow out the candles as though at a birthday party. Amazing! I didn't realise a vagina could be so versatile. How sheltered had I been? I shut my mouth and took a sip of my drink, trying to look nonchalant as though I saw this

242

kind of thing every day in my local pub. I could see the billing now on talent show night - '*Introducing, for one night only – Suzi and her multi-talented vagina.*' They would be transfixed. I was sure to win first prize if only for the shock factor.

As suddenly as she had started her act it came to a close and, after a feeble round of applause from the crowd, the woman walked off (without legs crossed or limping which would have been the least I'd expect in the circumstances) and disappeared behind a dark red curtain hanging at the side of the room.

'Well, what did you think of that?' Karl asked.

'Don't think I'll give up the day job,' I answered flippantly, feeling slightly queasy and crossing my legs. 'How much practise do you think she puts in? I wouldn't want to be her boyfriend in a clinch with her with those pelvic floors. He might never come out alive.' Karl screwed up his face in mock pain and nudged me. The bar suddenly flooded with scantily glad girls who made their way round the room draping themselves all over the men.

'They come round to persuade you to buy more drinks,' he explained. 'If you don't, you'll find you may have to pay an exit fee.'

My face froze. 'What do you mean?'

'You're alright here,' he added. 'But some bars have a scam where if you haven't paid enough throughout the evening, they try and prevent you leaving.'

I stared at him in disbelief. 'It's bad enough that they don't seem to like me,' I remarked as a petite, pretty girl walked straight past me making a bee-line for the steward next to Karl. 'But to make me pay to stay…'

'They'd like you if you were a lesbian,' Karl said out loudly. The next thing I knew a girl came over and leaned over me running her hands over my thigh as she asked me if I wanted another drink.

'They cater for everything here,' Karl said behind the back of the girl on his lap. 'As long as you can pay for it.'

I mouthed the word, 'Bastard,' back to him. I shook my head and refused the girl's attentions until she realised that I wasn't going to part with any money. Karl sat laughing. She gave up and disappeared to try her luck with the man sitting a few seats along from us.

'You bring me to the nicest places.'

Karl smiled and leaned over towards me as the music started up again. 'I thought you wanted to explore the city. Well, this is all part of it. Probably not the kind of place you'd usually go,' he admitted. 'I can show you the cultural bits tomorrow, but I thought you'd get the feel of the place from this.' He motioned towards the stage again where a young couple stood kissing and fondling each other. 'You haven't seen anything yet.'

I watched as they removed each other's clothes and started to have sex, right in front of me. They worked their way through an obviously set routine; left leg up resting on a waist height bar, then her right arm forward to touch her toes, slowly turn round and then he enters her from behind. Like a game of Twister they conjured up more positions than the Karma Sutra in their attempt to titillate the audience. Both looked so bored I wanted to go and buy them a drink just to cheer them up. I found myself switching off and concentrating on watching the bar girls plying their charms on the tourists who now surrounded the ring.

Karl caught my eye and whispered in my ear. 'Had enough sex for one night?' he asked.

'I think so,' I replied. 'There's only so much excitement a girl can take in one hit. They look so bored I feel sorry for them.'

Leaving the rest of the crew still finishing their drinks

we made our way outside onto the street.

'What do you want to do now?' Karl asked.

'You know, I think I've had enough for one night. My bed beckons.'

'Lightweight,' Karl smiled as he hailed a cab and we climbed in to make our way back to the hotel. 'I'll let you off for now as I'll be knocking on your door first thing tomorrow morning for breakfast. We have a full day sight-seeing.'

'You're too kind,' I replied, leaning back against the vinyl seats of the cab.

It didn't take long to get back to the hotel. Just as I closed my room door my phone vibrated in my bag with an incoming text. I swept the screen with my finger.

Hi Suzi, where in the world are you? Sorry I haven't been in touch. Things have been a bit tricky recently. When are you next at Heathrow? You fancy meeting up? I've got something I want to tell you. Ed.

I'd tried not to think about Ed since our walk along the beach. I needed to hold back from falling for him so completely that I would be mush in his hands. I still wasn't sure where he was coming from. How could I be sure it was really over for him and Candy? I've watched the 'bunny boiler' scene from *Fatal Attraction*; even supposedly committed married men can succumb to pleasures of the flesh. Ed might think it was over but did Candy? I'd had one encounter with her and that was before the abusive texts, I didn't fancy another. I had enough of my own baggage with Matt; I didn't need Ed to bring his into the relationship too.

But what did his text mean? What could he have to say to me? Maybe he wasn't interested in taking our relationship further? Maybe he was having second thoughts about staying with Candy, although he seemed pretty interested in an 'us' on the beach? Perhaps he was fed up with how long it was taking for us to get it together? We'd come pretty close on Dad's kitchen table that evening. It just seemed that everything was conspiring against us.

If there's one thing I've developed a taste for whilst flying the world, it's shopping. *'Confessions of a Shopaholic'* had nothing on me. There are so many opportunities to buy clothes, accessories and jewellery when passing through cities around the world that if ever I needed cheering up I was usually in the right place for a bit of retail therapy. Bangkok was the ultimate fix.

The next day Karl not only showed me the cultural delights but knew the secret passions of a girl's heart and took me to all the best retail hotspots too. It was just as we were entering Jim Thomson's to look at the silks that, turning round to see Karl overloaded with my bags making him look like a pack horse, I realised maybe blowing all my money was not the way to distract myself from all that was going on in my life. I hadn't replied to Ed's text. I need to know where I stood with him and I needed to know it now. I would test him. I would text him and ask him to accompany me to Matt's wedding. He knew very little of the history between us, but if he said yes, then he must be interested in something more serious than a fling. If it was a no, then I had a few more Baht's still to spend. I stopped and hunted out my mobile from my bag.

'Had enough yet?' Karl asked.

'Nearly. Just got to send this text then, depending on the reply, we may still have a few more shops to conquer.'

Karl raised his eyebrows and sighed, placing a handful of bags down by his feet and wiping his brow in mock exhaustion.

I tapped out my question to Ed telling him about the

wedding, outlining the details and pressed the send button. I had no idea in the world he was or even if it was the middle of the night for him. My phone buzzed back almost immediately.

Would love to. Coming in from 'Frisco that morning but will be able to make it. Will meet you there. Ed.

Result. My heart skipped. Ed *was* interested. Game on.

I looked at Karl and gave him the thumbs up. The look of relief on his face gave away his real exhaustion.

'Thank God for that,' he said picking up his burdens again. 'I've known some shoppers in my time but none surpass you. I need a beer.'

We left Bangkok the next morning. Karl was a delightful companion but after Ed's positive response I was desperate to get back to England and Matt's wedding. Even though I had mixed feelings, the trip couldn't pass quickly enough for me. It was going to be hard to see Matt and Debbie tie the knot but with Ed beside me it would be easier. If Matt was married that would be the end of it for him and me. I knew I didn't want a relationship with him any more but it would be closure on that whole period of my life. Also I wouldn't look like the sad ex, rejected and sitting all alone at the ceremony. Ed, I'm sure, would scrub up well. I wanted to show Matt that he wasn't my only hope.

Love Suzi x

29th September - Home

Dear Eve

It was only on our approach to Heathrow, with the familiar landscape beneath us, that I allowed myself to hope that Ed wouldn't let me down. I'd bought a new dress and was as geared up as much as I could be for this wedding. But the thing I most needed, more than a stunning outfit, was Ed by my side.

Two days to go till the wedding of the year!

In two days time Debbie would have a knot so securely tied around Matt he'd be gasping for breath. My ego needed a boost. If I, as an ex-girlfriend, was going to convince everybody that I had moved on, I had to sparkle. So almost as if I was the bride (well, it would be good practise for my own big day) I had to be ready for it. Not one part of my body was going to be left unattended to. I would be plucked, preened, waxed and coiffured to within an inch of my life.

Each time I ran my hand over my legs I could feel the sharpness of stubble equal to a bed of nails. If I was to have any chance of wedding guests not offering to plait the unsightly wig that seemed to have attached itself to my legs, they would have to be as smooth as the adverts, so that I could drop a silk hankie down them and it would whoosh off the end. So I booked myself in for a complete MOT at the beauty salon. As well as my legs, I booked the girls' equivalent of a back, sack and crack wax.

The moment I was handed the paper thong I realised that, in my enthusiasm, I might have gone too far. I had never had a Brazilian before and the pamphlet offering a vajazzle at a knock down bargain-half price, nearly made me choke rather than go for it. Really, what is the point of sticking jewels to your pubis when it has just been stripped of all its hair and resembles a plucked chicken? Especially as no one (sadly, in my case) was likely to see it. Wouldn't the jewels just get stuck to my knickers? What if one then made its way down my leg and plopped out on the floor by my feet. Try explaining that one to Matt's aged aunt as she stooped to pick it up. 'I think this is yours,' she would say. 'But you don't seem to have an earring missing?'

I lay on the couch at the salon and placed my hand over my groin as the woman came towards me with a large lump of wax stuck to the end of a spatula ready to baste me in the sticky stuff before laying a cloth on top and whipping it off. Yeowwwww! The effort of trying to keep everything in place so that a bit of my anatomy didn't come off on the cloth only distracted me momentarily from the excruciating pain. No wonder they use soft lighting, soothing music and sweet aromas. It's to lull you into a false sense of well being whilst you are being tortured. They say we women suffer for beauty and I can confirm, after enduring this treatment, indisputably that we do. When she came back for another try from a rear angle, I found it difficult not to bring my leg up in a swift knock-out kick to make her stop. Only the thought of having a landing strip with only one side suitable for landing and the other still wild bushland made me grit my teeth and let her continue.

I walked out, my body throbbing with the pain of the hair being ripped out from the follicles; so much so that it hurt even to have my knickers on. I resolved to do the sensible thing in future and stick to my tried and trusted razor method. No wonder they told you to give it 24 hours to settle down after the treatment. My groin looked as though it had done 6 rounds in the boxing ring with its crimson hue.

The next day I went for the softer option and ordered half a head of high lights at the hairdressers. By the time they had finished, my auburn tresses were rich and glossy; not a split end in sight. I would be able to toss my head for those photos and '*be worth it*' with the best of them. I had both my toe and finger nails French manicured, so that my little piggies could peep out of the new sandals with killer heels that I'd bought in Bangkok to make me look tall and elegant.

And just to make sure I was glowing, I decided on my first ever St Tropez fake tan. Well, my dress did have tiny spaghetti straps so I figured it would be better to have an all over glow than large, bikini strap marks that would completely destroy the effect. I came home from the salon after wearing more paper knickers and being sprayed like a criminal with a hose spurting brown stuff the size of a police water hose at a riot. It did make me wonder, as I duly waited the required amount of time to 'cook' for the process to complete, if I was being slightly over the top. Don't worry - it only lasted a second. Of course, I was completely within the laws of sanity in wanting to look tip-top and gorgeous at my ex-boyfriend's wedding.

One day to go!

It was evening and after having another shower to wash off the last traces of the spray tan and wrapped in my pink fluffy bath robe, I decided to celebrate my achievements. With the red wine open on the living room table, I was just catching up with a few of my favourite Soaps when the door bell rang. The other two girls were out. If ever a beauty treatment is undervalued it's the pedicure. Cracked heels, overgrown cuticles, chipped nails, now banished. My feet looked good enough to lick as I padded along the dimly lit hallway to the front door.

A figure stood on the other side of the half glass door. I half expected it to be Nanny McPhee from the silhouette. As I opened the door I had to quickly draw my robe closer around me as a breeze swept through. You'd never believe it Eve, but there, standing in front of me, with a bunch of garage forecourt chrysanthemums clutched in his hand, was Matt.

Love Suzi x

30th September - Home

Dear Eve

'Hi Suz. How's things?'

'Matt! What on earth are you doing here? Surely you should be at home getting ready for tomorrow? Or out on your stag do? You know Debbie's not here, don't you?' Why was he was standing on *my* doorstep?

'Hmmm…could I come in for a moment? It's you I want to see.'

Blimey. What was up? Last minute nerves? Surely he should be talking to his best man not his ex? Then I felt a wave of compassion. Oh, I know I've been saying I'd spit in his eye for what he'd done but surely you know me by now? I'm a pussy cat really. The guy looked miserable and he needed to get to a bin quickly. It was the only decent place for those awful flowers.

I stepped back to let him in through the door and he walked past me and into the living room.

'These are for you,' he offered turning as I came into the room and holding out the bunch of flowers.

251

Jeez! He still hadn't learned. Did I have to spell it out to him that *I hated bloody chrysanthemums?*

'Thanks,' I muttered as I took them from him. See, I am a pussy cat! 'Want a drink?'

'Yeah, sure.'

I went to the kitchen, got him a glass, and took it back to the living room where I filled it right to the top with red wine.

'Here, supermarket's finest,' I joked trying to make him smile. I sat opposite him on the sofa. I couldn't help flexing one foot. My toes really did look gorgeous. 'So, everything alright?' I encouraged.

'This is really difficult Suz,' he took a sip of his wine. Delaying tactics. What could be so difficult?

'Can't see what is. You're getting married to Debbie tomorrow. You have a baby on the way. You've got everything you ever wanted. Right in one hit.' There. I'd given it to him straight between the eyes.

'That's the trouble. I haven't got what I wanted, Suz.'

'What do you mean?'

'I haven't got you.' I stared at him whilst trying to gulp down a mouthful of wine without my usual choking. 'It's you I want.' He repeated.

I was stunned. I just sat staring at him like an idiot. What on earth did he think he was doing? He was marrying Debbie in the morning. Worse still, she was expecting his baby!

'Matt!' I sat up. 'You can't say that. Debbie's pregnant.'

'I know that Suzi. Don't you think I don't know that?' His voice was getting a touch squeaky and that vein. Oh, that vein was starting to pulse. 'It's all such a mess. I never meant it to go this far. I was only going out with her to make you jealous. Then before I knew it she announced she's pregnant and I had to do the right thing.'

252

Now I did feel sorry for him. Not because he's gone out with Debbie for the wrong reasons, but because he was trapped.

'But Matt. You are half to blame for getting her pregnant!'

'She said she was on the pill!'

Ohhhh. He's been caught by the oldest trick in the book. Whether or not Debbie had meant to do it I couldn't know, but Matt was truly sunk. But hey, what did he think coming here and confessing to me was going to achieve? My hackles rose.

'Why've you come to tell me? What do you think I'm going to do? Declare my love and run away with you?' This really was turning into a farce. Okay, so I did love the guy once but that was long over as far as I was concerned. Seeing him standing in front of me and admitting he didn't love the woman he was about to marry only made me wonder whatever I had seen in him in the first place.

My pussy cat side took over. He was once a friend.

'Listen,' I started, my tone getting softer. 'This is the situation. You either call it all off and suffer the consequences or go through with it and... suffer the consequences.' Put like that it was not much of a choice I have to admit. Somehow I don't think I was helping him.

'I don't know what I'm going to do,' Matt admitted. 'I just wanted to ask you one more time if there was any hope for us.'

How could I crush him at his lowest ebb? Easily. He was a grown man who should have known better. He was not my responsibility. I'd never led him along, played hot and cold, nor given him hope. Now was the time to crush his dreams and make him face his reality. Picking up the flowers that I'd placed on the table between us, I walked into the kitchen. Kicking open the pedal of the bin with my foot I thrust the ghastly bunch inside.

'I'm sorry Matt, but it's over between us. It has been for a long time.' Fair enough I thought. I couldn't be clearer than that. 'Would it be easier if I didn't come tomorrow?' It was the least I could do. I didn't want him to re-enact the scene from Hugh Grant's wedding in *Four Weddings and a Funeral* where he sees Andie MacDowell in the audience and calls the whole thing off.

Matt stood up and placed his barely touched glass on the table.

'Thanks,' he said miserably.

'What for?'

'For being honest with me and making me realise what I have to do.'

I'd done all that in five minutes? I must be good. Obviously the flowers and bin trick wasn't as harsh as I thought.

He quickly turned round and headed for the door. I put down my glass and followed him. 'Bye Suz,' Matt said standing on the threshold as he leaned in to kiss my cheek. I watched him walk, shoulders hunched, up the short path, leaving the gate wide open behind him.

I shut the door and returned to the living room where I refilled my glass and turned up the TV. Damn. I'd missed the best bit of my programme. The door bell rang again. Bugger. This was turning into a very busy night. What had Matt forgotten? Perhaps he'd had second thoughts about the flowers and was going to reuse them on Debbie? A small figure was silhouetted on the other side of the glass door this time. Definitely not Matt. Securing my robe about me I turned the knob and opened the door. Candy was standing there.

Love Suzi x

Later that very busy evening - Home

Eve

Blimey! Had she been sitting in her car outside stalking me? She must have seen Matt leave. Had she been there and watched him arrive and then waited to pounce? No, don't be so silly Suzi, you're just being paranoid now. So what if she did see Matt, it's got nothing to do with her.

'Don't you ever wear clothes?' she accused. 'Or is it more convenient for your business?'

Bitch! Stay calm, Suzi. Don't let her get you angry. 'Hi Candy, what a surprise?' Bloody cow insinuating that I was on the game. 'What brings you to my door? Again?'

'It's not a social call,' she started.

'Shame, that would have been so nice,' I said through gritted teeth. If ever I was going to have to bring my airline training into play, it would have to be now. My hand itched to slap her right across that overly rouged cheek. 'I would invite you in, but it's really not convenient right now.' My sarcasm was lost on her.

'I don't want to come in.'

'What *do* you want then, Candy?' Really! I'd just about had it with this girl. How dare she turn up on my door like this after what she'd done?

'I've just come to warn you once and for all to leave Ed alone.'

'What gives you the right to warn me of anything to do with Ed?' Breathe, Suzi. I could hear my voice rising. Don't want to give her the upper hand. Shouting at her like a fishwife is not becoming.

'Because, Ed has asked me to marry him.'

I leaned back against the door in shock. Christ! No! It can't be true. I quickly recovered and drew myself up to

255

my full height. Can't let her see she'd rattled me. How could he? He had promised to come to the wedding with me tomorrow. Surely he wouldn't be playing us one against the other? She must be bluffing.

'So he's back early from the States, is he?' I questioned. That would test her. If Ed was off the scene why would he tell her his itinerary?

'Yes, he got in from San Francisco this morning. But he'd already proposed. We're going round to my parents tomorrow to announce the news.'

I took a deep breath. Ed wasn't that nasty. He wouldn't promise to meet me at the wedding and then propose to Candy. Something was wrong. Surely my judge of character wasn't this far off the radar. Ed had told me it was all over between them. What had made him change his mind and when did that happen?

'Well, if it's all done and dusted then why you are here?'

'Because...you bitch...if you ever try and come between us again, I'll tell him what a tart you are.'

I laughed. But I had to grip my hands together to hold them down. I wouldn't stoop to her level and give her the satisfaction of degrading myself. 'What makes you think I'm a tart?'

'You're all tarts, you stewardesses. Think you can have any man you like, just because you fly the world and think you're better that the rest of us. I've just seen you. Just let the last client out, did you?' This time I really laughed. The silly cow was delusional and man, was she a disgruntled reject. The chip on her shoulder was so big I could see daylight through it. Maybe those recruitment selectors at the airline were better than I realised if she had been a candidate. Imagine Candy dealing with an incident at 35,000ft? The passengers wouldn't have a chance. They would have to restrain

Candy and strap *her* down to make it to their destination.

'Ahhh, I get you now,' I said leaning over her. 'You are still worried about me. Competition am I? Are you sure Ed has proposed or has it only been in your dreams? Don't think I don't recognise a last ditch attempt to put him off when I see one.' Slagging me off! Again! 'You think finding out I'm cheating on him will work? Really Candy, think about it, if I was truly on the game, do you think I'd be wearing something like this?' I gestured at my shabby robe with its flat fluff and wine stain on the hem. 'Surely I'd be able to afford something much better, the amounts I'd be charging for my excellent services?' If I was going to be a tart, at least I'd be a high class kind of tart. Candy was completely bonkers. What did she hope to achieve by coming here?

I was soon to find out. She thrust out her left hand, weighed down with a large sparkling solitaire on her ring finger. 'If we aren't engaged then why has he given me this?' she accused.

I'd had enough of this charade. If there was any truth in her words I had to hear it from Ed.

'I really haven't got the time for this anymore, Candy. Stop stalking me! Stop sending me abusive texts and stop trying to get me into trouble at work!' I stepped back and, nearly catching her outstretched hand in the wood of the doorframe, shut the door in her face.

Leaning back against the wall. I took a deep breath. I could still see her silhouette through the glass. I turned my back on her, walked into the living room and flounced down on the sofa. Really, what an evening. First Matt and his declaration and now Candy and her accusations. I was convinced she was making it all up as a last ditch attempt to hang on to Ed. But that was some rock on her finger. Ed needed to confirm or deny his involvement and another large glass of wine was in order to steady my nerves.

I kept pouring until the red liquid nearly overflowed the top of the glass. It had been quite an episode. I don't like confrontation. Why was it always so much easier to think of the smart things to say after the event? She really was a poisonous bitch. There was definitely a screw loose there; almost bordering on the psychotic.

I bit my thumb nail and wriggled around on the seat trying to get comfortable. I couldn't wait any longer. Time to confront Ed for the truth. I found my phone which had slipped off the arm of the sofa and onto the floor with all the recent activity and rang his number. The seconds passed until a connection was made. His voicemail kicked in. I quickly pressed the button to stop the call. It wouldn't do to leave a voice message the way I was feeling. I tapped out a text asking him to ring me straight away. It was too much to discuss in a text. I needed to speak to him direct. Only when I'd heard the words from his lips, that he and Candy were engaged, would I believe it.

In an attempt to banish the evening's visitors from my mind, I finished the bottle of wine and watched TV. It was much later when I was tucked up under my duvet that I heard Sam and Sarah-Jane return from their evening out. They were both obviously worse for drink as they giggled and banged about the kitchen making toast to appease the munchies.

Love Suzi x

2nd October - Home

Dear Eve

The big day dawned.

Anyone would think it was *my* wedding the amount of butterflies that were flitting about my stomach. The sun wasn't shining but there seemed to be only a thin layer of clouds so it looked like it would brighten up later. Shame. My vindictive side wanted thunderstorms and lashings of rain to hurtle down on the not-so-happy-couple. The wedding ceremony was at three which meant Sam, SJ and I could all get ready without too much fighting over whose turn it was in the bathroom. I, of course, kindly let the other two go first. I was too busy checking emails and stuffing cereal to feed those butterflies – it was worth a try, bombarding them with boulders of granola, to stop them taking off.

Standing in the shower after breakfast, I absentmindedly reached for the exfoliating cream and started to scrub my legs with rubble-sized granules. Bloody hell, I'd forgotten about my fake tan. If I kept scrubbing at this rate I'd rub off forty quid's worth in no time! I swapped the tube for my favourite coconut shower gel and finally stepped out of the cascade of water to dry myself down. My only hope of saving my investment was to slather enough of the orange and almond,make-your-skin-as-soft-as-a-baby's-bottom, moisturiser on. I finished my basting and checked myself over in the mirror. I looked suitably sleek and a tad shiny but was in danger of smelling like a fruit salad with the combo I'd liberally applied to my body.

Apart from a small patch across my middle, my skin still glowed with a faint brown hue. Result! Didn't want to overdo it like one of the stewards I'd met recently. His skin was a strange orange colour. When I questioned him as to the brand he'd been using for his fake tan, he told me it wasn't fake. He'd been eating a diet high in carrots which had turned his skin orange. He said it with a straight face but there are so many stories circulating around the airline that I never knew which ones to believe. Whatever he'd done, it had earned him the nickname of 'Orange John.'

I don't know about orange, but by the time I'd finished in the bathroom my cheeks were as red as a beetroot and the moisture from the shower was beginning to turn my hair into a deranged afro. I picked up the hair straighteners. They were going to have to rise to the occasion to transform me into the groomed, elegant creature I wanted to portray. God knows what I'll be like on the morning of my own wedding. That's if I ever have one.

I could hear the other two getting ready in their bedrooms. Sam was going to squash us all into her little car for the hour long journey to the venue. Not only did Debbie have to get married on a weekday but she was getting married near to her parents' house which was down the motorway and through numerous country villages. We were bound to get stuck behind a tractor which would only add to the tension which had already cranked up a notch when Sam found a hole in her last pair of stockings. In true stewardess fashion I scurried for the spare pair I always carry in my handbag and saved the day, and her temper.

I was ironing my hair for the third time in an attempt to get the fringe to lie flat when Sam appeared at my bedroom door.

'You nearly ready, Suz? We have to leave in five minutes,' she sniffed the air. 'Over done it a bit on the perfume, haven't you?' I ignored her remark. My appearance was perfect. I have to admit that I'd spent most of the time on perfecting the delicate line of black around my eyes. I wanted to go for the kohl-outline-your-eyes look, but the new liquid eyeliner that I'd bought to make sure I got it perfect was trickier than I thought. Some girls may be able to apply eyeliner without a mirror but it seemed I couldn't get it right even with a magnifying glass. I had to wipe my impression of panda eyes several times until I got a line that was suitably close to my eyes *and* flicked at the corners with just the right amount of aplomb.

Dashing to my cupboard I whipped out my new dress and slipped the azure blue silk over my shoulders. I wriggled into it until it slid down, clinging to my body in all the right places. I studied myself in the mirror. The panic attack I'd had at handing over such a large wad of bahts in Bangkok was so worth it. The stakes had never been higher. Slipping my feet into my new shoes I grabbed my only suitable clutch bag and checked its contents. Lipstick. Check. Purse. Check. Door keys. Check. Phone. Check. I swept the screen again before placing it into the pocket in the lining of the bag. Nothing. I hadn't heard from Ed since I sent my text last night asking him to ring me. Maybe Candy was right. Maybe he just couldn't face me with the truth. I had no idea if he would even turn up today. He hadn't texted to say he was back in the country, let alone free and single. I looked in the mirror for the last time and adjusted my left shoulder strap. I would have to go it alone. I would be the sad 'ex' sitting at the back of the church. All alone. Well, I would be sitting with Sam and SJ but that didn't count. Everyone who knew about Matt and me would be thinking what effect this wedding was having on me. With Ed by my side it would have been a clear indication that I'd moved on.

I also half expected to hear from Matt, that he had called the wedding off. His mood last night made me think he wouldn't go through with it. But I suppose he's not the kind to leave Debbie to bring up the baby alone. But why resign himself to a life with a woman he didn't love? This wasn't the eighteenth century where you had to get married and hope that love would grow. He could still support his child, just not marry the mother.

I thought back to the last time I'd been at a wedding. It was Ash and Katie's when Matt had been the best man and I'd performed a reading. Matt had proposed on the lawn in front of all our friends and I'd had to swoon to get out of it. I smiled at the memory. Well, no swooning today. Only if Johnny Depp happened to turn out to be Debbie's long lost relative.

The three of us climbed into Sam's Clio and she drove us at break neck speed to the Manor hotel where the wedding was to take place. Not one tractor in sight but we still arrived with only five minutes to spare.

SJ turned to me. 'I thought you invited that First Officer of yours to come with you today?'

Sam gave her a look that clearly said 'shut up.'

'He said he'd meet me here,' I replied as casually as I could muster. 'He's flying in from the States this morning so he may be a bit late.'

Sam, to whom I'd confessed about Candy's visit the previous evening, squeezed my arm. She got out of the car and whispered into my ear as we walked to the entrance of the hotel.

'Don't worry. I won't abandon you. He'll turn up. You'll see.'

'Wish I had your faith,' I answered as I scrunched along the gravel path. I may be able to walk at forty-five degrees uphill on a Jumbo whilst pushing a trolley and preventing the orange juice from spilling off the top, but I sure as hell couldn't master my new, four inch stilettos with any kind of dignity. I would be memorable at this wedding not only for smelling like an over-ripe fruit salad but for arriving like a squashed one too if I wasn't careful.

If I was worried about my butterflies ruining the wedding, the flock of fascinators perched on the heads of the wedding guests made me smile as I entered the panelled room. Like brightly coloured birds of paradise they waggled their feathers, hid behind blooms or dazzled with sequins as they chirped their gossip to each other. I've never understood the fascination with fascinators myself. Most just look as though they're the left overs from a haberdasher's shelf, randomly plonked on an Alice band – what's wrong with a complete hat? Okay, so the three of us weren't wearing any head adornment but that was no reason not to give up on hats. I looked for Matt's mum sitting in the front row. Yep, she had what looked like half a blue-bird's wing on her head by the amount of feathers that were flicking over her right ear. His sister sitting beside her mum had a hat to match, with a flimsy piece over her face like bird netting over a garden fruit cage. She turned to smile at me through curious mesh hanging half way over one eye - which I suppose was meant to be seductive but must have blocked half her vision.

In fairness I must give Debbie her due. Maybe my recent unkind thoughts towards her were me being miffed at the situation, but it was amazing to see what money can buy. The whole room looked and smelt glorious. Set against the backdrop of the dark wood panelling, the green and white arrangements of flowers were stunning. Interspersed with tiny snippets of yellow roses (not my first choice of colour but hey, it wasn't my wedding) the yellow theme was taken up in the small arrangements on the side tables and the button holes of the men wearing morning suits. About thirty people stood in their finery in the rows of seats neatly arranged to face a long white clothed table at the front of the room. The light from a large diamond pattern leaded window shone down almost as though God was shining his light on it (could have been mistaken for Matt's sacrificial altar?)

'Not bad, not bad,' SJ muttered beside me. 'Far more tasteful than I thought it would be. Perhaps there's more to Debbie than we thought?'

'Don't get carried away with the love,' Sam whispered sarcastically. 'It's all her mother's doing. Last time I spoke to Debbie she couldn't even decide if she wanted flowers let alone what kind or colour.'

We took our seats about three rows from the back. Sam discreetly left a gap between us. 'For Ed,' she said placing her bag on it. I smiled at her. What would I do without friends like her? Go and sit in the toilet and cry probably.

Bruno Mars's song *'Marry You'* started up from somewhere and we all turned to watch as Debbie and Matt walked in together.

'Her mother's idea,' Sam leaned over the empty seat to whisper. 'Afraid he wouldn't go through with it I suppose unless she organised him as well.'

'What, do you think he might do a runner if he was up the front and turned round to see Debbie walking towards him?' SJ said. We stifled a giggle and I playfully hit SJ on the arm to make her be quiet.

Debbie, carrying a small bouquet of yellow roses, beamed at everyone. 'She looks like the cat that's caught her mouse,' SJ remarked.

'A large cat,' Sam observed. Even I had to admit that Debbie had obviously taken to not only eating for two, but as a precaution upped it to what looked like four. Her boobs had doubled in size and the dress looked as though it was desperately trying to stop them escaping.

'She bought the dress a couple of weeks ago,' SJ confided. 'But it seems she's not managed to resist a few packets of crisps since.'

I smiled. With these two beside me maybe it wasn't going to be too bad after all. I looked at Matt. He had scrubbed up well himself, but his face was ashen and he wasn't smiling. He caught my eye as he walked past. Debbie followed the direction of his gaze and realised that he was looking at me. She let her smile drop for one moment. God. If ever I felt guilt it was now. How much did she know, or guess? I felt sorry for her. If she did know that Matt still hankered after a relationship with me then she was putting on a brave face. On the other hand, if she had tricked Matt into marriage through getting pregnant then maybe I didn't feel quite so sorry for her. I averted my eyes from their gaze and pretended to study the service sheet.

The music stopped and the registrar started her speech. I looked at the other guests. Most appeared to be Debbie's family. Matt's mum, in the front row, turned round just as I was looking in her direction and caught my eye and gave me a rueful smile. Lordy. Even she was conspiring to make me feel guilty. As she turned her head her fascinator bird feather waved from side to side with the momentum as though wagging its finger at me. I looked at Matt's sister standing next to her. Blimey. Don't babies grow fast? This one, who had been a newborn the last time I'd seen her, was now quite a chubby thing in her arms, upright and busily trying to get hold of the brightly beaded necklace around the collar of her mother's dress. She couldn't coordinate her arms and kept hitting her mum in the chin as her chubby fingers attempted to find their quarry. Suddenly a tinkling noise broke through the monologue of the registrar; the baby had pulled too hard on the necklace, causing the thread holding the beads in place to break, cascading them across the floor.

'Probably the most entertainment we'll get all day,' SJ observed a little to loudly as we watched the baby get passed to Matt's mum. Her daughter tried to retrieve what was left of her necklace from the floor without causing too much disturbance. 'Thank God someone thought to bring the baby.'

The woman in front turned round and frowned. Sam and I stifled our giggles again. It was like being in assembly at school, Eve, with the head teacher glaring at who was being naughty.

I was glad when the nuptials were over. Matt had said his words quietly but Debbie had smiled through hers and the awkward part when someone could have objected passed without a hitch. I wondered whether Matt secretly wanted me to stand up and make a declaration that I objected to his marrying her. Instead I kept my eyes glued straight ahead and counted the roses in the floral decoration that stood in front of the window.

'13.'

'13 what?' Sam asked.

'Oh, sorry.' I realised I'd been concentrating so hard I must have spoken aloud. '13 roses in that bouquet,' I motioned towards the object of my concentration.

'You alright?' Sam asked. 'I worry for you, I really do.'

'Best thing we can do is head for the bar,' said SJ as the bride and groom walked past us and out of the door as the ceremony concluded.

I looked out of the window towards the car park. Still no evidence of Ed. 'Best idea you've had all day,' I said to her. With Sam trailing behind us, SJ and I made our way through the door and along the corridor to where rows of drinks were laid out for us to choose from.

'To the bride and groom,' I announced handing Sam and SJ a flute of champagne before taking mine and downing it in one.

'Steady on,' Sam cautioned. 'It's not a shot of vodka. You're supposed to take your time.'

I picked up another glass from the passing waiter and took a large swig. 'Think I'll just get pissed,' I announced to the girls.

I saw Sam look at Sarah-Jane in her motherly sort of way as I finished that glass as well.

'I promise not to be embarrassing and vomit,' I offered as they both came either side of me and propelled me to the corner of the room.

'Take it easy,' SJ cautioned. 'At least wait until we've had something to eat to soak it up.'

I waved her arm aside and walked out through the French doors onto the patio as the happy couple had the photographs taken in the grounds beyond.

'At least she looks happy,' Sam said joining me. We watched Debbie smiling as she posed next to Matt in front of a large stone urn. 'Probably with relief that Matt went through with it,' I said. Bitchy. But what the hell. I felt bitchy.

I usually like weddings. They have the correct ingredients for a perfect event. Everyone's dressed up, alcohol and food flow freely and everyone's in a good mood, but as the afternoon wore on I found myself getting more and more fed up. And no, it wasn't due to the amount of champagne I was consuming. I'd spent the entire time trying to avoid bumping into Matt's family, especially his mum, which I found a little difficult early on when there weren't many guests, *and* it was a buffet. As more people arrived for the evening I found it easier to disappear among the jovial groups.

It was as I approached the buffet table for my umpteenth slice of French bread to smother with Brie after making sure that the coast was clear of Matt's relatives that I bumped into Debbie's mum, Cynthia. Literally. She backed into me and her champagne sprayed from her glass in a wide arc all down the front of her purple dress. I rushed for some of the white napkins piled high on the end of the table cloth then helped pat her down and soak up the worst.

'Least it's not red wine,' I offered. 'There, you can't even see it now.' I finished dabbing and stood up from my bowed position.

'I'd rather not be feeling it as well though,' she replied, her face resembling a dried up prune as she smoothed down the damp material. 'It's… er…Suzi, isn't it?' Cynthia gave me a look that made me wonder whether she had just crapped her pants. Or was it just me that smelt? Bitch. She knew damn well who I was. We had met on several occasions at the house and I'd even shared a tea towel with her as we washed up in the kitchen after a party Debbie had given. All sympathy for her wet dress disappeared. I wished it *was* red wine that I'd knocked over her and that had been a bucketful, not a glass.

'Yes, Debbie's housemate for the last year,' I replied without a flicker.

'Ah, yes,' she said as a bit of spittle sprayed from her mouth. I felt it land on my cheek. So here's the situation. We both know what she has just done. I can feel the wetness of her saliva as it slips down to my jaw line. She can easily see the evidence of her action. What to do? Should I just wipe it casually with the back of my hand and carry on? The least I'd expect from her was a profuse apology. But no, nothing, not even an admission of guilt.

Not one word came from her orange-coated lips. She stood staring at me as though I was dirt. I took her challenge.

'What a lovely bride she makes,' I said as I wiped my cheek with a spare napkin still in my hand and turned to where Debbie was bending over the buffet at the other end of the table. She was reaching for a chicken leg on the plate at the back that was proving difficult to secure. And, just to stab the knife in and twist it a little I added. 'You'd never know she was pregnant in that dress would you?' Touché. From where we stood we could see the side zip of her dress straining for mercy.

Debbie's mother walked away without saying another word, over to her daughter and whispered in her ear. I watched as Debbie relinquished her hold on the chicken drumstick, reluctantly leaving it on the plate, and picked up a piece of celery garnish that adorned the neatly cut sandwiches in front of her.

I walked out onto the terrace and leaned over the stone balustrade as I surveyed the extensive gardens laid out before me. Sam and SJ were seated at the far end of the terrace surrounded by our friends. I'd had enough of them all gathering round me and asking in hushed tones 'How was I?' whilst stuffing down a coronation chicken vol-au-vent. Anyone would think I was at a wake, not a wedding. It was only Ash's comment that he believed I'd made the right decision that gave me any hope that I had their backing.

Ed's non-appearance had really upset me. Why had he played it so keen on the beach if he didn't mean it? That whole time at my Dad's had convinced me he was genuinely interested in something developing between us. Well, I had definitely learned my lesson now. All male airline staff were off bounds from now on. Even the baggage handlers would be shunned if they dared wink at me whilst chucking my case from the hold and onto the trucks. Security staff would be the only ones to see me naked through their x-ray scanners and if a steward even hinted at anything even slightly romantic while serving at the other end of my trolley there would be an immediate incident of clear air turbulence resulting in whichever drink or meal was in my hand at the time flying in his direction.

SJ looked up and waved to me. I couldn't face another round of sympathy. Holding my glass up and gesticulating that it needed filling, I escaped to the Ladies. I'd lasted as long as I could, my face was aching in its fixed smile position and I needed to seriously consider having it botoxed to remain there.

Just as I opened the door I heard someone announce that the cake was about to be cut. Well, if they needed someone for Debbie to aim the knife at, best if I wasn't there.

I was in luck. The pale-yellow-walled cloakroom appeared empty. All four cubicles displayed their 'green for go' signs on the doors so I leaned against the basins and scrutinized myself in the mirror. Scent from the floral arrangement in the corner of the room filled the air with a heady, cloying smell. The room was far too small for such a large perfumed bouquet. I ran the cold water over my hands and pumped the soap bottle so that I could wash the remains of any champagne and Cynthia's spit from my fingers. The cloakroom door swung open and, as I looked up to see who had walked in, my face must have given away my feelings as Matt's mother met my gaze. Just my luck. I had successfully avoided her all afternoon only to have a private audience in the loos.

'Suzi. How lovely to see you. We've missed you.'

What could I reply to that? Non-committal and polite, that's what I'd be. 'Lovely to see you too, Evelyn.'

'You know,' she continued walking over to the wash hand basin and running the tap. 'Perhaps I shouldn't be telling you this but we did hope that you and Matt would one day…' she paused. 'You know, tie the knot. It was just your job I suppose.'

'What was my job?'

'Well we thought it would be a passing phase and that once you'd got the travel bug out of your system you'd see sense and want to settle down. But I suppose Matt couldn't wait. Silly boy. He should have given you a bit longer.'

I didn't know whether to hug the woman or slap her, Eve. At least she thought it was Matt's fault that we'd split up and that he'd got impatient with me. But the way she described my job as a phase that I would get over, a bit like a disease, made me want to scream. Why was wanting to see the world in all it's glorious Technicolor a flaw in my character? I wanted to experience more than her son's monochrome life.

'You must be pleased though, with a grandchild on the way?'

'Well, between you, me and the gatepost,' she said. 'It's all happened so quickly we're not convinced it's Matt's.'

We were both facing the mirror. Behind us a toilet flushed and one of the cubicle doors slowly opened. I just caught a flash of purple before I realised it was Cynthia standing there.

If ever there was a time for the ground to open up and swallow, it was now. I didn't know where to look Eve. We've got into a few sticky situations in our time but nothing as excruciating as this. Ignoring us, Cynthia walked straight past to the basin, doused her hands under the running water, not even bothering to dry them, and walked towards the door. She turned to face us. 'I believe the cake is about to be cut.' And with that she was gone.

Evelyn turned to me, her eyes wide open and raised her eyebrows. 'Think I've just put both feet right in it, right up to my armpits,' she announced. 'Ah well, not for the first time. Better go and face the music.' And with that she too left the room. There was nothing left to do but follow the two mothers out of the loo and back into the fray where I was met with a cheer. Hopefully it meant that Debbie and Matt had sliced into the cake and not that Cynthia had grabbed the knife and sliced into Evelyn, after her remarks.

I wandered back out onto the terrace, grabbing another glass of bubbly on my way. Everyone had disappeared to watch the cake-cutting and I could hear twanging from the band tuning up for the dancing. There was to be *more* merrymaking. Would this night ever end? I brushed some debris off the stone seat next to a round table and sat down, sipped my drink and kicked off my shoes. Despite consuming numerous glasses of the bubbly I still felt remarkably sober. Not the oblivion I'd hoped for. I would just have to try harder. Must have been the French bread soaking it all up. Music started playing with gusto, drowning out the volume of chatter from inside. I heard a tripping of high heels and Sam appeared at my side. She sat down on the seat next to me.

'So this is where you're hiding out. The band has started. Are you coming in? SJ's going for it on the dance floor, already.'

'Hmmm… not sure I'm feeling it at the moment. You know, I think I may just ring for a cab to the station. I think there's a train soon.'

'Oh, bloody hell, Suzi,' Sam chastised me. 'Just lighten up and enjoy the evening.'

'I can't help thinking that if I hadn't taken my job I would be standing there instead of Debbie?'

'Do you really want to be pregnant and married to Matt?'

'No,' I answered.

'Well, what is it then that's making you so moody?'

I couldn't evade the question anymore. I knew what the matter was and it wasn't Matt and Debbie.

'I can't understand where Ed is. Do you think he's really got back together with Candy?'

'I think,' Sam wisely counselled. 'That you won't know the truth until he appears and can tell you himself. In the meantime, you're becoming a real bore. Sort yourself out and take that bloody miserable look off your face. So my advice is,' she concluded in her best school-marmish voice. 'Smile. Come back in. Stick beside me and we'll get through this together.'

Okay, nobody likes hearing harsh words but I knew she was right. I had let the whole situation overwhelm me. No man was worth that.

'Just give me a minute and I promise I'll come and join you,' I replied.

'Promise? Otherwise I'll track you down again and force you to do a solo spot on the dance floor with Matt's dad.'

I smiled. Now that was a real threat, let me tell you. Matt's dad was renowned for his extrovert dancing after a few drinks.

'I'll just finish this and come and find you.'

Sam seemed convinced and got up, clip-clopping her way back into the building.

What a day! What was I getting so worked up about? So what that I'd thought things were going somewhere with Ed. I couldn't hold back my tears and I raised my hand to wipe them away. Well, there was nothing else for it. I needed to pick myself up and carry on. There was nothing I could do until I spoke to Ed. Even if Candy had

273

spoken the truth and they were engaged, there were plenty more fish in the sea. I was behaving like a wet fish and no one would want me like this. Whereas if I became a party animal I'd be bound to catch someone, maybe in that very room behind me if I was lucky.

Footsteps behind me made me quickly pick up my glass and swig it down. I searched for my shoe with my toe preparing to get up and disappear amongst the throng. I didn't need another confrontation. Before I could move, like in a game of musical chairs, Matt abruptly sat down beside me.

'Hi,'

'Hi. You alright?'

'I guess so,' he answered soberly twisting his bottle of beer in his hands.

'You scrub up nicely,' I added hoping to tease him into a better mood.

'Not bad yourself,' he said and leaned over to nudge me. 'Can we be friends again, Suz?'

'Of course, I thought we always were.'

'I realised it was insane of me to come round last night. I shouldn't have done it. I don't know what I expected you to do. Put it down to last minute nerves.'

'Okay. You alright now?'

'Yeah,' he said and grinned at me. 'Anyway what are you doing out here? Come and have a dance. Help me celebrate my incarceration.'

'Bloody hell. You're brave aren't you? Just had the first dance with Debbie and out here so soon.'

'I'm not afraid of her.' We both turned round as we heard someone call his name. Debbie had come out onto the terrace through the other set of French doors and was walking towards us. He grinned at me. 'Well, not too afraid.'

I smiled back. 'Go.'

Matt got up and went to join Debbie. He took her elbow and led her back into the room.

I pushed my seat back and bent down to search for my shoe which was stuck near the back of the wall. I lifted the seat forward until I could just reach the heel. More footsteps. It was getting busier than Piccadilly Circus. With my head under the table I was unable to turn around and see who they belonged to.

'Seems like I'm just in time, Cinderella,' a familiar voice said. Careful not to hit my head on the table as I straightened up, I turned round to see Ed standing beside me. He handed me a full glass of champagne and sat down.

'I'm so sorry I'm late, Suz,' he said. 'The flight was diverted from Heathrow and by the time we'd got to Gatwick, filled in all the paperwork, and sorted everything else out I just about had time to get home, change and get over here. Didn't think you'd want me arriving in uniform.'

I stared at him. My heart did a little flutter and I felt my mouth go dry. Damn him. I had to be cross, not this pleased to see him. He leaned against me and kissed me gently on the cheek. I smelt that familiar smell of *Eau-de-Ed*. If I thought Matt scrubbed up well, he had nothing on Ed. His jacket clung to his broad shoulders and his dark eyes twinkled against his tan. 'I really am very sorry,' he apologised again. I sat speechless. I didn't know what to say. Half of me was angry and the other half relieved. Luckily, right now, the angry side was more dominant.

'Why didn't you phone?' I said.

'Didn't you get my text?' he said, looking concerned.

'No. I haven't heard anything from you for over a week now. The last message I got was when you promised to be here.'

'Didn't you get my new number?'

'No.'

'I had to change my number to get Candy off my back. She was driving me nuts with her persistent messages. I decided the best thing to do was get rid of it and have a new one. Then the new one got stolen in 'Frisco, but I sent you a message telling you all this.'

'Well, I didn't get it. All I got was a visit from Candy last night telling me you were both engaged. I've been ringing you to find out the truth.'

'Bloody hell. I knew she was up to something but I didn't realise she would go that far. She's nuts, Suzi, honestly.'

'She was sporting a rather large diamond ring as well.' I hesitated. 'Ed tell me straight. Are you and Candy engaged? I need to know.'

It was then that Ed took me by surprise. Placing his arm around my back he pulled me to him encircling my waist. With his other hand he cupped my face and looked me straight in the eyes.

'Suzi Frazier. Lovely but completely mad, Suzi. I am not engaged to Candy, nor will I ever be. It's you I want to be with.' He leaned down and tenderly brushed my lips with his. I looked at Ed and knew this was my Mills and Boon moment. He couldn't mean what he said and have such genuine puppy dog eyes at the same time.

'I'm so sorry I'm late and wasn't here for you.' He released his hold on me and bent down. He removed the elusive shoe from under the table and knelt to fasten it onto my foot. 'Now, how about we go into that room and I show you my best dance moves.' He held out his hand to me. 'Coming to the ball, Cinders? It's time to party.'

Love Suzi x

5th October - LHR-MBJ - 37,000ft

Dear Eve

I have seen the light. Flight Deck *are* Gods. I know that in the past I've been scathing about all those stewardesses setting their caps on catching a pilot but, as I sat in my very large comfy bed-seat in First Class, I realised that those stewardesses were much cleverer than I thought. Why settle for less? First class darh...ling, was the only way to travel.

I had holiday time owing, so in an effort to make up to me for being so late to arrive at the wedding, Ed persuaded me to join him on his next trip. Not that I needed too much persuasion. Especially when he mentioned it was to the Caribbean. It was as I turned left instead of right on entering the plane that I knew Ed was a God. What I hadn't realised was that the flight was half-empty and he would easily be able to upgrade me to First Class. When he told me it seemed churlish to refuse. How shallow am I? An offer of extra leg room, endless champagne and I was putty in his hands.

The man in 1A needed a good slap, a colouring book and then told to sit down and be quiet for the rest of the journey. He had the stewardess running around him like an express train, scurrying back and forth to the galley to meet his every whim. He may be worth a bob or two, but that was no excuse to treat the crew like his personal servants. Unfortunately that's what some people think is included in the price of their ticket. One of the crew approached me.

'He's a bit of a pain,' I sympathised nodding in 1A's direction.

Kneeling beside me in the aisle the steward whispered in my ear. 'Tell me about it. Unfortunately he's high up in the corporate world so we have to bow and scrape. He's probably not even paying for his ticket. If he plays up any more I'm going to spit in his dinner.'

'Not if she's done it first,' I grinned as 1A rang the call bell once more making the stewardess scurry back to his side.

In contrast the man in jeans opposite me sat quietly waiting for the plane to depart. He was flicking through a magazine and only looked up to smile and thank the steward politely when he was handed a glass of champagne. For all 1A's pretensions my money was on Mr Jeans for having bucket loads of dosh. Those passengers that have to proclaim their wealth usually haven't got as much as the quiet ones. The steward passed by my seat again. I grabbed his arm.

'Anyone worth squinting at?' I asked.

'Only 2A.'

'Who is he?' I asked indicating Mr Jeans.

'Don't you know your rock stars?' He mocked. 'Only the lead singer of one of the biggest bands in Canada.'

I was well plied with champagne throughout the flight. Which was lucky as we hit a bit of turbulence along the way. I smiled as 1A turned a shade of green and reached for his sick bag. When the seat belt signs were finally switched off he staggered off to the toilets behind us. That would teach him to drink too much free champagne.

A short while later I felt the need to do the same. None of the toilets on aeroplanes are savoury but the first class ones are slightly better than those at the rear. For a start they have less traffic visiting them and, secondly, along with the other free First Class handouts, they have posh soap and usually smell good, or at least as good as a toilet on an aircraft can smell. I stood outside the door and waited patiently. A groan came from inside. Was he in pain or just dying in there? Another groan. I knocked on the door and inquired if he was ok.

A muffled voice replied.

I walked away and waited at the side so that it wouldn't appear I was stalking him. The door opened. I saw 1A walk out, rearranging his clothing and head back in the direction of his seat. I just hoped he'd read the sign about being kind to the next passenger and wiping the hand basin. Especially if he'd had a bout of sickness. As I walked towards the door I bumped into a smartly dressed woman exiting the same toilet. She apologised then walked off towards the back of the aircraft. Really! I'd heard about the Mile High Club, I just didn't expect to bump into it. I'm sure she wasn't just checking on his well-being. I don't know how they managed it. The toilets are small enough for one person, let alone two getting up to gymnastic feats. I suppose if you are going to become a member of that exclusive club, a First Class toilet has to be the place for the initiation ceremony. I'd rather miss out on the vomiting ritual beforehand though.

Just before landing Ed appeared. 'Nice to see you awake. Last time I came down you were snoring laid out there. Want to come up and sit in the cockpit for landing?' he asked.

'It's a tempting offer. But why would I want to swap the comfort of this very large seat to be squashed onto that hard jump-seat, in a tiny room where you three have been farting your way across the Atlantic, just to watch you do what I know you can do very well.'

Ed looked a little crestfallen that I had refused. 'Hmmmm…Was so tempting though,' I repeated. He smiled at my sarcasm. He turned to go and talk to the other passengers.

'Please yourself.'

I watched as he walked about the cabin doing his P.R. routine; chatting to the passengers and enquiring after their well being. I thought about the man in 1A and what I'd witnessed. Best not to mention it to Ed at this moment.

On our arrival in Montego Bay I found myself being driven in the crew mini bus along a familiar driveway and up to the front of a hotel.

'I've stayed here before,' I exclaimed as I turned to Ed excitedly.

'Have you?' he questioned. 'I thought crew didn't darken these hallowed doors. Unless…'

'Unless what?' I smiled knowing that he was inferring that I'd have had to hook up with a member of the Flight Deck to stay there. 'They cocked up once with our inferior accommodation,' I laughed. 'And they had to move us here. It's got the most amazing infinity pool.'

'I know.'

'And the hugest beds,' I added. I grinned and watched as the porter opened the door for us to get out of the minibus. The four, tall, white stone columns of the hotel entrance stood before me; the large oak doors open in welcome. 'With petals strewn all over them.'

'I know,' Ed repeated grinning at me.

We walked into the lobby and I hung back as Ed checked-in at the marble reception desk. We made our way along the pale yellow painted corridors looking for his room on the ground floor. He opened the door with his room key and stood back gesturing me to enter. A small lobby opened out into a large sunlight room. A long cabinet lined one wall with a large flat-screen TV sat on the end of it.

'I'll tell you what,' he said walking over to the patio doors and unclasping the hooks top and bottom to push them open to the beach beyond. He returned to his luggage left by the door and reached into his bag. 'You open this,' he said as he took out a bottle of champagne and two glasses. 'Then we'll go down to the pool to check it out.'

'Do you do this every time you land?' I asked.

'Do what?'

'Produce a bottle of bubbly from your bag.'

'No, only when I want to impress someone special.'

I took the bottle from him and started to peel off the paper top and the wire cage surrounding the cork. There was a loud popping noise as I twisted the bottle. Ed held the glasses out for me to pour in the sparkling liquid.

'Come here, Suz.' Ed took my hand and led me out onto the patio with its stepping stone path that wound down to the beach. I felt the soft white sand beneath my toes and the late afternoon sun's warmth on my limbs. The azure blue sea was twinkling. Small clear waves rippled on the shoreline. Stopping and taking my arm to entwine it with his, he raised his glass and looked me straight in the eye. 'Now, Suzi, what would you like to do whilst we're here?'

Do you remember my last visit here, Eve? It was only a few months ago but things were so different. I was in such a dilemma about my life. Things seem so much clearer now.

'Well,' I started. 'Tomorrow I want to climb the Dunn's River Falls. Last time I was here I had to do it on my own.' I took a sip of my champagne. 'There's a natural slide half way up and I want you to stand at the bottom and catch me.' Okay, Eve, I know it's cheesy but something in me just wanted a bit of what that other stewardess had when her First Officer caught her at the Falls.

Ed raised his eyebrows questioning.

'Don't worry it's just something I saw last time and I wanted it to happen to me, although I wouldn't ever admit it at the time.'

'Not quite what I had in mind first,' he said encircling my waist and pulling me close to him. 'But okay. And before that?'

I stared at him as I felt the nearness of his skin and smelt the sweet aroma of champagne on his breath. 'Before that I want…' I reached up and gently kissed his lips. '…before that I want to try out that rather large bed in there. Last time…'

'Last time, last time…' Ed smiled as he pulled me even closer and held me tight. 'No more last time, Suzi.'

I smiled at him, wrapped in his embrace. 'This time… ' I said, but my words were lost in his kiss.

Love Suzi x

Dearest Evie

Firstly I want to say sorry for neglecting you these last few months, but I know you would forgive me. Things have been so exciting recently! Ed and I are an item now; he's even said 'I love you'!

I know we always vowed we'd NEVER dump each other for a boyfriend, but I was sure you'd understand. I'm all loved up. I think this is the real deal. That trip to the Caribbean cemented it. I realised then that he meant every word he said and so far he's done everything he can to prove it to me.

It's been tricky with our work schedules but so far we've managed to get a few trips away together. They've been so much fun. Ed knows all the best places to go. He even took me to where the Atlantic and the Pacific Ocean meet on a trip to South Africa. How cool is that? We stood on a high cliff overlooking the sea. It was so romantic. We didn't get to climb Table Mountain when we were in Cape Town because the cable car wasn't running, but on the way home he was flying the plane and circled over the top so we could all peer out of the window at it.

I try hard not to think about him when he's away in some far-off exotic location without me. I know other stewardesses look at him. There will always be the ones looking for their pilot to ensnare, but if I don't trust him Eve, there's no hope for us.

My landlord is chucking us out soon and I'm hoping

that when I tell Ed he will ask me to move in with him. Better still we might buy somewhere together. You know how I always dreamed of owning my own home. I might finally have the three C's we used to laugh about – country house, cocktails and cleaner! Maybe not straight off but it's worth aspiring to.

I would never have got through these past few months without you, Eve. You've always been my best friend. I can tell you anything - just like the old days. I really wasn't going to spill the beans to your mum about you taking a drag of that boy's fag in the corner of the field after school. I know we were having one of our spats that always ended up with one of us making the other laugh at how silly we were being. I just wanted you to realise how stupid it was to smoke, but you always had to have your own way.

I can't believe that I was the last person you spoke to. I just wish I could have been there with you when it happened. I've played it round and round in my head. How you must have felt. How you must have been frightened. I hope you weren't in pain. They said that it was very sudden. That you wouldn't have known anything about it, but I still don't like to think of you on your own. It was such a shock when your Mum came over to our house to tell us you had a brain haemorrhage. Just after you put the phone down to me. They didn't know the condition ran in the family. I cried for weeks. I couldn't understand it. How could you leave like that? Why you? You were only thirteen, Eve. Thirteen! That was no age at all. You were so young. They said it could have happened at any time and that you were lucky it hadn't happened earlier. *I* was the lucky one to have had you for a best friend up to that point. I've never found anyone to replace you.

But Eve, you hadn't even been kissed. Well, you had

that quick snog with Ross Courtney after the school disco, but that doesn't count. I know that now. Now that I've really been kissed. I've tried to get out there and see things for the both of us. Tick off our wish list that we used to add to nearly every day. Every time I went somewhere new I'd enjoy it for *us*. It was only when my life started getting complicated that I needed to write it all down. It helped to get the worries out of my head. You were the natural choice to write to. I tried to think what you would reply to all my rantings; something sensible but always with your sense of humour. You always were so much more rational about our problems and I know that you would have supported me all the way, whatever I chose.

I want you to know that I will never forget you. Do you remember how we used to promise each other that when we got married we'd be each other's bridesmaid? I still haven't forgotten. If Ed asks me to marry him (I will *not* wear a meringue) I will come and lay my bouquet on your grave to prove that –

you will always be with me in my

heart,

all my love,

your best friend,

Suzi x

The End

If you enjoyed *Love, Suzi x* perhaps you may also like *Choices*, the first of my 'hen-lit' novels:

CHOICES

A second before Lauren Harding hit the midnight blue car in front of her, she had been thinking about what on earth to serve at Ellen's surprise birthday party at the weekend. The shock of the bump focused her mind, along with the sight of the irate woman getting out of it.

She couldn't believe what had just happened. How on earth had they hit each other with the traffic going so slowly? The car in front seemed to stop for no reason. Sitting very still for a moment to gather her thoughts, Lauren was aware of a surge of nausea creeping up from the bottom of her stomach. It had only been a small bump. Surely not enough to cause her to be sick?

Gulping back the excess saliva that had pooled in her mouth she felt a slight tingling in her head. This was crazy. She hadn't been sick for years. Why should such a small collision cause this reaction? Lauren scraped back her hair from around her face tucking the stray blonde strands behind her ears. Then she reached into the glove compartment and hurriedly took out a tissue from the packet that was squashed up against the half empty bag of mints and held it against her mouth.

Lauren opened the door and, using the handle for support, slid out of the grey, leather seat just in time as another wave of sickness caught her. Now the liquid feeling in her stomach felt on the move. Gulping desperately, she stood up and watched as the woman from the car in front walked over to her and started gesticulating. Although she could see the woman's mouth moving, for some reason Lauren couldn't make sense of the ramble that was issuing forth. Instinctively, grasping the tissue firmly to her mouth, Lauren knew without a doubt that this time there was no turning back. As though caught up in someone else's movie, unable to rewind or fast forward, Lauren gulped. Trying desperately to wave the other woman out of her line of fire, Lauren turned her head to the side, just as the woman, who finally seemed to grasp the significance of Lauren's actions, moved in the same direction as the liquid missile that issued from Lauren's mouth.

'Oh, my God, what the hell are you doing?' the woman shouted staring at her feet in disbelief as she lifted, first one exquisite red stiletto, then the other to survey their condition as the multi-coloured mixture squelched down the side of her shoe. 'Not content with smashing into my car, you have to throw up all over my feet as well.'

Feeling relief from the nausea flood over her, Lauren wished that the buzzing noise in her ears would subside so that she could hear properly. She wiped her mouth with the damp tissue, and looked at the cars as they sounded their horns in protest at having to negotiate the two vehicles causing the congestion. Knowing that unless she sat down immediately she would fall down, Lauren slowly backed away from the scene and reached for the small wall beside the pavement and lowered herself onto it. Her hands instinctively brushing the top of the brickwork to clear the loose stones and dust. What had Rob said on the phone last night about someone in the office being laid low with a bug? She tried to think back to when she'd last eaten. Some soup at lunchtime the day before, a couple of biscuits with a cup of tea in the afternoon, and after that some chocolate ice cream. There wasn't anything unusual in that to make her feel this bad.

Breathe, breathe she chanted to herself as she felt her skin prickle and her stomach lurch. Trying again to get some assistance from the limp ball of paper in her hand by frantically dabbing her lips, Lauren looked at the young woman in front of her. For having eaten such a small amount of food there seemed to be an inordinate amount of vomit on the woman's ankles.

'Oh, that's great,' Miss Red Shoes proclaimed, extracting herself from the unsavoury pool at her feet and hopping from one foot to the other. 'I'm late for work and have a car crash with a mad woman who vomits on my shoes. What a day!'

'I'm so sorry,' offered Lauren pathetically as she watched the younger woman stride to her car to take a cloth from the pocket in the driver's door and start to wipe the sticky mess that clung to her ankles.

'Ugh, it smells disgusting!' was all that Lauren could hear through the noise in her ears. 'What on earth have you been eating?'

Lauren sat on the wall and endeavoured to gather herself together. The nausea seemed to have subsided for the moment but she was aware of feeling slightly light-headed. A white van honked its horn in protest as it found its way blocked by a single-decker bus coming in the opposite direction. The road through the busy market town was easily wide enough to let two cars pass each other but the collision was starting to cause a tailback.

Feeling the eyes of everyone upon her, Lauren sat calmly watching the two vehicles gingerly edge past each other just skimming the van's wing mirrors in the process.

Vaguely conscious of Miss Red Shoes, having cleaned herself up as much as she could, slowly walking towards her, Lauren shifted in her position and looked down, absentmindedly wiping her coat. There was something in the ungainly way that the woman moved that made Lauren wonder whether she had been able to walk in the shoes in the first place. She was distinctly aware of a revolting taste in her mouth. This was evident as her prey backed off as Lauren looked up and gulped again.

'I'm a reasonable sort of person,' Miss Red Shoes delivered from a safe distance. 'But you'd better have a pretty good excuse for what you've just done. I'd only just got those shoes. Hundred quid they cost me. The most I've ever paid for a pair. How the hell I'm ever going to get them clean again, I just don't know.'

'I'm so sorry,' Lauren repeated. She squirmed in embarrassment. 'I'll reimburse you for them.'

'You're bloody right you will, and let's not forget the damage you've done to my car. It'll be at least a thousand by the time that dent's knocked out,' Miss Red Shoes replied, placing her hands on her hips in defiance.

Her strength returning, Lauren pushed herself up from the wall and walked over to where the two cars were still locked together. She bent down and ran her hand over the small dent on the bumper of the other car. It was obvious that it was only slightly damaged; she could only feel a small indent with her finger, most of the impact being taken by the large knock in hers.

'I take full responsibility for the accident,' she started, her voice getting louder by the second as she walked over to her passenger door to retrieve the bottle of water she always kept there. The sickness seemed to have subsided for the time being but she needed to get rid of the foul taste in her mouth. 'It'll only take a few knocks to bash out that dent. I'm not that stupid.'

The strength in her voice obviously took the other woman by surprise. Dropping her hands from their lofty position on her hips, Miss Red Shoes hurried over to her open car door and retrieved her handbag from the opposite seat, delved into it and extracted a large piece of lined paper.

'Well if that's the way you feel, I'd better have your name and address so that we can let the insurance companies sort it out.' Lauren calmly took the pen from her outstretched hand and leaning on the roof of her car, started writing.

'Take your shoes into the cleaners and send me the bill,' she said without looking up. 'I can let you know of a good one if you have trouble getting the stains out.' Ending her writing with a flourish of confidence that she didn't feel Lauren looked up into a piercing pair of green eyes.

'I'm really sorry I threw up on you, Miss...?'

'Debbie Wells.'

'Debbie, I'm just on my way to the doctors now. I think it must be the bug that's going around at my husband's office. If you'll excuse me I must hurry or I'll miss my appointment,' she concluded handing back the piece of paper. Intent on getting out of such an awkward situation quickly, Lauren hurried into her car seat. She manoeuvred the car into the steady flow of traffic. Looking into her rear view mirror she caught sight of Debbie standing aghast, her mouth wide open, watching her depart.

'Hello, Mrs Harding,' the young woman opposite her said whilst indicating a chair for Lauren to sit on. 'I'm Dr

Engle. I'm new to this practice; it's lovely to meet you. What can I do for you today?'

'Well, I wouldn't normally bother you, Doctor...'Lauren hesitated feeling a little foolish that she had come in the first place. Most women her age must feel tired and a little fed up some of the time. This young woman wouldn't understand what it was like to feel worthless. Lauren sank down onto the hard fabric of the chair and placed her handbag carefully down out of the way beside her feet.

'I can see from your records, that you don't often bother us, as you put it, Mrs Harding. In fact the last time you came to the surgery was over five years ago when you had that scare over a lump in your breast. Is that alright or is that why you've come today?' the doctor encouraged.

Oh God, Lauren thought. She'll really think I'm wasting her time when I tell her.

'No everything's fine with that, thank you,' Lauren continued. 'It's just that I've been sick.' Oh no, why did I say that, she chastised herself. 'In fact I bumped into another car on the way here and then threw up all over some poor woman's shoes.' She added in a hurry to give her visit credence. Lauren twisted her fingers and stared at the woman opposite her.

'A bump you say, how much of a bump?'

'Oh nothing much, I'm fine really. I wasn't paying as much attention as I should. I was fighting off a wave of nausea at the time.'

'How long have you been feeling sick and how often?'

'It's the first time.' Oh shit, now she did really sound pathetic. Who makes an appointment at the doctor's before they're ill? Why can't I just come out with the real reason? Lauren thought. She's a doctor, for goodness sake. 'It's probably a bug or something that's going around,' Lauren concluded folding her arms, stretching out her legs to lean back in the chair.

'Mmmm, I'd like to examine you, if that's alright, just check that no damage was done with your bump, as you put it.' Dr Engle continued decisively. 'It won't take long, would you go behind the screen and lie on the couch for me?'

Lauren meekly did as she was told and walked over to where a clean white couch was covered with a long strip of blue paper towel. She slowly took off her coat and folded it carefully over the back of the chair at the end of the couch. Pulling the curtain across to screen them the doctor continued to busy herself in the corner of the room as Lauren began to remove her shoes and place them neatly under the chair.

She perched anxiously on the side of the bed. This new doctor must be straight out of medical school to be this conscientious. What was she examining her for? It was only a minor bump, she felt fine. At least she'd managed to divert the doctor from what was really bothering her. It all seemed so ridiculous now. She had a lovely home, a husband who provided her with everything she could ever want, a daughter with a fine career. What had she, Lauren Harding, have to complain about? Her friend, Marsha, had only reminded her of that this morning during their weekly catch up conversation on the telephone.

'So how long is Rob away for this time?' Marsha had questioned.

Lauren had let out an involuntary sigh before she answered. 'Oh, only a week. He's promised to be back as Alexa's coming down for the fiasco at the weekend. She's got something to tell us, apparently.'

'Any idea what?' Marsha inquired.

'No,' Lauren snapped as she lay back on the white

duvet covering her bed and stared up at the ceiling. 'As much as I hate to say this about my darling daughter, it's bound to involve money if she wants her father to be present. You know she sees him as her own private banker… I don't know where I went wrong,' Lauren paused curling over onto her side tracing the embossed pattern on the material with her finger, the phone wedged to her ear. 'I might as well be dead for all she cares.'

'Lauren, don't say that!' Marsha exclaimed. 'She loves you really, she's just got a weird way of showing it,' she added as a way of compensation. 'When she's older she'll appreciate all that you've done for her.'

'Marsha, she's twenty-four, how much more growing up has she left!' Lauren screeched down the phone, sitting up in indignation. 'Anyway, it doesn't matter, she's got her own life, I just wish sometimes she would treat me with a little more respect.'

'Perhaps, if you hadn't let her get away with it for so long, she would?'

'It's lucky you're a good friend, Marsha, otherwise….'

'I know… I know... you'd tell me to mind my own business.' Lauren smiled as the woman on the end of the phone finished her sentence.

'Well, anyway, Alexa is coming down on Sunday and Rob is due back from New York that morning. We've got Ellen's surprise seventieth, remember? Hopefully there won't be any sparks flying except from the candles…maybe we'll all get along.'

'Like happy families..?'

'Yes, you skeptic, like happy families. Maybe Alexa's got some good news for us?'

'What… like she wants to leave her job and settle down?'

'No, she likes it; it's just not really the kind of career for settling down.'

'Is that what you want her to do? 'Marsha asked.

'Yes… no… not really,' Lauren continued hesitantly. 'It's just that I don't really think I know her any longer, she's always on a trip somewhere around the world. I know she has an enviable lifestyle, I just wonder where it'll all end. She never seems to have a boyfriend or even be interested in making a home for herself. The flat Rob bought her hasn't been touched since I went up and decorated it for her and that was five years ago.

'You worry about her too much,' Marsha reasoned. 'You need to do more with your own life and then you won't be on her case so much. You always told me to warn you if you were getting over protective. Well, now is the time. Get out more, take up a new interest. Anyway, I heard somewhere that once you've been an in flight attendant for over five years, you're so immersed with the lifestyle that you can't give it up.'

'You are such a comfort, Marsha. I don't know why I put up with it.'

'You put up with it my dear friend, because I'm the only one who can tell you the truth. Anyway enough of your unappreciative daughter how's your unappreciative husband?'

Lauren's heart sank but she forced her voice to remain light. 'Oh, he's the same as ever; brought me a lovely handbag back from his last trip to the Far East. It's been really busy for him at work recently, the office sent him all over the States last month and I know he's away for most of next month. He's really stretched at the moment. It'll be nice to spend some time together at the weekend.'

Lauren had climbed off the bed, holding the phone between her shoulder and ear, her head at an uncomfortable angle as she stared at herself in the floor length mirror on the wall. She was only forty-five but looked young for her age, being what her mother-in-law always so charmingly reminded her as, well covered. Lauren had read once about how women had to choose between their face and their bottom. Well, even she had to admit that now her bottom was making the choice for her, as she turned to inspect her backside. She hadn't realised just how fleshy she'd become. Lauren picked up a handful of thigh and squeezed it; the mottled dimples fused together. Moving over to the glass she stared closely at her face in the mirror, stroking the pale flesh of her cheek. Her skin had always been one of her best features, but now it seemed dry and pallid; large hazel eyes stared back from a sallow face, revealing more wrinkles than she remembered. Maybe she should start wearing foundation and get some of the grey strands covered; it would give Rob a surprise if he came back at the weekend and found the blonde that he'd once married.

It wasn't long before Dr Engle had finished her examination of Lauren and the two women were seated opposite each other once again. Lauren fidgeted with the buttons on her cardigan as she waited for the doctor to finish writing her notes and say something.

'I can't see anything at the moment that would indicate a problem from the crash, Mrs Harding. But, I wonder if I might ask you a few questions.'

Lauren nodded her consent and grasped her hands firmly in her lap, twiddling her thumbs.

'Have you also been feeling tired lately?'

Lauren nodded her head, her mouth open.

'And maybe a bit emotional, more tearful than usual and you don't know why?'

Lauren's head resembled a nodding dog.

'And when did you last have your period?'

Lauren gasped. 'Why do you ask? Is there something wrong? It hasn't been for a couple of months now, but

I'm not bothered. I just thought it may be the start of the menopause.'

'I've got an idea what I think might be the problem but I'd like to do a few more tests. Would you mind if we took a urine sample and some blood?'

Lauren felt her palms get sweaty and a prickling feeling crept up over the back of her head.

'What could it be? Do you think it's anything serious?' she questioned, her throat tightening. Maybe her breast lump wasn't a scare after all, maybe it had just been hibernating inside her, waiting to grow and now had manifested into something else. Perhaps that was why she had started to be sick. What if she now had stomach cancer? How would Rob and Alexa cope without her? Feeling her panic getting out of control she stared intently at the young woman's face.

'Now, calm down, Mrs Harding,' the doctor reassured. 'As to serious, it would depend on how you view these things. I can see from your age that you could be right to expect that a loss of your monthly cycle could be the start of the menopause but after examining you, I have reason to believe that there maybe another explanation for it.' The doctor paused and was obviously waiting for the penny to drop. Lauren continued to stare at her in confusion. The doctor leaned forward and placed her hand over Lauren's white knuckles.

'Mrs Harding...Lauren, have you ever considered that you may be pregnant?'

Printed in Great Britain
by Amazon.co.uk, Ltd.,
Marston Gate.